Our Cause, It Is Just

Frank Becker

Greenbush Press
Spring, TX

Published simultaneously worldwide.

Becker, Frank
Series: "The Chronicles of CC"

Book Four
Our Cause It Is Just / Frank Becker

ISBN:
Paperback. 978-0-9766720-8-1
eBook, 978-0-9766720-7-4

Library of Congress PCN 2014938517

Printed in the United States of America

Dedicated to
Sandra, Cheryl, Jamieson, and Matthew

The Star Spangled Banner
Francis Scott Key, 1814

Oh, say can you see by the dawn's early light
What so proudly we hailed at the twilight's last gleaming?
Whose broad stripes and bright stars thru the perilous fight,
O'er the ramparts we watched were so gallantly streaming?
And the rocket's red glare, the bombs bursting in air,
Gave proof through the night that our flag was still there.
Oh, say does that star-spangled banner yet wave
O'er the land of the free and the home of the brave?

On the shore, dimly seen through the mists of the deep,
Where the foe's haughty host in dread silence reposes,
What is that which the breeze, o'er the towering steep,
As it fitfully blows, half conceals, half discloses?
Now it catches the gleam of the morning's first beam,
In full glory reflected now shines in the stream:
'Tis the star-spangled banner! Oh long may it wave
O'er the land of the free and the home of the brave!

And where is that band who so vauntingly swore
That the havoc of war and the battle's confusion,
A home and a country should leave us no more!
Their blood has washed out their foul footsteps' pollution.
No refuge could save the hireling and slave
From the terror of flight, or the gloom of the grave:
And the star-spangled banner in triumph doth wave
O'er the land of the free and the home of the brave

Oh! thus be it ever, when **freemen shall stand**
Between their loved home and the **war's desolation!**
Blest with victory and peace, may **the heav'n rescued land**
Praise the Power that hath made and preserved us a nation.
Then conquer we must, when **our cause it is just**,
And this be our motto: **"In God is our trust."**
And the star-spangled banner in triumph shall wave
O'er the land of the free and the home of the brave!

"...and this desire on my part, exempt from all vanity of authorship, had for its only object and hope that it might be useful to others as a lesson of morality, patience, courage, perseverance, and Christian submission to the will of God."

—Johann Wyss, 1812
Author, "The Swiss Family Robinson"

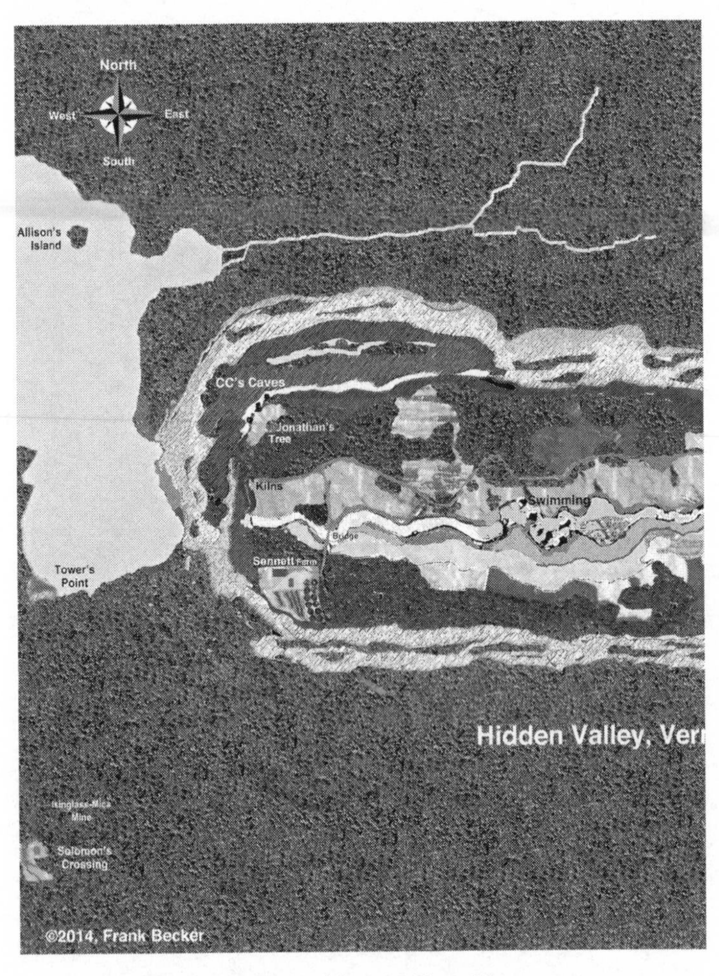

West end, Hidden Valley, Vermont

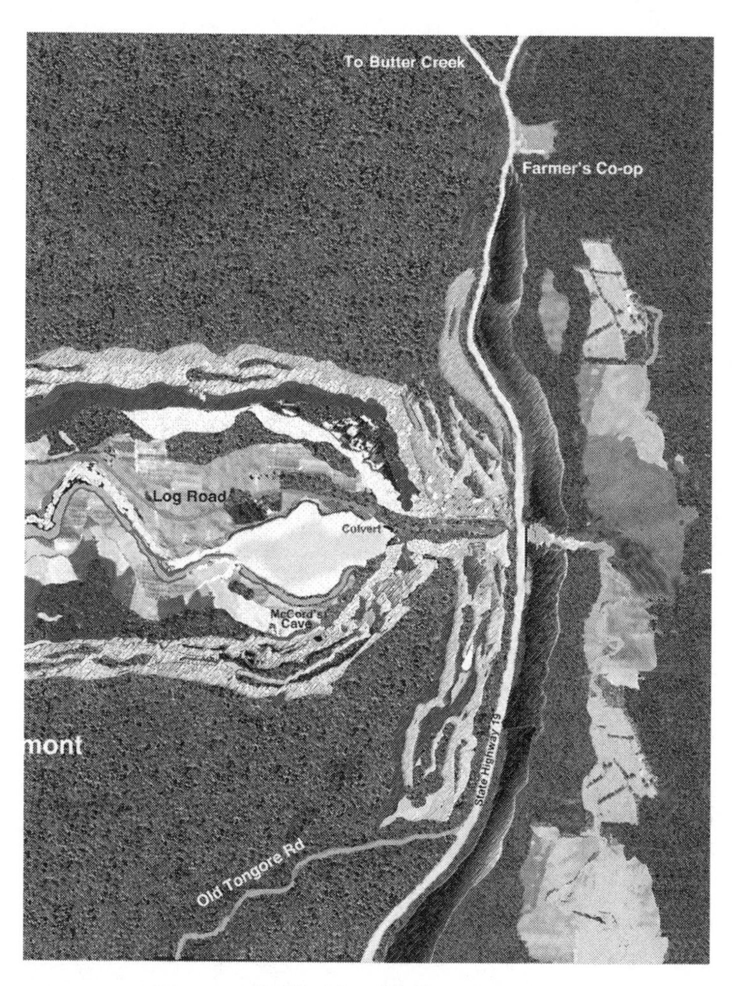

East end, Hidden Valley, Vermont

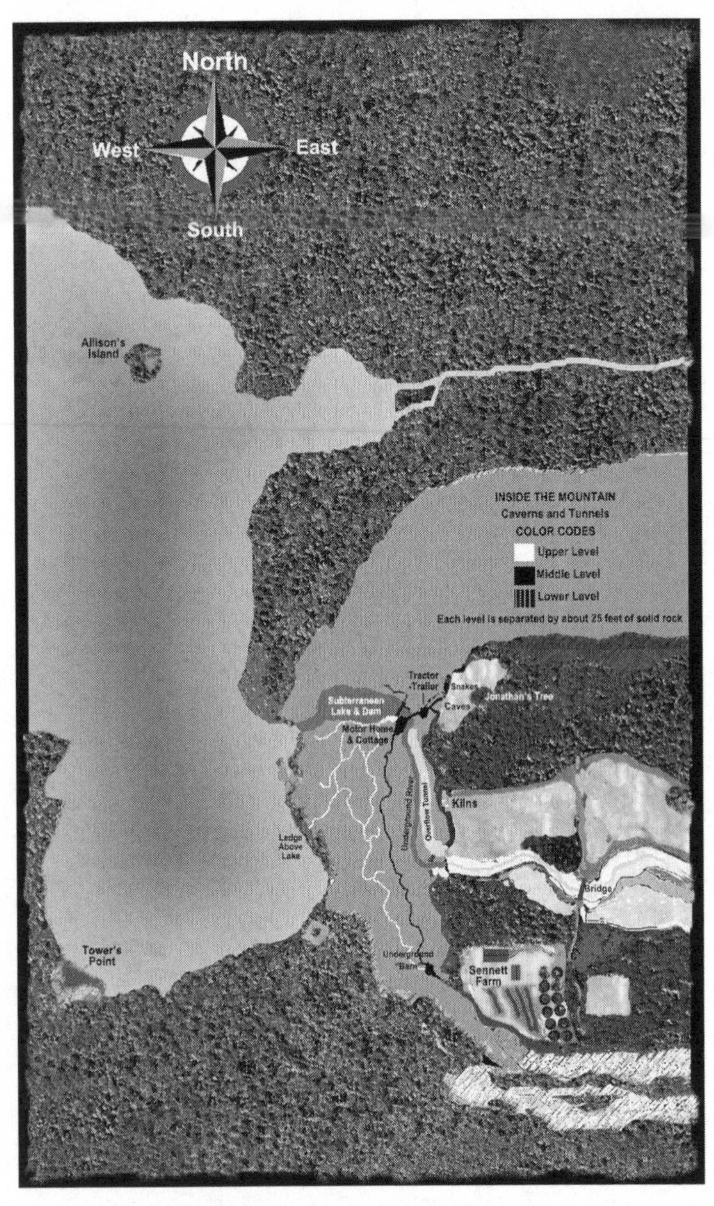

Elizabeth's Drawing of the Main Caverns

Eviction Day

Hidden Valley Caverns
April 30th, 9 a.m.

CC jogged down the cave past the hot tub. Not five minutes before, he had been soaking in that bubbling water with not a care in the world.

Well, he thought, *if I have to run again, at least I've had one last hot bath.*

He'd done a lot of running since he'd awakened in a hospital a year earlier, alone and the victim of amnesia. His efforts to overcome the pain and confusion at that time had paled with the realization that the distant rumblings that had awakened him were the sounds of nuclear weapons being detonated in distant cities. Even now, a year later, he had few clues to his real identity, and no idea where his wife might be, or even if she had survived the war.

When, after two weeks, he had finally left that hospital, it was at the wheel of a tractor-trailer loaded with food and equipment that he had pillaged from various abandoned businesses around town. He had driven that truck north into the mountains of central Vermont where he was blessed to discover the hidden valley in which he had survived for the past year.

Within months of establishing this new home, he had found himself caring for two children. They too had managed to survive in a country poisoned by war and occupied by ruthless invaders. Later that year the three of them had been joined by three additional adults. The going hadn't been smooth, but by the grace of God, they had enjoyed a relatively good life

That was over now. Some of America's invaders had stumbled upon their hidden valley, and as a consequence their lives were now in danger. CC was about to run for his life again, and the question he was asking himself was, *Will the God who has helped me this far still be with me?*

He was comparing his feelings with the hopelessness he felt on the day he had left the hospital. He had come here alone, but with enough food and supplies to last him for several years. Now there were six of them, and they would have to abandon this home and all their precious resources, and wander off into an inhospitable forested wilderness with only the small quantity of food they could carry on their backs.

He rebuked himself. *I can't allow myself to question God's love or his care. He has brought all of us through numerous trials, and we must not entertain the possibility of failure now.*

The mouth of the tunnel he was in opened abruptly above the valley floor, thirty feet below. A moment before, he had taken a final look and he had seen several soldiers wandering around the edge of the wood. Now he was jogging down the sloped tunnel toward the lower cavern. He found his little group waiting at the door to their cottage storeroom.

Jonathan, their teenage prodigy, was there too, which was a surprise, and CC realized that the stranger who was independently battling the soldiers must have helped him escape from the immense hollow tree that had served as the teenager's tree house and crow's nest. Any explanation of how the boy had gotten safely to the cave without the enemy seeing him would have to wait. CC just hoped the stranger who had helped the boy wouldn't be able to follow him into the caverns, even though his assistance seemed to indicate that he wasn't an immediate threat.

CC examined the members of his little troop, and noted that their backpacks and firearms were stacked at their feet.

Jonathan turned to him.

"CC," he said, loud and demanding.

"I know."

"You know about the man? It was the guy who was here last winter, the guy you call *G.I. Joe.* "The boy went on. "There I was, way up in the crow's nest, and a soldier crawled into the opening at the bottom of my tree. He began laughing and shouting that he knew I was there and that he was going to kill me."

The boy's experience was obviously news to the others because his words captured their attention. Little Sarah took his hand possessively, as though to somehow protect or encourage him, but Jonathan seemed oblivious to her presence.

"I could see him through the cracks in the trap door beneath my feet." "He was pointing his rifle up at me, and I figured I'd had it. But then someone reached into the hollow tree, stabbed him with a knife, and dragged him away."

"I was watching from the upper cave. I saw it."

"Did you hear what he hollered up to me."

"He spoke to you?"

"Yes. He told to me to climb down quickly, but to stay hidden inside the tree trunk. Then he told me to wait until the coast was clear, and run to the cave."

CC didn't know how to process that. *Is this guy somehow on our side, or was he just feeling so sorry for the kid that he had discovered hiding up inside a tree?* It was something else he didn't have time to dwell on.

He took one last look around. Even though he'd built this cottage, it still seemed incongruous to him to see a structure built inside a cavern. He frowned. *It's been a good home,* he thought with regret.

He turned to Jonathan. "Have you shut down everything mechanical?"

Jonathan nodded.

"Okay. C'mon," he ordered, and turning away from the entry tunnel, he led them toward the cottage.

"Wait," Jonathan cried. "I have something to show you." He held out a crumpled page of newspaper.

"We don't have time to read old newspapers." CC brushed it aside and turned back toward the cottage door.

Jonathan caught at his arm. "You'd better look at this one," he insisted. "Over here," and caught CC's sleeve and pulled him away from the others.

"Very well, show me," he said.

Jonathan pointed his flashlight at a picture that headed a brief article. It was a photo of some jewelry. In the poor light, CC found himself squinting. He realized that it was a picture of a necklace, a necklace that looked vaguely familiar. In fact, if memory served him correctly, it was remarkably similar to the one that Elizabeth had been wearing the night they'd found her asleep in the motorhome, the necklace that had been conspicuously absent from her neck ever since. CC was about to hand the paper back, but Jonathan persisted.

"Read the article. It's short."

Almost beside himself with impatience, CC grabbed the paper and scanned the words. He read it twice through before he understood.

"Where'd you get this," he asked.

"It was used for packing material in a carton of canned goods."

"O.K. Don't say anything to anyone about this."

"Right."

The group hadn't been able to overhear their words, and when they returned, everyone looked bewildered.

Why is CC taking time to chat with Jonathan when all our lives are at stake? Rachel wondered.

CC crumbled the clipping and stuffed it in his pocket. Then he shrugged into one of the emergency packs that had been prepared weeks before, pulled the strap of a water bottle over his shoulder, grabbed his rifle, took a final look around the cave, and surprised everyone but Jonathan and Sarah by leading them into the living room of their little cottage.

The others hesitated in confusion, then followed them into the little building. Jonathan carefully closed the door behind them. "Leave it unlocked," CC ordered. To forestall any questions, he explained. "We don't want anyone thinking there is anything special about this little building. If we lock it, they may think we have something to hide."

CC opened a closet, slid the hanging clothes aside, and lifted a cunningly disguised trapdoor in the floor.

He heard exclamations of surprise from McCord and the women. The dog slipped alongside him, looked down a long stairway that led to a cavern below, then skittered around and slipped back into the bedroom. Jonathan caught him by the collar.

"It's okay, boy. I'll help you down."

Jonathan led the way, holding the dog's collar, and one by one, the others moved gingerly after him, climbing down the steep stairway into the enormous cavern that they had never suspected lay beneath the one in which they'd lived for months. Each of them nervously gripped the wooden railings until they reached the bottom.

CC had let them all precede him. He stood on the top tread of the stairs inside the closet, and reached up to slide the clothes on the bar above his head until they were evenly spaced across its length. Then he tucked some loose clothes in the gap between the wall and the hinged trap door so that when he dropped it down into place, the garments would spread out and help hide it from casual examination. *We need as much time as we can get,* he reasoned.

When the trap door dropped back down, he reached up and slid a barrel bolt, making it far more difficult for anyone in the cottage above to raise the portion of the floor that served as a trap door.

Reaching the bottom of the staircase, he found that Jonathan was preparing to lead the others away. McCord and Ross seemed dazzled by the electric lights glaring off the surface of the water, and were clearly amazed at the existence of the underground dam and water wheel that had provided the electricity to the cavern above, but had been kept secret from them.

CC crossed the top of the dam, then made his way down a stone stairway to the ledge beneath the dam that housed the waterwheel and generator. By that time he reached the bottom, Jonathan had all of them turn on their flashlights. CC hit a switch, the incandescent lights around the dam glowed a dull orange, and then went dark, leaving everyone temporarily blinded. The absence of the lights would place anyone who might later follow them at a distinct disadvantage. As their eyes began to adjust to the darkness, their flashlight beams seemed to make a pitiful glow in the vastness of the dark cavern.

CC rejoined them at the top of the dam and they all moved upstream along a wide ledge that ran along the left side of an underground river. After about a hundred yards, they climbed over a shelf of rock and entered a narrow low-ceilinged tunnel. CC led them around the turn so they were well out of sight of the main tunnel.

Then he insisted they all take time for something to eat while he checked everyone′s gear. "It's an old axiom for soldiers," he told them. "Eat, sleep, and get a shower whenever you have the opportunity." *It's not exactly the way the military phrased it,* CC thought, *but it is certainly more fitting for innocent ears.*

So, in spite of the fact that they were excited and certainly a bit frightened, they all tried to eat something. With the exception of Sarah, they were all despondent. Even for Jonathan, war had lost any possible charm. He had already been thoroughly disillusioned by death, disease, hunger and grief. And now it was coming home to all of them that they were being forced to vacate one of the most wonderful places that could be imagined in this broken land. In spite of any differences they might feel toward one another, none of them wanted to leave this shelter.

Nothing more had been said to mar their fellowship since the night they′d begun the Bible readings, and, for now at least, everyone seemed to be working together.

It's amazing, CC thought, *what a little common adversity can do to bind people together. But we need to face facts. Matters are now out of our control.* He studied each of them, hopelessness evident in their dejected stares, and noted that even Sarah was beginning to reflect their despair.

Strangely enough, he was able to sleep for a few hours, but when he awoke he still felt exhausted and was beside himself with anxiety. He felt that he had to do something, to take some action. *I can't just sit here doing nothing!*

"I'm going to take a look around," he suddenly announced. "Wait here until I return, and try to rest while you can. Whatever happens," he warned them, "we must not get bottled up inside this mountain." Apart from himself, only Jonathan was familiar with the alternate escape route, and CC had told him to keep it to himself, not knowing whom they could trust.

Before he left, CC had sent Jim back to the junction of the tunnels so that he could watch downstream, keeping an eye on the area around the dam. If their enemies did locate the trap door, and make their way down into this tunnel, they would have to run. Without drawing attention to himself, Jonathan had followed Jim, staying out of sight, but monitoring the man's movements. The teenager had good reasons not to trust the man.

CC moved in the opposite direction, and when out of sight, took the tunnel that would lead to the cave where he'd found seven-year-old Sarah a year earlier. It was over a half-mile away.

That cave exited the sheer side of the mountain behind her grandfather's farm on the southwest corner of the valley. Sarah's grandfather had sheltered his wife and granddaughter her in the cavern to protect them both from any possible nuclear fallout. Regrettably, the old man didn't make it back before he was himself exposed to a deadly dose.

When he didn't return to the underground barn, his wife went to search for him and discovered him in their house, just a couple of hundred yards from the cavern. By the time she'd found him, he was too ill to walk with her back to the cave. She spent a lot of time with him, trying to ease his suffering. When she finally returned to the cave, she was also sick with radiation poisoning. She passed away just moments after CC entered the cavern and discovered her with her seven-year old granddaughter.

The distant cave held additional fascination because the elder Sennett not only used it as an emergency shelter, but also to ensure the safety of his livestock during bad weather. It had served as an underground barn. And when CC entered that cave, weeks after the limited nuclear war, he found a variety of discontented animals – small and large – living in the illumination of one 40-watt light bulb.

The Overlook

April 30th, 5:48 p.m.

CC passed through the underground barn and exited the cave at the farm. The entrance was screened by trees and shrubs, and he peered between the branches to study the barn and the burned remains of the house that had once served as the heart of the Sennett farm. There was no one in sight. After walking a few yards he found a steep narrow trail that climbed the steep south wall of the canyon.

Careful to stay behind rock outcroppings and in the shelter of the bushes that grew along the pathway, he climbed about halfway to the top before he found a small ledge from which he could survey the valley below.

There were perhaps a dozen men visible along the north shore of the stream that ran down the center of the valley. Using his binoculars, he spotted another group far down the valley by the narrow entrance. There were another half dozen men much closer to him. They were moving past the huge boulders near the swimming hole. It was no swimming hole now, for the roaring water, nourished by the spring snow melt, had created a wild stream that spread far beyond its regular banks.

The group that was just across from him posed the greatest danger to his little group's security, as they weren't more than a quarter mile from the entrance to the caverns where they were hiding.

The soldiers had started a fire and it looked like they were brewing coffee. *I could sure use a cup of that,* he thought idly. *They obviously believe themselves secure, as they appear very relaxed and indifferent to any possible danger.*

CC studied them. A couple of men had their boots and socks off and were soaking their feet in the slack water of a small cove. Another was lying in the grass, shirt off, taking advantage of the weak sunlight. As far as CC could tell, they had no one keeping watch.

For a moment, he permitted himself to hope that these lax soldiers might somehow overlook his cave, but it proved a forlorn hope. He heard shouting from that direction, and raised his binoculars to look out across the end of the valley.

A soldier was running out of the woods that hid the entrances to CC's caverns. The man was waving his arm and shouting something, but the others obviously couldn't make out his words. One of the men who had been soaking his feet climbed up onto a massive rock formation and shaded his eyes so that he could peer up the valley toward the source of the shouting.

The setting sun is in their eyes, CC realized, *and the noise from the stream is preventing them from making out his words.* He figured that it would be several minutes before the man who was raising the alarm could make his way through the rubble and undergrowth to reach his compatriots.

CC again focused his binoculars on the group by the swimming hole. The two men who had been soaking their feet had pulled on their socks and boots, retrieved their weapons, and were starting up the valley toward the larger group. In their hurry, they left their packs and coffeepot behind.

CC swung his binoculars back up the valley to focus on the soldier who was hurrying toward the stream. His elevation enabled him to see what those below him could not. The man was walking near a copse of thick underbrush and was momentarily hidden from the sight of his comrades. Intent on reaching them, he did not see the shadowy figure that slipped from behind the trunk of a large tree as he passed.

The field glasses gave CC the illusion of being within a few feet of the two men, and as the attacker drew a knife, CC caught himself starting to shout, to warn the soldier of his danger. Even as he realized that he shouldn't want to help his enemy, and that he was, in fact, too far away to be heard, he saw a hand snake out, grab the man around the neck, and jerk him back behind a tree. CC was unnerved by seeing the soldier killed, and was unable to steady the binoculars that were now gripped in shaking hands.

CC tried to comprehend what was going on. Apart from his little group, two competing forces were evidently in competition here. But no matter which group proved the victor, he could see no advantage to his own little community

One thing was certain, however. This place he was hiding was an excellent overlook from which to observe the valley, and he could see things that he never could have seen from the mouths of the caves or the floor of the valley.

The man whom CC thought of as *G.I. Joe* had lowered his victim's body to the ground and was dragging him back into a small meadow. When he reached a tall boulder, he bent down, took the corpse by the ankles, and lowered it head first down into what was obviously an opening in the earth. He then knelt down, laid his rifle on the edge, and dropped down into the hole. He disappeared just before a half dozen well-armed troops drew near.

It was easy to see who was in charge of the troops. In spite of the confusion over the disappearance of a soldier who had just been shouting for their attention, he quickly asserted his leadership. Using hand signals, he ordered his men to fan out into a widely-spaced line along the edge of the stream. Then he raised a walkie talkie to his ear.

CC searched up and down the valley to see who he might be contacting.

Please, God, he prayed, *not a helicopter.*

He noticed that the troops who had been lolling down by the small lake near the bottleneck, over half a mile away, were slowly getting to their feet, picking up their weapons, and starting the long walk up the valley. The guy with the walkie talkie had evidently ordered them to join his troops up here at the west end. CC measured the distance with his eye. It would take them at least fifteen minutes to reach their comrades.

Two other men near the swimming hole suddenly turned at right angles to the stream and dashed toward the long north wall of the valley. They finally dropped to the ground about half way between the stream and the cliffs. In the meantime, the larger group was now standing at wide intervals alongside the stream. A command was shouted, and they turned and began walking toward the woods in the northeast corner of the valley.

Those trees are the only thing standing between their skirmish line and the entrance to my cave, CC thought, trying to hide his bitterness.

The officer in charge had spaced his skirmishers about fifty feet apart, thus forming a line over four hundred feet long. CC thought he understood what they meant to do. As the skirmishers started working their way toward the cliff on the north side of the canyon, each man would examine the ground before him, his eyes probing under bushes and behind rocks, like bird dogs attempting to flush out their prey. If their quarry were to try to slip away, he would find himself under the guns of the two snipers who were hiding off to the right end of the skirmish line.

The troops moved slowly forward, but no alarm was raised, and it was soon apparent that the man they were searching for had somehow disappeared.

CC again looked down the valley to see what progress was being made by the troops at the east end of the valley. They didn't appear to be in any hurry, and CC realized that they'd probably prefer to avoid combat. He began to hope that all of the Americans who had signed on as mercenaries to the Chinese invaders now found their work equally distasteful.

He had been concentrating on the safety of his unknown benefactor, *G.I. Joe*, when he suddenly realized that he was also at risk of being discovered, and was grateful that he was separated from the troops by the swollen stream and probably safe from discovery for the time being.

Dear God, he thought, *how did I get mixed up in a real life action-adventure like this?* He shook his head, half hoping he'd wake up in another time and place. *Truth really is stranger than fiction,* he thought.

Then he spoke out loud. "The whole world has gone to hell in a hand basket, so why shouldn't I find myself running for my life again?"

Hearing his own words, it was as though a pawl had dropped into the notch of a ratchet wheel, and the eternal clockwork that sets the times and seasons of our lives made just one more infinitesimal and immutable clank forward, and in so doing, forever fixed his destiny in time. He stood perfectly still, just one word from his spoken sentence burning into his thought processes.

"Again!"

I'm running for my life again? His mind raced. *So before I woke up in that hospital, I was running for my life? But from whom? And why?*

He tried to order the sequence of events, then shook his head in a vain attempt to drive away the confusion. He just didn't have enough facts. He couldn't remember!

Then, as though to steady him, one portion of scripture after another flitted across the mirror of his mind. "*Be sober, be vigilant; because your adversary the devil, as a roaring lion, walketh about, seeking whom he may devour.*" And a seemingly disparate verse. "*Marvel not, my brethren, if the world hates you.*"

CC found the second passage no more illuminating than the first. Nor did he find comfort in the one that followed. "*Man is born to trouble as sparks fly upward,*" although it brought the memory of smoke and flame to his mind, causing him to mentally reel.

The scene playing out across the valley was forgotten, and he pressed the palms of his hands to his ears as though to shut out the words that were bursting like flames across his consciousness. He felt both confused and anxious. Then the nightmare was dispelled.

They say that misery loves company, but why? There's little comfort in comparing one's miseries with those of others. It may help to put them in perspective, but it certainly doesn't reduce them. He smiled wryly as he again focused his binoculars on the soldiers across the valley. His hands were steadier now. *This definitely wasn't what I had in mind.*

Looking up at the clouds, he again spoke aloud. "How about bringing to my memory a verse like, oh, *Be strong and of a good courage, fear not, nor be afraid of them: for the LORD thy God, he it is that doth go with thee; he will not fail thee, nor forsake thee?* He laughed aloud. "That's the sort of promise I need right now."

And then he wondered, *Where in the world did that passage come from, and how did I spout out that entire verse without faltering?*

And a voice seemed to answer, "Where in the world? Why, nowhere in this world."

Then another verse ran through his mind: "But the Comforter, which is the Holy Ghost, whom the Father will send in my name, he shall teach you all things, and bring all things to your remembrance, whatsoever I have said unto you."

The voice seemed so real that he jumped at the sound and had to look behind him to confirm that he was still alone.

And then he was brought rudely back to the present as his attention was caught by the faraway shout of one of the infantrymen. The soldier seemed to be trying to get his officer's attention. CC was suddenly aware of his own exposure, and sank down behind the boulder against which he'd been leaning.

Those guys might not be able to get across that roaring stream to capture me, he realized, *but a sharpshooter's bullet could easily reach me at this distance.*

CC crouched down behind the large boulder, and rested his elbows atop it to steady the glasses. From this position, perhaps one hundred feet above the valley floor, he was able to focus on the shouting infantryman. The soldier was pointing down at the ground near the tall rock where CC had seen *GI Joe* disappear.

The soldier was quickly joined by several others, and they appeared to know what they were doing. Four men took positions around the spot, as though standing at the corners of a square. Each man stood about ten feet back from the dark area that CC imagined to be a hole in the ground, their weapons pointed down into its depths. They were obviously searching for someone.

One man suddenly pointed down into the hole, then turned his head to shout something at the officer. The officer in turn began haranguing them. One of them knelt and began to climb down into the opening. After a minute or two, another man set his rifle aside and followed the first down.

A moment later, they both reappeared, their arms wrapped around the body of the man who had been ambushed. They were laboring hard to lift the body up over the edge of the hole. One of them climbed back to the surface and knelt there, pulling on the dead man's wrists, while his mate was evidently pushing up from below. CC saw the man kneeling by the hole suddenly release his hold on the dead man's wrists, press his hands to his own chest, and topple headfirst into the hole. A fraction of a second later, CC heard the muffled report of a rifle. The body, and the man in the hole who'd been lifting it, immediately slid down out of sight.

The officer shouted at the other men, gesturing vehemently toward the pothole, but it was obvious that none of them was willing to approach any closer. *So much for the discipline in the new order,* he thought.

Apart from the officer, they were all dressed in filthy, ragged uniforms and looked half-starved. Another man crawled to the edge of the hole, and was pointing his rifle down into the shadows. There was a loud crack as he fired down into the hole, followed more muffled discharges. The rifle slipped from his hands and fell, muzzle first, down into the hole. Then he in turn fell slowly forward, like his comrade before him, following his weapon headfirst into the darkness.

CC realized that there must be some sort of underground tunnel or cavern leading away from the bottom of that pothole. The assassin had to have remained hidden while awaiting his opportunity to fire on the other three men. It followed that he must know a great deal about this valley, and that such a tunnel must serve as a bolt hole from which even now he was probably making his escape.

He shook his head in grudging respect. *G.I. Joe* had already accounted for four of his own enemies, as well as helping to save Jonathan's life. In spite of the fact that he appeared to be working alone, he was obviously smart, fearless, and extremely dangerous.

CC focused the glasses, returning his attention to the soldiers across the stream. The four men who had been standing by the hole were now lying on the ground, but in spite of the threats shouted at them by their officer, none of them would approach any nearer to that hole. CC focused the binoculars on him.

Who can blame them? he reasoned. *There are now three seriously wounded or dead men down in that hole, and it seems probable that hidden somewhere in a tunnel near the bottom, a skilled marksman is waiting for them.*

He could now see that the man he had mistaken for an officer was wearing sergeant's stripes on his sleeve. He had ceased screaming at his men, and instead approached within a couple of yards of the hole. The sergeant positioned himself behind the large boulder, then leaned forward for just an instant to look down into the hole. CC actually saw a bullet take a chip out of the boulder near his head.

The sergeant ducked back, then unhooked something from his belt, and fiddled with it a moment. His men were screaming at him, clearly furious, but he ignored them. He reached around the big boulder, and flipped it down into the hole. Suddenly there was a muffled explosion. Rocks, dirt, and other things that CC dared not guess at, blew out of the hole and fell to the earth around them. The use of a grenade made it clear that, in the hope of killing the assailant, the officer had pretty much ended any possibility that one or more of his own men might have still been alive.

The sergeant again pointed at the hole, ordering another of his men to climb down, but when CC turned his glasses toward him, he could see the man vehemently shaking his head in refusal. The muzzle of his weapon was no longer pointed down toward the hole, but in the direction of the sergeant.

Mutiny? Well, why not? CC thought. *The sergeant has demonstrated nothing but contempt for the lives of his men.*

This time, however, the non-com seemed to exercise a little prudence and tolerated the man's refusal to obey orders. He had obviously pushed his troops too far, and the next step might be to discover that one of his subordinates would be all to happy to shoot him in the back.

With the game temporarily stalemated at the pothole in the ground, CC scanned the surrounding area. The persistent back and neck pain that he'd experienced for as long as he could remember came to his attention, and he tried rolling his shoulders to alleviate it. *I wonder whether I've suffered this all my life,* he asked himself, *or whether it's the result of the constant stress I've lived with since the war began?*

He noticed a couple of troops who had been hiding behind some smaller boulders further downstream. They were well away from the violence and out of their officer's sight. They appeared to be engaged in a heated discussion, for CC could see them waving their hands. After a moment, one of them seemed to nod his head in grudging acquiescence.

Without rising, they twisted their bodies and began crawling down the valley, away from the action. After they'd gone about ten yards they reached the cover of several huge boulders that bordered the stream. Now, well hidden from those who had been involved in the fire fight, they rose to their feet and jogged into the trees that paralleled the log road, remaining out of sight of the other soldiers who were slowly making their way up the log road. It was obvious that they had little taste for this kind of warfare, and had decided to desert.

Two less to worry about, he thought, and then condemned himself for being crass. But the math was undeniably important. His life, and the lives of his friends were in danger.

So, what does that come to? Four dead and two deserters. Six down, and six to go? And the most dangerous of all is the big guy who altered the odds, but he is also the guy who helped Jonathan escape.

CC looked across the stream to where the remaining troops surrounded the hole in the ground, two of them were now lying near the rim of the opening, rifles held awkwardly as they attempted to remain back from the edge, yet somehow aim down into the cavity. The hand grenade should have been the equalizer, and unless the assassin had found some other way out of that pit, he too should be dead. But CC didn't think that he was.

He's still very much alive, and he obviously knows more about this valley than I do. Even as CC continued to study the scene below, his mind wandered. *I wonder who he is, and why he came here? And why is he alone?*

An idea was taking shape on the edge of his consciousness, but it eluded him, and he did not have the luxury of time to pursue it.

CC swung the binoculars to the northwest corner of the valley, searching the distant cliffs for the portals to his caves. He could imagine that he saw a shadow about where the upper tunnel would be located, but it was obscured by brush and vines.

The sun was sinking in the west beyond the top of the cliffs, and CC was now hidden in the shadows, and the risk of discovery had become less of a concern to him.

He wasn′t surprised that the sergeant hadn′t tried to force his remaining men down into the hole to gather their dead. The risk was too great. CC was surprised, however, when the remaining troops didn′t head through the woods toward his caves. He had little doubt that they would have quickly found the entrances. Then he remembered that the first man had been killed before he could report what he had discovered. They still didn't know that the caverns existed.

Still, he reasoned, *it's only a matter of time before they find the entrance and get past the artificial wall that I built to hide the caverns beyond. And that discovery will take their attention off GI Joe and place it squarely on us.*

He made his way back down the narrow trail in the gathering gloom. The last glimpse he had of the ragged squad of soldiers was of the officer withdrawing his men for the night, leading them down the valley toward their camping site by the swimming hole.

Perhaps they don't realize that it wouldn't make any difference what time of day or night they enter the caverns, he thought. *It's perpetual midnight underground. On the other hand, they are certainly shaken by their losses, and that murderous swine who is leading them probably realizes that he needs to let them take a break. Besides, they are probably waiting for reinforcements.*

Our little group is already overwhelmed, even without the enemy bringing in reinforcements, but the additional time they are allowing us will be helpful. One way or another, we need to be well away from here before they arrive.

Into the Abyss

The Caverns
April 30th, 6:55 p.m.

He decided not to reenter the caverns by using the entrance that lay behind the farm, and he succeeded in avoiding detection by making his way back across the west end of the valley under the shadow of the cliffs. He crossed the rocky shoreline where the underground river roared out of the side of the mountain, then passed the old cement kilns that stood at the base of the cliffs.

CC was nearing the entrance to his cave when a lone soldier spotted him through the twilight gloom. As CC ducked into the cavern, he turned to see the man racing after him. He realized that the soldier was fumbling to unsling his weapon while trying to keep up with him, and he put on all the speed he had.

He reached the false wall that he'd built to close off the larger cavern beyond, and fumbled to open the hidden door in the darkness. Slipping through the narrow opening, he purposely left the door slightly ajar. He then ran the length of the tractor-trailer he'd hidden in the tunnel a year earlier, and raced toward the big underground room where they'd built the cottage. He could only hope that the others wouldn't hear their approach or would stay out of sight. CC was carrying a penlight, but extinguished it as soon as he found his way into the dark tunnel that he'd warned everyone to avoid.

He could hear the soldier's boots clattering on the cave floor as raced after him. The beam of the man's flashlight penetrated the darkness, and CC continued moving up the inclined tunnel floor away from him.

To make certain that the soldier was following, he turned his penlight back on for an instant, and a shot immediately rang out. The bullet ricocheted off the cavern wall, and CC found himself breaking out in a cold sweat in spite of the chill of the cavern.

This was the tunnel in which he'd almost lost his life the day he'd discovered these caverns. No longer daring to use his penlight, he slowed to a walk and began sliding his hand along the left-hand wall, hoping to safely bypass the big hole in the floor that lay somewhere ahead on the right side of the tunnel.

CC could hear the soldier cursing as he followed him up the tunnel in the darkness.

It's not an elegant plan, CC thought, *but it's a simple plan, and it's all I've got. I can only hope that he doesn't have a night scope on that rifle.* As he continued taking mincing steps and moving slowly up the tunnel, he could hear the soldier's pace quicken, and realized that the man was gaining on him.

CC was reasonably certain that he had passed the chasm in the floor because the sound of rushing water that ran through the tunnel far below began to fade. He went a few yards further, then decided to cross the tunnel. It was vital that his pursuer stay to the right side of the tunnel, and that meant that CC would have to make such an inviting target of himself that the man would come straight on toward him. In other words, he had to position himself so that the crevasse was between him and the oncoming soldier.

Carefully reaching out the toe of each foot to test the rocky floor, he moved as quickly as he could to the right side of the tunnel. When his hand made contact with the far wall, he knelt down and then lowered himself until he was laying flat on the floor of the cave, facing back toward his pursuer.

He could now see the soldier's silhouette in the backsplash of the flashlight he was carrying, and CC realized he was already dangerously close.

Conscience struck, and he realized that he was double-minded. He didn't really want to be responsible for anyone's death, but he didn't want to become a victim either. So he risked shouting a warning: "You'd better not come any further!"

His words reverberated through the caverns, making it almost impossible for his pursuer to ascertain his position. Nevertheless, his words were immediately answered with a deafening burst from an automatic weapon.

Well, I tried to warn you, CC rationalized. Taking a chance, he cupped a butane lighter in his hand, ignited the flame, and immediately flipped it up in the air toward the hole in the tunnel floor. If he were wrong, he knew it was unlikely that he'd live more than a few seconds. *The momentary glare might be enough to lead the man on,* he thought, *but might also help him target me.*

There was another burst of gun fire, the bullets striking the wall just above CC's head and ricocheting up the tunnel. Since he didn't return fire, the soldier evidently believed that he was either unarmed or dead, and that it was safe to close with him. He began running toward CC's position.

Suddenly the sound of his footsteps ceased. There was a scream of terror, and the scream became a wail as the man plunged downward toward the underground stream far below. A second or two later there was the sound of a distant splash and his scream was snuffed out like a candle. For a few moments CC heard the sound of the man thrashing about in the rushing stream. Then there was just the sound of the stream.

CC was sick to his stomach. He felt both terribly guilty and immensely relieved.

The Best-Laid Plans

The Caverns
April 30th, 7:20 p.m.

CC made a stealthy approach to the place deep in the caverns where he'd left the others. He was worried that enemy troops might already have chased his little group off, or worse, captured or killed them.

But they were still there, all of them, which was unfortunate because Jim had deserted his post near the subterranean dam and rejoined the group, evidently to play politics during his absence.

The underground dam that McCord was supposed to be guarding was a remarkable structure. It lay at the lowest level of the caverns, and impounded a long, narrow lake that ran through the mountain from west to east.

At least, I think the dam is in the lowest level of the caverns, CC thought. *This mountain is so riddled with natural tunnels that it's impossible to tell how many levels there are.*

He had discovered the dam a year earlier. The discovery was the happy result of a near-fatal accident. He had been scraping footings for the cottage that he and Jonathan had been building in a large underground room when a pothole had opened beneath his feet and he had fallen through the floor, landing in a large pool of water about thirty feet below. That pool lay just beneath the dam's spillway, and for a brief period the discovery changed their lives. They were able to install a generator and operate modern electrical appliances such as refrigerator, range, and clothes washer.

It was highly likely that their enemies would soon locate the now year-old cottage. When they did, they'd also probably discover the trapdoor in the floor of the bedroom closet, the trapdoor that hid the stairway leading down to the dam.

The dam itself impounded an underground river that served as the drain for a lake that lay to the west of Hidden Valley. It was a beautiful lake in the center of a vast forest, and was unknown to most people because access was limited by huge tracts of private property.

The underground dam had evidently been built many years before by the Sennett family. The water that crossed the dam's sluiceway powered a waterwheel that had once been used to grind grain and convert limestone to cement.

CC and Jonathan had been able to convert the water power to electricity by hooking up a large, semi-portable generator they had discovered on a trailer behind the hospital at Black River Junction. It had enabled them to operate all sorts of electrical equipment, including a water pump, lighting, home appliances and power tools, and it had made their lives infinitely more comfortable than the lives of most survivors of the recent holocaust.

No one noticed CC as he approached the little group. He stopped just outside the glow of the kerosene lantern that sat on the cave floor in their midst. He remained unseen in the deep shadows and listened as Jim McCord attempted to convince the others that something disastrous had happened to him. McCord's voice came clearly to him.

"As difficult as it is to accept," McCord insisted in his pedantic manner, "he won't be returning."

When CC stepped out into the lantern light, McCord's voice trailed off. He was obviously upset that CC had returned, and probably wondered how much the man that he had been trying to supplant might have overheard. The others, however, all began speaking at once, pleased and excited that he had safely returned.

CC held up his hand to call for silence, totally ignoring McCord, and wasting no time explaining where he had been or what he'd been doing.

"There are enemy troops approaching our caverns, so we have no choice but to leave. If, however, we can create some sort of diversion, it will give us a much better chance to make good our escape."

Never doubting that what CC was saying was true, Rachel asked, "What can we do?"

"We're over a half mile upstream from the narrow east entrance to the valley," he replied. "If we can flood the lower end of the valley, we might be able to keep any more of the bad guys from moving in or out of that bottleneck."

The idea surprised them, but it was McCord, characteristically, who questioned his suggestion.

"How can you do that?" he demanded, his arrogance and contempt thinly veiled.

CC weighed the question carefully before replying. *McCord obviously wants to precipitate a showdown,* he thought, *but this is not the time to go to war with him, though that war might be only moments away.*

So instead of responding in kind, CC treated the sarcasm as though it were a reasonable question, and he offered a quiet and reasonable response, making it clear that he was addressing his explanation to the entire group, not yielding any authority to McCord.

"We cannot remain here any longer. There's a squad of soldiers in the valley and more are on the way. They'll soon know where the entrance to our caves are. We need to slow them down and try to leave them with no reason to hang around here."

CC's even-tempered response momentarily disarmed McCord, and he went on without interruption.

"It was something I considered doing some time back," CC continued, "but I kept putting it off because I didn't want to destroy the electrical power plant. In retrospect, it seems as though it might have been a good trade-off."

He had anticipated the looks of confusion that appeared on their faces and began to elaborate.

"If I had carried out my plan, it might have discouraged people from entering the valley. On the other hand, it would also have raised the question of who or what caused the flooding, so it might have drawn their attention anyway. And it would definitely have cost us the convenience of having our own electrical power plant."

"That seems like a small trade-off," McCord snapped in derision, "if successfully pulling off such a thing were possible."

Rachel winced. It was becoming increasingly clear to everyone that McCord was being intentionally confrontational rather than seriously addressing the practical challenges facing the group as a whole.

"It might seem so," CC replied evenly, "but keep in mind that the electricity served us by pumping and heating our water, operating our appliances, and keeping us warm. In short, it provided all of the comforts and conveniences of our pre-war lives. He was silent for a moment, which helped punctuate the obvious. Understanding came into the faces of the others.

Rachel voiced the loss for all of them. "We're not apt to enjoy such luxuries again."

"No," CC responded. "Having a source of electricity kept us from moving back into the 19th century in terms of comfort, convenience, leisure time, and health." He shrugged.

"Well, we don't have the time or luxury to cry over spilled milk," he continued. The bad guys are here." Even as he spoke, he was excoriating himself for not having made that trade-off earlier. *Better to have lived without electricity,* he reasoned, *than to have made it easier for the enemy to enter the valley.*

Oddly, Elizabeth would have none of CC's apology. She saw a flaw in his reasoning, and wanted to encourage him.

"First," she said, "you are right. This is no time for regrets. Besides, you've done a wonderful job, and if we hadn't had the electricity, we would have had to cut and burn firewood, and that would certainly have attracted attention."

Everyone but Jim nodded agreement, and it made CC feel better to realize that they were on his side.

But Elizabeth wasn't quite through, and she asked the question that was on all their minds.

"But how would destroying our source of electricity help keep the enemy out of the valley? I don't think that any of us makes the connection."

"Do you remember the huge slopes of scree and loose rock along the side of the valley at the bottleneck?" he asked.

Before he could continue, McCord interrupted him, still with that surly contempt in his voice.

"Sure we remember. There are mountains of rotting stone on both sides of the entry. In fact, my cave" he said in a superior voice, "is just a short way up the valley from there on the south wall."

He seemed to have forgotten that CC had already pinpointed the location of his cave. McCord's memory wasn't that faulty. Did he think that everyone else's was? Elizabeth's certainly wasn't.

"We all know where your wonderful cave is located, Jim. Perhaps you should go there now, and resume living the high life, while leaving us to our fate."

But McCord ignored her and went on in his overbearing manner. "The cliffs are disintegrating, and the fallen rock forms steep slopes of scree beneath them. That's why I avoided the bottleneck. It's ready to collapse." He sounded like a self-important lecturer reiterating the obvious to a group of sophomores.

"Correct!" CC snapped, realizing that his temper as well as their time was growing short. "The first thing anyone finds after passing into this valley through the bottleneck is the lake. Vehicles can just get around on the north edge of the lake by following the narrow logging road that lies at the base of those mountains of rock, although men on foot may also get around the left side through the narrow strip of woods that your cave looks down on."

"How do you know where my cave is?" McCord demanded.

CC laughed, but still made an effort to maintain the peace. "I told you months ago exactly where your cave is located." Then he added unnecessarily, "I know a good deal about this valley."

"Yes, I suppose you do," McCord grudgingly conceded. "Have you been sneaking around behind my back, checking up on me?"

"No," CC snapped, his patience fraying. "Though it was certainly justified. Besides, what could possibly interest us?"

"We can discuss your paranoia later. What about the end of the valley?" McCord challenged.

That was my line, CC thought. He held McCord's eyes until the other man finally broke and turned away, and CC continued. "If we can dynamite those cliffs, the fallen rock might close off the entry road and maybe even dam the culvert pipe at the end of the lake."

McCord shook his head, offering a mocking smile for what he wanted the others to perceive as CC's impossibly stupid plan.

CC ignored him. "If," he persisted, "we can create an earth dam that closes off the bottleneck, that entire end of the valley will fill with water."

Everyone except McCord was obviously intrigued by the idea, and CC ignored him and pressed on.

"At this time of year, there's already an enormous amount of water flowing down the valley. If we can destroy the underground dam here at the west end of the valley, and simultaneously create an earth dam by blowing down the cliffs, we may succeed in creating a lake at the east end of the valley. Once the lower end of the valley floods with water, any overflow will be channeled down the narrow bottleneck. Hopefully, that would keep people out at least long enough for us to make our escape."

All the while he was speaking, McCord had been shaking his head in an exaggerated fashion.

"Any thoughts?" CC asked, looking directly at McCord.

"Yeah, what's to keep them from bringing people in by helicopter?"

"Nothing, except the only copter I've seen so far is a two placer, and therefore they can only bring one or two men at a time, and not much equipment.

"McCord looked like he was going to say something more, but turned away.

"Of course," CC offered, "we not only have to blow the dam here, but we'd also have to simultaneously set off a number of charges on both sides of the bottleneck at the far end of the valley."

McCord sat there, again shaking his head slowly from side to side, but now everyone ignored him. He'd made no friends in this little company.

"For the plan to work," CC continued, "we must accomplish three things." He held up his index finger. "First, we must destroy the dam here in the cavern." A second finger was raised. "Then we must create a dam at the far end of the valley by blowing the cliffs down into the bottleneck. And third," he concluded, we must bring down enough rock and dirt to fill the end of the lake and seal off the culvert pipe that drains it."

He examined each face, his own lips forming a wry smile. "And," he added. "if that's not asking enough, we have to accomplish those three little miracles at pretty much the same moment. The problem is that, while I'm down the valley setting the charges there, someone here will have to blow up this dam."

Jonathan had been absent during the beginning of this discussion because, immediately after CC's return, he'd walked down the tunnel to check the area around the dam. He returned just as CC began speaking about dynamiting the dam. When CC saw him, he smiled and asked, "Everything okay out there?"

"So far," the teen answered, looking accusingly at McCord. "I was just wondering why Mr. McCord left his post a half-hour ago?

"How could you know that?" McCord challenged.

"Because I was standing at the end of this tunnel, and I could see you standing on the dam."

"So?"

"So, I saw you searching the area with your flashlight, then you took off running up the river walk."

"Well kid," McCord responded, "not that it's any of your business, but I had some personal business of my own to attend to."

"Yes, I saw that, too. You were carrying a package, and you took it up another tunnel."

"Your eyes must have been fooling you in the dark, kid. I didn't take anything anywhere." Then, in a bullying tone, "You'd better watch what you say about me in front of others, or it could go hard on you."

"That's enough! CC snapped. I won't have you trying to intimidate anyone here."

McCord subsided, but continued to scowl at Jonathan, obviously trying to do exactly that.

The teen ignored him, causing the man to seethe.

CC, on the other hand, directed his attention to McCord instead of returning to the discussion of his plan.

"What's with you, Jim? You seem to hate everybody."

"Yeah," he half joked. "I hate everyone regardless of race, color, ethnic background, national origin, religion, or sexual orientation."

"Sadly, I almost believe that."

"In point of fact, I only hate certain groups."

"Such as?"

"Christians and Jews."

"So that's why you were angry that we were reading the Bible."

"Absolutely."

"Okay, that covers Christians. Why Jews?"

"Because most of the problems in the world were caused by Jews."

The remark left them all speechless.

It was Jonathan who broke the silence. He sounded very adult, very cold, even dangerous.

"So what did the Jews do to you?" he asked.

"Nothing special. But I've studied them, and Hitler was right. The world would be better off without them."

Jonathan was suddenly shaking with anger. "That's it! I've had enough of you. You're evil!"

He snapped his rifle to his shoulder and pressed the muzzle against McCord's ear, and CC was afraid to touch the teen for fear the lad would pull the trigger.

He spoke very softly.

"Jonathan."

The boy didn't seem to hear him.

"Jonathan?"

"I'm going to kill him."

"Jonathan. If you murder him, what makes you any different than him?"

"That's easy. It would be like killing a mad dog."

"No, Jonathan. I don't disagree that he might deserve killing, but we must not lower ourselves to his level."

"You don't understand!"

"What don't I understand?"

"My great-grandparents...." The boy choked, and there were tears in his eyes.

"What about your great-grandparents?"

"The died in the gas chambers at Auschwitz."

"Oh, dear God," Rachel whispered.

McCord screamed, "Get that kid away from me!"

CC ignored him.

"So you're Jewish, Jonathan?"

"On my father's side."

"Well that's just fine, son. We're honored that one of God's chosen people – a Messianic Jew, and a descendant of those who suffered under the Nazi evil – is part of our company."

Tears ran down Jonathan's cheeks, and he pressed the muzzle of the rifle so hard against McCords ear that his head was pressed down against his shoulder. "I've got to do this."

"No, Jonathan!" It was his little shadow, Sarah who spoke. "You would be a murderer. I don't want my big brother to be a murderer."

"I'm not your brother," he sniffed.

"You are my big brother. Jesus said so."

The boy was silent, but he moved the muzzle of his weapon about an inch from McCord's head.

CC put his hand gently on the teen's shoulder. It's okay, Jonathan. Remember, "Vengeance is mine; I will repay, saith the Lord."

The boy turned to look at him. "What vengeance did God take against the Nazis for the millions of people they murdered?" But after a moment the boy submitted, stepped away, and pointed the barrel of his rifle at the ceiling of the cave. While everyone remained stunned by what had just transpired, Jonathan got down on his knees so that he was eye-to-eye with Sarah. He put his arm around her, and said, "Thanks, sis."

"I love you, Jonathan."

"I love you too, sweetheart."

With that situation temporarily defused, CC turned back to the issue at hand, but not before warning McCord.

"Open your mouth once more, and we'll hold a trial right here." Then he turned back to the others.

"Let me recap. I want to try to dam the lake at the end of the valley. In order to have enough water to fill the resultant dam quickly, we'll also have to destroy this dam.

"You mean our dam?" Jonathan asked. "If we destroy the dam, we'll lose our electrical power and everything."

"That's right," CC answered, "but I'm afraid it's already too late to save our little home. And, if we don't make this sacrifice, we'll lose everything anyway." CC searched the faces of each of them in turn. They all understood that he was referring to losing more than their home and supplies.

"Look," CC said. "You've had no way of knowing this, but there are two groups of enemies out in the valley."

"Jonathan suggested that possibility," Elizabeth said, surprising him, "but Jim laughed him down."

"Well, Jonathan was right," CC confirmed. "I saw the big guy who paid us a visit last winter, and he's obviously opposed to the soldiers.

"You're talking about my new friend, 'G.I. Joe,'" Jonathan guessed.

They were all startled by his remark.

"He's the one who saved my life when I was hiding up in my crow's nest," the boy explained.

His statement brought a look of surprise to the faces of the two women, but clearly shook McCord's composure.

CC's next statement seemed to bring a look of fear to McCord's face.

"I saw him kill four of the men from the other group."

"Nonsense!" McCord said, but with little conviction.

"Nonsense? I actually saw him kill them," and CC tapped the binoculars that hung from his neck. "He's one very clever and very dangerous man, I can tell you that."

For once, Jim did not argue with him.

"What did this 'big guy' look like?" he demanded.

As CC described him, McCord's face paled, but no one noticed the change in the dim light of the tunnel.

"I don't know why he's after those other soldiers," CC mused, "but I suspect that, like us, he hasn't been conforming to their demands."

"It doesn't really matter what his reasons are," Jonathan commented, bringing them all back to reality. "If he led them here, our security is gone."

"He does seem to know a lot about this valley," CC commented. "I saw him jump down a hole in the ground near the stream, and it soon became clear that it opens on an underground passage of some kind."

"What do you think they're doing now," Elizabeth asked.

CC held his watch toward the lantern and tried to focus on its face. "It's past eight o'clock," he finally replied. "I saw the squad making camp as the sun was going down, so I think we'll be safe from them until early tomorrow morning."

"Why do you think they gave up the hunt?" Jonathan asked.

CC took a moment to answer. "The troops that were doing the fighting were obviously angry and frustrated. They had suffered four dead, plus two more who I saw deserting. And the sergeant in charge had to realize that his men were ready to kill him"

"Why would they be angry?" McCord asked in a mocking voice.

"Because he threw a hand grenade into the hole where several of his men were laying either either wounded or dead."

"Why would he do a thing like that?" Rachel asked incredulously.

CC gave an ironic laugh. "Because the guy that we've been calling *GI Joe* had been hiding down in that hole, and shot two of them when they obeyed the orders he gave them. Then, when his men began refusing to go near the hole, instead of venturing into it himself, the sergeant simply threw a hand grenade into the hole."

They were all struck dumb by CC's account of the sergeant's cold-blooded behavior. Even the atheist McCord muttered, "My God!"

Elizabeth caught CC's eye. "So that's why you think they are holding up the search?"

"That and the fact the officer is almost certainly waiting for reinforcements. And he probably expects them to arrive first thing in the morning." CC gnawed his lip. "Even if they don't already know about us, they'll keep searching for the guy who killed their comrades, and sooner or later they are bound to stumble onto our hideaway."

Rachel had been sitting on the cave floor, a blanket wrapped about her. "What do you think we ought to do?"

"One thing's certain," CC replied. We can't stay here." He had a habit of grinding his teeth, and it was obvious that he was doing so now. He looked around at their faces. "I'm sorry," he said. "We have no place left to hide."

Elizabeth nodded her understanding. They all appeared despondent.

"Perhaps if we destroy the dam as you suggest," Elizabeth offered, "it will discourage them." She sighed. "Maybe they'll think there's no reason to search further."

"I hope so," CC replied, "but I honestly doubt it."

He was mentally exhausted, and barely able to respond in a civil tone to what he considered inane conversation.

And if we are able to blow down those cliffs, he thought, *they'll search long and hard to find us. They won't like it at all that someone had both the explosives and the know-how to accomplish such a task. They won't want their enemies running around with that kind of potential, and they will wonder what we were trying to accomplish, or what we were trying to hide.*

He exhaled audibly.

"I will be the first to admit that destroying the dam and blowing those cliffs at the end of the valley represents an almost impossible challenge."

"Then why attempt it?" McCord demanded.

"As I was saying," CC went on, visibly controlling his temper, "it's almost an impossible challenge, but it's a necessary one. And, as someone once said, 'All things are possible to certain individuals.'"

"And who might those certain individuals be?" McCord sneered. "You?"

CC stared at him for a moment, but before he could answer, Rachel replied.

"All things are possible to them that believe."

McCord turned his malice on her.

"And you think you are one of those *certain individuals?*" McCord mocked. "A believer?"

CC had reached the end of his patience. Raising his voice slightly he said, "Shut up, Jim! I won't tell you again. Shut your mouth and keep it shut until you are spoken to." He waited for some sign that McCord would submit. "Do you understand me?"

He stared unblinking at McCord until the man looked away. Then he went on. "The problem is that, if we pull it off, it will seem like a very impressive piece of work to our enemies, something that only trained explosives' experts might accomplish. So, they'll want to find the people who did it. In fact," he added, "it might result in their trying to bring a lot more men here."

Jim looked up, about to make another acidic remark, but CC's icy stare forestalled him.

It was Elizabeth who spoke. "If they'll react by bringing a lot more men here, why go to the trouble?"

"Because," CC added with a false brightness, "it may hold them up for a day or two, and provide us time to get away undetected."

Jim was staring at the floor. He was clearly hesitant to say anything, but doggedly shook his head.

But Elizabeth persisted. "I don't understand. What difference will that make? Why not just go now?"

"Because they've got a lot of men out there who will soon be searching through these caverns, and without question, they will follow us when we leave. Unlike us, they have a supply chain, and at least one helicopter. They have sources of food and weapons, and those supplies can be delivered to them in any handy meadow by air. We, on the other hand, have to carry everything we might need on our backs. They will not burdened...," and he looked at Sarah, and hesitated while he framed his thoughts. "Those men will not be burdened with women and children, or with carrying medical supplies and food and clothing and other survival gear. We, on the other hand, must carry everything we can in order to survive even in the short-term."

He realized that he might be frightening them, but he was so tired he could scarcely think. He rubbed his eyes. "We need to create a diversion that will provide us with at least six or eight hours head start," he said. "We need enough time to get ten or twelve miles through the forest before they work their way through these caverns to follow us. We need a day's head start, not a few minutes. That's why we've got to try."

It was clear that CC was adamant and intended to attempt this, but they were only marginally satisfied with his explanation.

"Well, what good will that diversion do?" Elizabeth pursued. "How will that slow them down?"

McCord was still looking at the cave floor, but he wore a slight smile.

"It's not just slowing them down that is important," CC answered. "If we blow the dam, it will deprive them of the generator. Electrical power – particularly electrical power that is generated without fossil fuels – would offer them an enormous advantage. They could hide an army inside these caverns, and even an atom bomb wouldn't dislodge them. And the electric generator would run their communications systems and lighting."

He realized that he was raising his voice, and he fought to maintain his temper. *I've earned their trust,* he thought. *Why do I have to fight for it?* Then he noticed McCord's sly smile.

He's smiling because he thinks that they don't trust my judgment. How can a man of such intelligence be so oblivious of people's feelings?

In the months since McCord had stumbled on their cave, he'd been nothing but trouble. At this juncture, none of the others appeared to have any respect for him at all. CC wanted to say something to McCord, but he realized it would be an exercise in futility, so he picked up the discussion where he'd left off.

"If we succeed," he replied in a voice made sad because of the necessity of having to explain this to a group whose trust he'd felt he'd earned, "we may be responsible for drowning a few of those men out in the valley who are hunting us. But they are here to take away our liberty, and even our lives. So we need have no regrets."

The women nodded their heads in agreement, while Jonathan gave an enthusiastic "Amen."

"On the other hand," CC continued, "we might interrupt their shaky communications with their base. And we'll make it more difficult for them to regroup and enter the valley to reach the caverns, and to search for us. And, finally," he concluded, "if we create a lake that goes from cliff to cliff at the east end of the valley, we will keep them from bringing more people in on foot or by vehicle."

"So what?" Jonathan asked, earning a smile from McCord.

That angered CC.

"So what? They'll have to use their small helicopter to bring in one or two men at a time, plus minimal supplies. While they're doing that, they can't be chasing us. It could take them quite a while to get a viable force together, and that will assure us of more time to get away. And," he added, "if they are using the copter to ferry people into the valley, they can't be using it to search for us."

Everyone but McCord nodded his understanding.

"That's a lot of ifs," he mumbled.

"And that's the last time you'd better open your mouth without permission," CC warned.

McCord didn't seem prepared to challenge those words, and he subsided from further comment.

"Well, it is obviously a lot of ifs, as Jim pointed out," Rachel put in, "but it seems clear to me that we must attempt it." Then she added in a near whisper, "God help us!"

"Yes, we've got to try," Elizabeth agreed.

McCord snorted.

Elizabeth turned to him, and saw him gazing at her with loathing, as though she were a traitor who'd changed colors.

She intuited McCord's thoughts, and with some surprise realized that she had changed significantly since she had met him three months earlier. She no longer felt intimidated by him. She smiled to herself. *It feels pretty good.*

Rachel looked at CC. "So, who's this *we* that you're referring to?"

"Hm, what?" he asked somewhat distracted, for he had been trying to decipher the exchange of looks between McCord and Elizabeth, wondering whether this was a case of thieves falling out.

"Oh, yes, the *we*," he acknowledged, mentally replaying the conversation. "Well, that's the problem."

He rubbed his eyes and gazed off into infinity, attempting to make his weary mind work, scarcely aware that he'd moved from rubbing his eyes to scratching his two-day growth of beard.

"There's no way around it," he mused.

"No way around what?" Elizabeth persisted.

He dragged his eyes back to focus on her.

"It will take two of us to get this done." He gnawed his lip. "We can place the dynamite charges on the dam here now. Then one of you will have to detonate the charges at the agreed on time. In the meantime, I'll have to get to the far end of the valley, set the charges in the cliffs on both sides of the bottleneck, then be prepared to detonate them at the same time that you set off the explosives here."

As he spoke, he was using a stone to scratch a map of the valley in the fine silt on the cave floor. Pointing at his crude drawing, he indicated the area where the steep slopes of scree hung above the log road, then moved his finger to a point on the southeast corner of the valley where Jim's cave was located.

"We will have to blast thousands of tons of rock and dirt across the end of the valley, and especially into the mouth of the culvert pipe. If I can close off the bottleneck" – and he emphasized his point by scratching back and forth across the place where the valley narrowed and the small lake flowed into a massive culvert pipe – "we might create a large enough lake to flood the lower end of the valley and prevent vehicular traffic in or out."

As CC outlined the plan, he realized that he was repeating himself. A couple of them nodded their heads in understanding, but Jim stood aloof, his very posture an expression of contempt.

"What happens to the person who sets off these explosives?" Rachel asked, refusing to accept CC's declaration that it was his job. "Does he or she drown with Pharaoh's army when the sea rises?"

There was uncomfortable laughter.

"No," CC answered. "I plan to climb to Jim's cave before I detonate the explosives.

"That all sounds simple enough in theory," Rachel persisted, "but implementing it might be something else again. Do you have the skills necessary to accomplish it?"

"It's got to be me," CC answered flatly.

"Well, none of us would question that," Elizabeth replied. "Your success in building this wonderful home-away-from-home," and she smiled at her little joke, "should convince everyone that you can accomplish anything you set your mind to. The problem is," she pursued, "that we can't afford to lose you. You're indispensable!"

"Flattery will get you everywhere," CC intoned piously. And that brought another polite laugh, except from Jim who simply uttered a flat, "Ha, ha."

Jonathan surprised everyone by challenging CC. "I bet you've never handled explosives in your life, have you?"

CC didn't have an opportunity to respond before the boy continued.

"Because," he stated emphatically, "I have!"

They all looked at him in surprise, doubt on the women's faces, disdain on McCord's, but Jonathan went on undaunted.

"My dad's mushroom business was very successful. We owned over fifty acres of mountainside, and when we needed more space to accommodate larger crops, we blasted through the rock to make more tunnels. I've been drilling holes and setting explosives charges since I was twelve years old."

"And your point is?" CC asked in a very quiet voice.

"My point is that I know how to do what needs to be done, and you don't." Then he realized that he might have overstepped his bounds and grew silent.

"Well, Jonathan, I guess you've answered the question."

"What question?"

"Who's the other person?"

"So I'll go down the valley and plant the charges."

"No. I'll go down the valley. You'll stay here and blow up the dam."

"That's not right," the boy argued. I know how to do it. You don't. And not only that, I could also set the charges here before I go down the valley."

Rachel turned to CC, "You can't let him try that! It's too dangerous."

"You're right," he agreed. "I can't let him go down the valley and attempt that."

Jonathan's look had changed from hopeful to belligerent.

"On the other hand, I can't reject his help either." Jonathan's head snapped up, hope again illuminating his eyes.

"Jonathan, you'll stay here, and set the charges on the dam." The boy's disappointment was unmistakable.

"I'll be glad for you to help me set the charges here, but it will be your exclusive responsibility to detonate them. I'll be the one who goes down the valley. And," he hesitated, trying to carefully shape his thoughts, "if I don't get back... in time, you'll lead our little family out through our secret passage."

"Why shouldn't I lead the group?" Jim whined.

CC wanted to say, *Because we can't trust you,* but he decided that wouldn't be prudent, so he answered, "Because Jonathan knows where everything is hidden, and he knows the way out. It's complicated."

Then he realized that they all needed to know the truth, and he backtracked, "No, that's not really it."

He moved to within a few inches of McCord. Their eyes locked, and CC spoke very quietly. "You can't lead because we can't trust you."

That statement was met with silence, but there was no mistaking the malice on McCord's face.

Jonathan interrupted, indifferent to his discomfort. "When do you plan for us to do this?"

"Just a few hours from now, about three tomorrow morning, hopefully before the bad guys are up and around. It will mean a tough night for all of us."

Jim mumbled, "I don't agree with this, so don't plan on my help."

"This isn't a democracy, Jim."

"So I noticed. It seems to be more of a popularity contest."

"If it were, it's not one you'd be apt to win," snapped Elizabeth. Having begun, she couldn't seem to hold back her contempt. "Are you always going to let other people do your dirty work for you?"

"As often as possible, yes," he answered flatly. His unexpected confession, though it should have embarrassed him, was the first that they considered honest. But he didn't stop there. "Since I don't want any part of this, and I'm completely opposed to this plan, nobody is going to make me do any of the dirty work."

Rachel stared at him with contempt. "If it's any comfort to you, none of us has ever counted on you for anything."

Jonathan diverted their attention by grasping CC's arm, the fever of adventure in his eyes. "I can do it." He was not discouraged by the momentary confusion in CC's eyes. "I mean it," Jonathan said. "I should be the one to blow the cliffs. It will be more difficult than the dam, and I'm young, strong, and know what I'm doing."

That may be, CC thought, *but you're not going down that valley, kid. I want you alive tomorrow morning!*

But that's not what he said to the teenager. He sought to maintain an even voice as he attempted to appease the eager youngster.

"I'm sure you are young, strong, and knowledgeable, Jonathan, but those gifts don't make any difference."

"Why not?" the boy asked, disappointment warring with rebellion.

"Because that valley is full of heavily armed, highly trained, very nasty men, and I'm not sending a teenager to do my job."

"Teenagers are who they send to fight wars."

"Teenagers *were* sent, yes. Past tense. But they were under the command of older men. And I sometimes thought it was the politicians who should have gone in their place."

He wrapped his arm around the boy's shoulders, cupped his chin in his hand, and forced his head around so that the teen's eyes were just a few inches from his own. He smiled sadly at the boy. "Thank you, Jonathan. You're one in a million, and I couldn't be more proud of you, but this is my job to do."

The boy stared back, tears in his eyes. He knew better than anyone how poor CC's chances were of pulling this off, let alone of his returning to the caverns. And CC had become like a father to him. This was a bitter time, a time that would probably end with their being separated forever.

The boy forced a smile, then said, "Okay, CC. Whatever you say."

"I think I can handle the other job," CC continued, without much conviction in his voice. He threw his poncho on the damp floor and seated himself near the others.

"I'll go out of the tunnel by the Sennett farm, sneak down the along the south side of the valley, work around the east end beyond Jim's cave, and set the charges."

"What about being caught?" Rachel asked. "You said there are still at least six of them."

"I'll be on the south side of the stream," he replied. They have all gathered around the big boulders on the north shore near the swimming hole, a long way from where I'll be setting the charges. The stream is more like a wild river now, flooding the low ground and actually flowing over the log road in places. I think they'll be more concerned with staying on high ground, and right now there's no way they can get from the north side of the stream to the south without going around either end of the valley. What's more, I don't think anyone will see me in the dark."

He began planning aloud. "We'll need all of the dynamite that Sennett had stored in the cavern near the farm. You'd better go get it, Jonathan, then we'll talk some more."

"Okay," the teen replied.

"I'll go along to help him carry everything," Elizabeth offered, thinking the boy might decide to head out on his own once he had the explosives. CC gave her a nod of thanks as she turned to catch up with Jonathan.

Rachel looked up at CC. "Do you really think that Jonathan can handle dynamite?"

"Yes. Far better than I can."

The two of them returned about an hour later and told CC that they had actually exited the tunnel to check out the farm. They were concerned because they had seen a man sitting in the barn, reading by lantern light, but they didn't think he'd seen them. Jonathan thought it might have been G.I. Joe.

The two of them had immediately returned to the subterranean barn, where they found two cases of dynamite, a box of detonators, a coil of blasting wire, and a magneto to fire them.

McCord risked asking, "What was the farmer doing with all these explosives?"

Elizabeth wheeled on him. "You have a great deal of curiosity for someone who refuses to become involved."

Jonathan answered. "The Sennetts business was mining cement. They needed the dynamite for that work. The problem is that it might be pretty old."

"What's wrong with that?" Elizabeth asked.

"It becomes unstable over time."

McCord's loud laugh rolled around the cave.

Jonathan was annoyed by the unnecessary racket, and put his hands to his ears to indicate the risk of their voices carrying through the caverns. Surprisingly McCord subsided.

There had only been a little desultory conversation while Elizabeth and Jonathan had been away getting the explosives. When they returned, Sarah awakened and they heated a few cans of soup. While they were eating, the women discussed with Jonathan where they might situate themselves when he detonated the explosives.

After that, Elizabeth headed back toward the farm to make certain that none of the bad guys came up the south side of the canyon and discovered that entrance to the caverns.

Jonathan and CC sat down apart from the group to estimate how much dynamite each of them would require, then divided the explosives into two piles. CC knelt on the floor of the cave, conversing with Jonathan as an equal. In this matter, however, there was no question that the boy was now in charge. "I'll need a quarter of the dynamite to blow the dam," he told CC. "You'll need the magneto to detonate your charges." He seemed to be working things out in his head, step by step. "I'll figure some way to detonate the explosives here."

"What if something goes wrong?" CC asked.

"Better hope it doesn't. I guess I could always try hooking up a bunch of flashlight batteries in series."

CC meant, *What happens if one of us blows himself up?* but decided the question was superfluous. *I'm more apt to blow myself up,* he concluded.

So he instead asked, "Okay, what's next?"

"After you've set your charges," he told CC, "You should climb up to Jim's cave and detonate them from there. I'll need two hundred feet of cable to do my job. You'd better take all the rest. There's well over twelve hundred feet on the coil that we brought from the farm."

Elizabeth assisted them by helping pack the explosives in watertight plastic bags and putting them in two separate backpacks. CC inserted his small emergency overnight packet into his knapsack, along with the dynamite, detonators, wire, and magneto. Altogether, it weighed about fifty pounds. He taped the sheath of his knife to his ankle, and strapped a belt and holster containing a handgun around his waist. He could barely carry the lot, so he quickly removed a bottle of water and the cooking implements from the emergency pack, keeping only two energy bars, a space blanket, fire-making tools, and a small first-aid kit. Frowning, he removed the gun belt, and set it atop the rejects. The loaded gun and holster was simply too heavy, and if he were to run into any of their enemies, it was unlikely that it would improve his chances of completing his mission.

He looked up from his chore to speak to the boy.

"Jonathan."

The boy looked up, sensing the gravity in his voice. "I want you to understand, this is not a suicide mission."

The boy looked away without speaking.

"Do you understand me?" CC was emphatic.

The boy toed the ground.

"Do you understand me?" CC repeated.

The boy frowned.

"If I can't count on you to obey my instructions to the letter, then I'll have to count you out."

Then, so quiet CC almost didn't hear the grudging response, Jonathan whispered, "Okay, but what about you? Is it a suicide mission for you?"

CC ignored the question, and continued.

"If we run into trouble, we throw down our weapons and surrender. Is that clear?"

The boy just stared at him.

"Is that clear?"

Before Jonathan got an opportunity to respond, Elizabeth came running back down the tunnel.

"A couple of soldiers have discovered the underground barn behind Sennett's farm," she gasped, out of breath.

"All right, let's go," CC said.

They all got to their feet, scrambling about, picking up their possessions, turning on their flashlights, and heading for the walkway that skirted the stream above the dam. Their only hope was that the men hunting them would get lost in the labyrinth of tunnels between the farm and the dam. CC was now sorry that he had marked the turns with fluorescent paint in order to keep from getting lost.

Elizabeth helped Jonathan carry his share of the explosives down the river walk toward the dam. They arrived out of breath, and she sat down to rest while he rushed down the stairway to the base of the dam where the generator was located. He hit a switch and the lights came on.

When he returned to the top of the dam, most of them had their flashlights on. CC knelt down beside him. He had to shout to be heard, the roar of falling water making normal conversation all but impossible.

"Well, Jonathan, that's that!"

"What do you mean. 'That's that'?" the boy shouted back.

"The plan was for me to exit the cavern at the farm, then head east down the side of the valley, but, as you know, the bad guys are in those tunnels now." Then CC pointed toward the end of the dam where a wooden staircase led up to the next level. "And I can't go up the stairs to our cottage and out that tunnel, because there's an entire squad camping near there. So there's no way out. I'm stuck here."

It didn't take a genius to see that Jonathan was again angry because their plans appeared thwarted.

"I can do it!" the boy repeated insistently.

"Jonathan, your pride exceeds your reason and experience."

"No! You should listen to me, CC!" There were tears of frustration in the boy's eyes. "I've been right more often than you, and I know I'm right now."

CC stared sadly into the distance.

"See!" the boy shouted. "You aren't even trying to deny it."

CC turned back to him. "I didn't realize you felt that way."

"Well, I do," the boy responded.

CC didn't pick up on the uncertainty in Jonathan's voice because his own pride was bruised by the boy's seeming contempt. And his repeated response simply hardened the boy's resolve.

"Jonathan, your pride exceeds your reason."

"You should listen to me, CC! I've been right a lot of the time, and I know I'm right now."

CC's next words simply escalated the conflict.

"Let me offer you a little home-grown proverb."

"I don't need any more Bible."

CC gazed sadly at the teen. Then, after a very long moment, he said, "It's not from the Bible. It's just something I thought up from my own experience."

"So?" the boy replied, his contempt adding fuel to the fire.

"Okay, it goes like this. *Trusting a bridge of pride is a very dangerous way to cross a river of fire.*"

Ironically, it would be quite some time before CC remembered this conversation and realize that he should have applied his proverb to his own pride. Instead he blustered on.

The boy gave him a look of disgust. His love and respect for this man were temporarily forgotten. He was driven by a belief that he had to be the hero of the day.

"Look, Jonathan," CC struggled to explain. "Since I can't get past those guys in the tunnel from the farm, we'll have to give up this plan and just try to escape. And we'd better do it soon, because they might take a turn that brings them out between us and our bolt hole at the back of the mountain."

The teen didn't appear to be listening. He suddenly leapt to his feet, scooped up CC's backpack and threw it over the railing, then leapt out into space to follow the backpack down into the pool below.

Everyone stood frozen in place, stunned by the boy's action, trying to comprehend the disaster that had overtaken them. Then CC found himself following the boy over the edge of the dam, the end of a rope gripped loosely in one hand.

The View Beneath the Dam

Hidden Valley
April 30th, 10:03 p.m.

Immediately after CC broke the surface of the water, he was swept out and away from the base of the dam. He tried to swim against the current, but it was nothing like the lazy summer stream he'd found himself in when he'd fallen through the pothole in the cave floor months earlier, and that was terrifying enough.

Things look a lot different from down here in the water than they did when I was standing on top of the dam, CC thought. *My perspective has changed from one of detached interest to one of absolute terror.*

He was floating in the pool below the dam, and although the surface looked smooth, he was just a few yards from a torrent fed by winter snow melt and spring rains. He was being rolled over and over, and he realized that he was being drawn toward the whirlpool that lay just downstream.

When he had viewed the whirlpool from above, CC had concluded that it was caused by the water being sucked down into a subterranean cavern. He pictured it like the drain of a giant bathtub. The river came through the mountain from the lake on the west. It roared over the dam, gathered in this pool, then was sucked down into the whirlpool, flowed through a tunnel, and was spewed out to become the headwaters of the stream in the valley. Not that it mattered. To a man who believed he was about to drown, any explanation seemed superfluous.

As he was being swept away from the dam, he fought to position himself so that he might catch sight of Jonathan in the murky light cast by the bulbs hanging above the dam. The surface of the water was surprisingly smooth, but as he was drawn closer to the whirlpool, he could see that it was like the inside of a funnel that was spinning counter-clockwise, and the surface of the water actually sloped steeply downward toward its vortex.

The powerful current was inexorably sweeping the two of them toward its center and would ultimately suck them under. Jonathan had entered the water first and was a couple of feet closer to the whirlpool than CC. They bobbed about, fighting the flow as it dragged them around on opposite sides. CC swam a couple of strokes toward the center, sacrificing time and distance in hopes of getting closer to Jonathan. It worked. The whirlpool's smaller radius caused him to be whipped around faster until he came opposite the boy. There were just a few feet separating them.

CC realized that Jonathan had probably thought it would be a daring thing to try to complete his mission by casting himself off the dam. It was soon apparent that the boy no longer suffered from that illusion. Now that he was faced with the terrifying power of the relentlessly flowing water, he'd obviously realized that his impulsive act was foolish.

As he was spun around, CC saw Jonathan's face for the first time. His hair and eyebrows were made even darker by the water, and contrasted with a face bleached white with fear. He was clearly terrified, but to his credit he wasn't letting the fear control him. For his own part, CC hadn't had to think about the danger. If he could just save the boy's life, it would be enough.

They were being swept in diminishing circles toward the vortex of the whirlpool, but since CC was now a little closer to the center, his revolutions were becoming smaller and more rapid, and he knew he would soon be separated from Jonathan again.

He was still holding the end of the rope, the other end of which was fastened to a stanchion on the top of the dam. He immediately stretched out his arm to pass it to the boy, but Jonathan's eyes were too blinded by the water to discern his gesture. CC tried to take a breath and instead got a mouthful of water. Somehow he choked out, "The rope!"

Jonathan reached out, trying to catch the knotted end that CC was pushing toward him, but he couldn't quite reach it. It was no good. CC realized that there was no way that he and Jonathan were going to join one another on the end of that rope.

He had been gripping the knot in his right hand, and suddenly pushed down hard with his flattened left hand in order to lift himself a little higher out of the water, then threw the knotted end at the boy, sacrificing his only possible hope for survival.

The rope hit the water between the boy's flailing hands and he quickly snatched it to himself. With no thought for his own safety, Jonathan held onto the rope with one hand and immediately reached toward CC with the other, but they had already drifted too far apart.

Suddenly CC was dragged under, and when he surfaced again he was choking and gasping for breath. He thrashed at the water, and his hand thumped against something solid. He felt fabric, and thought he'd somehow struck Jonathan's body. Then he realized it was his knapsack, buoyed up by the waterproof plastic bags that contained the explosives. He slipped his arms through the straps on the pack, pulling it up beneath his chest, and its buoyancy helped raise him a little from the surface of the water.

One final time he faced Jonathan. They were about six feet apart now. He might as well have been reaching for the moon. But while the vagaries of the current had swept the two of them further apart, it had also spun Jonathan over and over in the water, causing the rope to wrap several times around his upper body just beneath his arms. He still held the knotted end with one hand while reaching futilely toward CC with the other.

The rope was stretched in an almost rigid line to the railing at the top of the dam. Jonathan again screamed at CC to grab his hand, and he actually tried, freeing one hand from the backpack's straps and extending it toward the teen.

Just as their fingers touched, the boy was inexplicably jerked out of reach, and a startled look swept over his face. CC's eyes followed the rope up to the top of the dam. In the glare of the lightbulb, CC saw that Jim, a malicious smile on his face, was yanking Jonathan toward the dam with short, jerky pulls. Elizabeth was futilely pounding her fists against his back, and Rachel was trying to pull her away, obviously concerned that Jim might let go of the rope which was Jonathan's only lifeline.

CC pushed down on the pack a second time to lift himself clear of the turbulence. He shouted to Jonathan in clipped words, "Blow the dam at five." Jonathan twisted himself in the water so that he could see him, the boy's face a mask of despair. When he tried to answer, a wave splashed over him and he choked. He disappeared from sight as CC slid further down into the vortex of the whirlpool.

CC's body had already begun to ache from the icy water. As he felt the maelstrom dragging him down, he gripped the backpack beneath his chest, pushed down hard to get his head clear of the water, and took three quick breaths, each one slightly longer than the preceding. Then the river's suction caught him like a giant vacuum cleaner, and jerked him bodily under.

He became disoriented the moment he was sucked into the void. He was spinning downward, and he allowed himself to go with the current, his arms twisted in the straps of the knapsack. He drew his knees up around the pack, pulled his chin down, and rolled along in the fetal position, holding his breath and trying to relax in order to conserve oxygen.

The underground river, born of the melted snows from the slopes of the Green Mountains and fed by the thawing ice of northern Vermont streams, nearly paralyzed him. His only hope was that the water was moving fast enough to spew him out into the valley before he drowned. He would have let go of his precious package if he had not instinctively pulled himself into a tight ball to ward off the cold. It was only the slight positive buoyancy of the backpack that kept him from being dragged along the bottom where the rough surface might have crushed his skull or caved in his ribs.

Fortunately any boulders that had been carried by the stream had dropped out long before reaching the dam. He was so cold that he didn't even notice the bruises to his elbows and knees. Once, his shoulder banged against the tunnel roof and he almost lost his grip on the knapsack, and again he considered it miraculous that he hadn't been knocked unconscious. He began to spasm from the radical temperature change, and was convinced that he would never escape this racing madness.

Facing his own death, he had a moment of unusual clairvoyance. He thought of the heroism of the boy, jumping into the unknown in a misguided attempt to save his friends. Jim would probably have described Jonathan's dive as "*an existential phenomenon, a leap into darkness, a gesture of defiance, a childish and impulsive act.*"

CC now thought of it as a leap of faith, a dive of hope, and a sacrifice of love. And he wanted very much to survive this trial in order to share that one thought with the boy. Survive? It was a forlorn hope. How could he even imagine such a possibility? It would have been enough to have traded his life to help them escape.

Then the noble thoughts died. There had been a few times during his life that, while swimming, he'd stayed under until he'd exhausted his air, but he had always been able to get back to the surface. There was no chance of that here. His body seemed to scream for air, and he was near panic. He knew that he was in some kind of subterranean tunnel that carried the huge flow of water from the lake within the mountain out into the valley to the east.

If it were late summer, there would have been very little water flowing through this passage. He might even have been able to float playfully along on the surface of the stream and perhaps look up toward a vaulted ceiling above. Things were different now. The melting snows and spring rains had filled the tunnel, transforming it into a submerged raceway. The numbing cold and chaotic racket began to stifle what little thought he might have managed. It was an eternity or two before he realized that the deafening noise was being produced by the banging of small stones as they were swept along the bed of the stream by the awesome current.

He was nearly incapable of thinking, much less doing anything for himself. Had he fought the current, he might well have been propelled against the tunnel's walls and smashed into oblivion. Instead he was carried along in the deepest and fastest part of the channel. *Please, God,* he prayed, *I'm drowning.*

The icy water probably saved him. It slowed his respiration and reduced his need for the precious and rapidly consumed oxygen. The air in his lungs was nearly exhausted, and he was exercising his last expedient. In order to capture every last molecule of the remaining oxygen, he began to slowly let the air dribble out from between his lips. He knew that once his lungs were emptied, his body would demand air, and he would be unable to stop himself from inhaling. And when he finally succumbed to that irresistible impulse, he would fill his lungs from the killing flood.

Help me, Lord, he prayed. *If not for my sake, then for the people back there.* But it was too easy to accept the idea that his survival wasn't in God's will, and his remaining determination was rapidly slipping away. It seemed like an eternity to him, and his head felt as though it was going to burst. His lungs cried for air!

He had an almost irresistible desire to surrender himself to the warmth that seemed to be suffusing his body. *I can't make it,* he thought, and began to relax his hold on the pack. At that moment, some object in the water slapped his face, perversely filling him with a raging indignation. His lungs were starved for air, and he silently accused God, then relented, and finally submitted himself to His will.

The Maelstrom

Hidden Valley
Central Vermont
April 30th, 10:14 p.m.

CC's situation had become critical. His limbs were relaxing from the numbing cold, and the forgotten knapsack had begun to drift free of his nearly lifeless hands. He had unconsciously opened his lips and the last of the exhausted air dribbled out between them. The need to inhale was now nearly irresistible. At the instant he began to draw in that fatal breath, he was thrust out and upward into the twilight of evening.

Instead of his lungs filling with water, he sucked in delicious, life-giving air. Still just this side of unconsciousness, he fought to get another breath, but started choking when he inhaled a mouthful of water. This brought him close enough to consciousness to terrify him and cause him to again struggle for life. He propped his head above the swirling water by centering the backpack beneath his chest, the raging stream thrusting him forward.

It was twilight, almost dark, when CC was swept out of the submerged cavern to find himself beneath the overhanging cliffs at the west end of the valley. He remembered the prayer he'd uttered moments before, and if his eyes weren't already filled with water, he might have noticed them being flushed with tears of gratitude.

He was confused by the sight of trees and rocky shoreline as they seemed to spin about him under the darkening sky. He now resisted the effort to breathe regularly, frightened that he might again find himself choking on water.

I must be hallucinating, he thought, as he found himself making eye contact with the big man who had killed the enemy soldiers. *GI Joe* was leaning over the edge of a flat boulder, filling his canteen, only a few yards from where CC had been spewed up by the churning maelstrom. The man was obviously shocked to see him appear out of the depths, but reacted incredibly quickly, dropping his canteen onto the rock and leaning out to reach for him. But CC, almost paralyzed by the cold, couldn't lift his arms out of the water and was swept past him into the darkness.

His impression of the man, as if caught in a photograph, remained with him. He was dressed in a camouflage suit, an assault rifle propped against a shrub at his side. Dark hair spilled down over his forehead, emphasizing eyes made more intense by his high, broad cheekbones, his lips a tight line above a square jaw. It was a strong handsome face, but one that seemed both drawn with tension and dissipated with illness or with the excesses of inordinate living. He nevertheless gave an appearance of enormous energy and power, overshadowed by a sense of despair.

CC was dragged under again, and the torrent swept him around a curve and out of sight. He still had one arm slipped through one of the straps on the knapsack. He grasped the other strap with the same hand, and held it like a shield, manipulating it beneath him to keep his face above water, using his other arm to try to guide his movements.

Now another glorious breath. Again, swept under, but this time back to the surface sooner, and two wonderful lungs full. Then, just one more time, driven under, and CC found himself, by chance, swept into in an area of slack water at a turn in the stream where a tree had been undercut and was trapped against the shoreline.

He was being swept alongside the huge trunk which was still rooted to the bank, just within his reach. He caught feebly at a limb and missed. Something tore at his numbed legs, and he realized that he had been driven against one of its submerged branches. Reaching out with fingers stiffened by the cold, he dragged himself up onto the log, then clumsily pulled the knapsack up beside him. The pack was light in the water, but felt immensely heavy when he tried to lift it up onto the log. He looped one of the straps over a broken limb that rose vertically in front of him, then grasped it as he tried to catch his breath.

He was breathing raggedly, choking as his body fought to expel the water from his lungs. He recognized the need to somehow get out of the water and get warm, but his numbed hands defied him. They felt like broken sticks, useless, totally incapable of performing the simplest task. He arm bent a small branch as he brushed against it, and its recoil whipped it across his frozen fingers. He winced with the pain. CC began to feel as though his entire body was on fire, the reaction from coming out of the icy water into the relatively warm night air. His teeth were chattering so hard that he thought they might break, and he was still breathing in and out with deep violent gasps.

He wrapped his arms around the two broken branches, and dragged his midriff onto the log. Using the broken limbs that protruded from the fallen tree for support, he pulled himself up the log toward the shore, dragging his numb and nearly useless legs through the water. As he moved, the tree began to rock, and the drag of the water against his legs threatened to pull him back into the sucking torrent. CC fought to stay atop the slippery trunk, his face almost submerged in the ebbing water on the downstream side. Each time he reached another branch, he had to lower himself back into the water to maneuver around it, or he had to squirm around on the log to lift his legs over it.

He'd already made his way past two such limbs when he noticed a length of rope that trailed off downstream. It was tied to a broken limb a few feet from his hand. Gazing longingly at the shore, he recognized this as the old tree that they had used the preceding summer to swing out over their swimming hole. Its roots had obviously been scoured free by the creek's erosive power, and now it floated here, vanquished by the flood, its usefulness seemingly ended. *Well, maybe not ended,* he thought. *It's saving my life.*

As his eyes moved up the length of the log toward the shore, the stars above provided just sufficient light for him to see that the tree was only anchored to the shore by one or two twisted roots, and he realized that the dark watery hole in the creek bank must be where it had stood for at least a hundred years. *That means that I've already reached the old swimming hole, and I must be nearly opposite the soldiers' camp,* he thought with alarm.

As he returned his gaze to the cavity where the tree's roots had been ripped out of the shore, he realized that they seemed to be shifting. The trunk was swinging downstream under the pressure of the flood, and the roots were being twisted free from the muck. He heard a root popping apart under the enormous stress brought on the huge trunk by the swift current.

Perhaps, he reasoned, *my added weight has provided the drag necessary to finish tearing it loose.*

It was obviously too late to make his way up the log to the shore, but he did manage to straddle the trunk and nest his chest on the log, his hands gripping two smaller limbs on either side of his head, like the horns on a bull. He was just in time. The tree ripped free of the bank and slipped out from the shoreline where it began rocking so violently that he could barely hold on. The log accelerated as it was drawn into center stream, and he found himself careening down the raging creek.

Out of the corner of his eye he saw a group of soldiers huddled about a campfire. Rolling his head to the side, he saw a guard, sitting on the bank of the stream near the fire, throwing stones into the racing current. CC didn't think the man could see him through the rapidly deepening gloom, huddled as he was on the log. He couldn't have cried out for help even if he'd wanted to, for his teeth were still chattering in a vicious staccato rhythm.

The soldier appeared to lean forward to stare at the log on which CC rode, then shrugged his shoulders indifferently, leaned back, and skipped another stone over the waves. The rock made a hollow sound as it bounced off his racing log, and dropped back into the stream. CC couldn't help thinking that the man skimmed the stones very well, and was surprised at himself for taking time to make such an absurd reflection while fighting for his life.

It was the appearance of the soldier that refocused CC's thoughts on his purpose. I'm here to do something, he remembered, but it took him a moment to remember what that something was. *Even if I can keep from freezing to death,* he thought, *I don't see how I can accomplish it.* Then he thought of his adopted family, and his concern for them helped focus his thoughts. *A lot depends on Jonathan,* he realized, *but I've got to do my part!*

He felt woozy. It was so strange. He thought he saw radiant letters appearing before his drenched eyes, so he blinked them in an effort to clear them of the water, and the words immediately faded. He relaxed, and some of the words reappeared. *"I can do all things through Him who strengthens me." Huh! Probably brought on by the exchange I had with McCord a few hours ago,* he thought. The words faded away, but the message was enough to make him fight on. *If it was an illusion,* he thought, *it was certainly a heavenly one.*

On the River Bank

Hidden Valley
April 30th, 10:16 p.m.

Shocked to see the man pop up through the surface of the stream out of nowhere, like a cork out of a champagne bottle, the man that CC called GI Joe reached out for him, then watched helplessly as he was swept past him into the darkness.

There's no way I can help him. And I can't imagine him surviving for more than a minute or so. On the other hand, he made it through the underground tunnel, so only God knows.

He looked downstream where the remaining soldiers had built campfires to warm themselves. *They are stupid,* he thought with disdain. *They could have sheltered in the caves out of the rain.*

He noticed one soldier, illuminated by one of the fires, tossing rocks into the stream. The big man stood, picked up his weapon, and began moving in his direction.

The Flume

Hidden Valley
April 30th, 10:20 p.m.

CC heard the roar of the flume ahead. He'd forgotten about those terrifying rapids until now, for even in mid-summer he couldn't imagine surviving their passage. "O God," he mumbled, "please...." There was no time for more than that.

He wrapped his arms around a large branch as the log began to heave and twist in the boiling water. At first it didn't seem much worse that what he'd already experienced, with the log occasionally scraping the shore, but then it almost capsized, and once it even turned end-for-end so that he found himself looking back the way he'd come with no idea what lay ahead, or rather, behind him. Then it thumped into the river bank, spun around again, and he was temporarily submerged as the log tipped on its side. When it righted itself, he blinked the water from his eyes and realized he was again looking downstream, and still somehow straddling the log.

He tried pulling himself into a sitting position, like a horseback rider, so that he could breathe more regularly and maybe even see what was ahead, but he quickly decided he was far more secure on his belly, knees straddling the log, squeezing it for dear life, his hands gripping the two limbs. He resumed his prone position just as the log stood nearly on end, and was swept down the first of two racing slopes of water. Somehow the log remained in the center of the cascade, and he realized he was clawing at the bark with his fingers. He was amazed that the log didn't flip over, and wondered if a heavier limb might be hanging beneath the log, acting as a keel. If so, he was grateful for small favors, but it was all he could do to hang on as the tree bounced from wave to foaming wave.

He sought to pull his legs further out of the water, pressing his knees against the log, hoping that he would not be crushed between it and a chance boulder or another tree. As it turned out, those broken limbs were serving as buffers, protecting his legs.

Although time seemed to stand still, he was through the flume in less than a minute. The log's movement had become far less jarring, and he realized that he must have entered the little lake at the east end of the valley. In just a few minutes, he'd almost reached the narrow bottleneck that formed its entrance.

How could I have traveled to the end of the lake so quickly? He wondered. *This is where I need to get out of the water so that I can begin setting the charges.*

But the lake wasn't little now. Moonlight had penetrated the heavy cloud cover for an instant, and his bloodshot eyes widened in fear as he realized he'd almost reached the maw of the huge culvert pipe.

Oh God, he prayed, thinking back to the horror of the subterranean passage he'd traversed just minutes earlier, *have mercy!* The memory of his miraculous deliverance was eclipsed by this new challenge. *I'm going to be drowned in that pipe.*

He tried to drag himself to a kneeling position, hoping that he might leap for the bank and pull himself to safety, but he quickly dropped back onto his stomach. His head and shoulders cleared the sharp top edge of the huge corrugated steel culvert pipe with inches to spare as the log accelerated and began its underground passage beneath the valley's narrow entrance. It slowed as one of the log's broken limbs scraped against the corrugations on the arched metal roof. The sound was like a jackhammer, magnified in the enclosed space. Despite the fact that it was intensely dark within the culvert, he realized that he was being propelled at an enormous speed through the conduit.

Grateful that the space between his uncertain perch and the curved galvanized roof above provided adequate air for him to breathe, CC found himself in total, terrifying darkness, with not even the faintest hint of light ahead. Now his fears turned to the possibility of his log somehow hanging up in the pipe, leaving him to freeze or drown out of the sight and memory of man. But it sped relentlessly on.

He suddenly remembered that the conduit ended just beyond the east side of the mountain highway, and that there was a waterfall not far beyond the end of the conduit. He had no difficulty picturing the log rocketing off that ledge, swept by the cascading water down the face of the irregular cliff, and crashing to the valley far below. And he knew he was helpless to do anything about it but pray. The early part of the journey through the conduit seemed to take hours, but when he remembered what was at the other end, the time raced by. It could have taken only a minute or so to cover the eighth mile from one end of the huge cylinder to the other.

He realized that his log had exited the pipe when the drumming of the branch against the corrugated pipe suddenly ceased. At the same time, the pain in his ears lessened because of a reduction in the air pressure around him. Shooting free of the long tunnel, he felt the log pitching sideways. It slammed against the decaying stone abutment of a bridge that had been removed when the new highway had been built a dozen feet higher over the end of the culvert.

The log spun, and the end on which he was perched slid rapidly toward the center of the stream. There was a cracking, tearing sound, the tree jerked to a halt, and his nose was smashed painfully against the trunk.

The darkness, the reduction in the noise, the swirling water, and his pain, all consorted to disorient him and magnify his terror and confusion. But he'd become resigned to death, and somehow he still lived. *Perhaps,* he thought, *I've exceeded my capacity for suffering.*

A new thought gripped him.

This wild ride has more significance than my mere personal desire to survive. Someone mightier than I am has taken a special interest in my life, so I can only conclude that there's a purpose in my surviving this long. He tried to cling to that thought.

It would seem that I might be meant to survive a bit longer. And, on the basis of that epiphany, he resolved, *If God is for me, I've got to do my part. Nothing else matters. All the pain and terror haven't beaten me.* Then with more hope than faith, he resolved, *And they are not going to beat me now! I've come this far,* he reasoned, *and I'm still alive, so I'm going to make it!*

Through chattering teeth he stuttered aloud, "Thank you, Lord!"

He laughed hysterically, unable to control his emotions. Maybe his reasoning seemed convoluted, even insane, but it was all he had. He didn't feel the blood dripping from his nose because it had coagulated in the cold. His clothes were soaking wet and he was shaking in the breeze. He raised his eyes and looked around.

The log's movement had been arrested because its fractured end had been driven into a fissure in the broken masonry of an old abandoned bridge abutment. The log had spun in a slow, dizzying end-for-end circle, and its great root ball, now flushed clean of the soil in which it had once been anchored, had come to rest against the bank thirty feet downstream. It lay almost parallel to the shoreline, and was held just a few feet away from the bank by its short, broken limbs.

CC would not play the fool twice. He remembered how this insecure perch had quickly broken free at the swimming hole. He fully expected it to do so again. But this time there would be no reprieve from death, for in mere seconds it would be swept over the brink.

Slowly, desperately, a prayer on his lips, he scrabbled up the log toward the embankment. Almost forgotten were the frozen fingers and cramped legs. Roaring death lay just beyond the end of the heaving log, where the water cascaded down the face of the cliff for nearly two hundred feet.

He was past pain now, his fright driving him in his extremity toward his deliverance. He found himself standing on the end of the thrashing log, the night chill stiffening his clothes. He was shaking as much with fear as with the cold. Finally he was able to reach out and brace one hand against the abutment. He reached out one foot and found himself stepping into shallow water. Then he stumbled to the blessed shore.

He was exhausted, and his thoughts were muddled. He tried to remember what he was doing here. The epiphany he'd experienced mere seconds before was nearly swept away. All he knew was that he had to get warm. He had to have a fire.

But something was gnawing at him. Something vitally important. And with that awareness came instant denial. He suddenly remembered, but he didn't want to remember. His eyes turned of their own volition toward the precarious perch he'd just abandoned with such a great sense of relief. The log still laid there along the shore, leaping slightly with each errant wave, its splintered end stuck precariously in the crack between two huge stone blocks in the old bridge abutment.

The realization of his blunder chilled his heart more than the wind. His oversight would likely cost him his life. He hesitated, then turned back toward the log. Halfway down its length, exactly where he'd left it, hung the backpack that contained the explosives.

"Dear God," he mumbled, shaking with the cold, "I can't go back out there."

He looked around, trying to find an excuse to flee this place, seeking an alternative to this unthinkable challenge, trying to imagine some other way, any other way, that he could accomplish the task he'd set for himself. His eyes were drawn involuntarily to the edge of the waterfall that lay just yards beyond the end of the log. The crashing of the water as it fell down the mountainside punctuated his terror.

Yet he had to get that dynamite or all he'd been through would be for nothing.

His mind was numb, and he was mesmerized by a snake that lay slithering in the slack water near the shore. His eyes stared indifferently at the undulating serpent, waiting for it to make a move toward him. Then the truth penetrated his conscience. His eyes focused, and he realized that it wasn't a snake. It was the old rope that they'd used to swing out over the swimming hole on happier days.

He tried to run down to the shore, but stumbled and fell, the victim of cramped legs. He realized that he was kneeling on some sort of a ledge that lay just a few inches beneath the surface, and he crawled the last few feet through the shallow water to reach the rope. Grabbing the end, he scrambled to his feet, then turned to stagger back up the bank where he wound the rope several times around the trunk of a tree before tying a knot, thus precariously anchoring the floating log to the shore.

It's not secure, he thought, *but it's safer than it was.* He snorted. *Safer? I'm an idiot!*

Nonetheless he grabbed a broken limb and pulled himself back up onto the rocking log. Reaching out to another of the branches to steady himself, he again pulled himself along its slippery surface. He squatted slightly, baby-stepping over the slick bark, gripping the broken limbs to hold himself erect, and sensing the log settling beneath his feet as he moved out along its length.

As soon as he was close enough, he attempted to grab the pack, but his fingers wouldn't obey his mind, and it was simply too heavy. What was worse, the soaking wet canvas had begun to freeze in the wind. He laughed inanely. "*Bridge surface freezes before highway,*" he quoted.

CC squatted, placing his bent knees on either side of the thick branch to anchor himself, then put both hands beneath the pack and lifted it over the top of the broken limb. He didn't remember it being that heavy. Almost dropping it, he slipped his arms through the loops and pulled it against his chest like a mother hugging her baby.

Then he very carefully turned and started to make his way back up the tilted, slippery surface. It seemed a lifetime before he reached the ledge on which the other end of the log was precariously resting. He almost fell backwards into the deep water when the log rocked violently, but again caught his balance, and continued on as quickly as he dared, using just the one hand to pull himself from branch to branch.

He was perhaps two long steps from the end of the log, balancing dangerously, when another tree came tearing downstream out of the end of the culvert and struck his perch. He was nearly thrown from his log as it broke loose from the bridge abutment. The upstream end of the log slipped free of the shore and began moving in an arc toward midstream, just a few yards above the brink of the waterfall. He took a quick unsteady step, leaned toward the shore, and used both hands to heave the pack toward the bank.

With the release of the pack's weight, his feet slid off the downstream side of the log, and he fell forward, slapping his shins against the top of the log as it was swept away from beneath him. The pain was almost as great as his terror as he fell face first into the water.

He struck the ledge, banging his elbows, and choking on another mouthful of water, and he was immediately aware that the current was dragging him away from the shore. A sob was wrenched from his throat. The log he'd been riding began to tip over the edge of the precipice, and the rope that had been restraining its movement snapped with the report of a small-caliber rifle, freeing his log to be swept away over the cliff.

The end of the rope that he had secured to the tree whipped over his shoulder and dropped into the water beside him. He grabbed savagely for it, and began pulling himself across the submerged rock. The backpack lay in shallow water, and kicking and dragging himself across the ledge, he grasped one of its straps, praying that the knot he'd tied at the base of the tree would hold. After what seemed like an age, he gained the safety of the shore. Catching up his pack, and fighting his way to his feet, he stumbled up the bank away from the water's edge.

He did not look back, so he did not see the lifeless body of the soldier who'd been skipping stones on the water sweep past and disappear over the edge of the escarpment.

Desperation

Vermont Highway 19
April 30th, 10:29 p.m.

Warm... I gotta get warm! he thought as he clawed his way up the steep gravel slope that lay between the waterfall and the highway. Anesthetized by cold and fear, he was nearly oblivious to the sound of a rapidly approaching vehicle.

He stopped to crane his head back, and looked dumbly upward as the beams from the headlight swept over the top of the wall just above his head. When he reached the base of the wall, he heard the vehicle slow and its tires crunch as it turned off the highway.

Dragging himself up with his free hand, he was just able to peer over the top of the wall in time to see a battered pickup truck bounce across the shallow ditch on the far side of the highway, then pull under the cover of the trees before stopping at the entrance to the bottleneck.

Having spent what seemed an interminable period in nearly total darkness, CC was dazzled by its stop lights, and when the driver shut down the engine and extinguished the lights, he found himself momentarily blinded.

He heard the truck doors open, then slam shut, and he could almost interpret their coarse banter as two men walked up into the bottleneck. Then he realized that their unexpected appearance meant that he might well be cut off from returning to his valley.

Prudence warred with necessity. He was no longer shaking with cold and his thinking was fuzzy. He seemed to remember that this indicated that he was suffering from hypothermia. It was obvious that he couldn't wait much longer to find shelter. His mission temporarily forgotten, all that now mattered was that he find a way to get warm.

Hoping that they'd left no one behind to guard the truck, he dragged himself up onto the wall, slid across the top, and tumbled over the other side, falling hard onto the narrow shoulder of the road. His body was already stiff from the cold, and it was painful to reach up and grab the edge of the wall in order to pull himself erect. He slowly made his way across the road, tottering like an infant. Every step was a trial, the knapsack still half-forgotten in his hands.

He realized that the darkness was now his friend. He could only hope that no one had spotted his silhouette against the starry sky as he'd crossed the road, for he barely had the strength to walk, let alone run away. Heedless of the danger, he stumbled toward the pickup truck. It took nearly all his remaining strength to lift his pack over the side and drop it into the bed of the truck.

Then he fumbled with the handle on the passenger door and scrambled up into the cab. The truck cab was still warm, and he felt his body soaking up the heat. He told himself that he must not allow himself to remain there, but exhaustion overcame him, and he slipped into a dreamless sleep.

About twenty minutes later, after the cab had cooled down, he awoke. He stepped outside and felt around the back of the truck until he located his backpack. Unzipping the smallest compartment, he rummaged around until he found his LED headlamp. Fumbling with numb fingers to push the button, he finally got a dull red light to come on. He stretched the elastic band around his forehead, at the same time unconsciously bracing himself in anticipation of a shout or a gunshot. When he realized that his presence was undetected, he began to rummage through the stuff in the back of the truck.

He couldn't believe his good fortune. There were several backpacks stacked against the cab, as well as a couple of rifles in padded canvas bags. He struggled with the buckles on one of the larger packs, dumped the contents onto the floor of the truck bed, sorted through them, found a can of baked beans, ripped the lid off, and wolfed them down cold. He then grabbed a pair of flannel-lined slacks, a shirt, and a sweater, and climbed back into the cab where he stripped off his still wet clothing, patted himself down with a clean undershirt, and pulled on the dry clothes.

Stepping back outside, he picked up the large backpack that he'd emptied, and fumbled his own, including its load of explosives, down inside it. Then he resumed sorting through the items in the bed of the truck. He discarded a bottle of whiskey. *I need a stimulant, not a dangerous depressant!* he thought. He did add a couple of cans of baked beans and some beef jerky to the top of the pack.

Dragging it out of the cargo bed, he balanced it on the tailgate, got his arms through the straps, and pulled it up onto his shoulders. Then he snapped the belt that snugged it to his waist. The short sleep and the food had restored something of his determination if not his physical strength.

He turned back to the truck, unzipped one of the fleece-lined rifle cases, drew out an assault rifle, removed the magazine to make certain it was loaded with cartridges, snapped it back into the rifle, and staggered away into the bottleneck.

Leaving his headlamp on, he followed its dim beam up the wood road, oddly indifferent to the possibility that he might be seen. He had come to the seemingly illogical conclusion that since he had been brought safe this far, he was for the time being, pretty much indestructible.

How else, he asked himself, *could anyone explain my incredible survival?*

For an instant, his frozen lips twisted into the rictus of a bloodless smile.

Luck?

He shook his head in the negative.

A series of amazing coincidences?

This time a smile of contempt.

Not likely!

But his sense of wonder at his survival was already fading, and the reality of the challenge facing him was intruding on his confidence. He certainly didn't feel indestructible, and realized that he had little strength – emotional or physical – to produce a sense of bravado. He was battered, bruised, scraped, and scratched. His head ached fiercely. He was again shaking from the cold, his stomach hurt, and he was ravenously hungry. Yet, in spite of all that, he couldn't deny the inexplicable confidence that seemed to embrace him.

I'm moving like an old man, he thought, *but at least I'm moving.*

As beat up as he felt, he was surprised that his thoughts turned again to his all-but-forgotten purpose. He had almost reached the far end of the bottleneck. Just a few yards further and he would reach the place on his right where he had planned to start placing the dynamite charges. With his need for warmth, however, and the fact that the two men in the truck had probably followed the log road in that same direction, he decided he'd better keep to the left and head for McCord's cave. At least he might be able to warm himself up there.

As he passed out of the bottleneck, he turned off his headlamp. He turned left around the end of the little lake, and pushed deep into the scrub, frequently stumbling in the darkness, once even dropping his rifle. When he reached the evergreens that grew along that corner of the valley, he turned the red LED headlamp back on. Aiming it just in front of his feet, he shrouded it from potential observers by cupping his hand around it.

There was very little underbrush beneath the towering pines, and the going immediately became easier. He had worked to his left, away from the lake, and soon found himself deep in the southeastern corner of the valley. As he neared the base of the towering escarpment, he stumbled over the rocky scree that had broken free from the cliffs above, and shortly after found himself sliding down into a small depression beneath an overhang in the cliff.

He had no idea how he could find McCord's cave in the dark, but he knew that he had to find a means to get warm, even at the risk of being discovered. He dropped his pack on a flat rock in the bottom of the hollow, scrabbled back up the side of the hole, and used his light to locate and break up some driftwood that had been left high and dry by earlier flooding.

Returning to the hollow, he piled the kindling together in the darkness, and started rifling his emergency pack, looking for a match. There were none. He realized that he must have removed them back in the cave when he had rushed to reduce the weight of his pack. He choked back a sob, then caught hold of himself.

It began raining, a light drizzle that rapidly turned to a soaking rain. This increased his suffering, but more importantly decreased even more any chance of lighting a fire. It was little consolation that his enemies might also be cold and wet. He must get warm or he knew he would die. He was already suffering disorientation and sleepiness, and he stumbled back against the cliff in an attempt to get out of the driving rain.

He wiped the water from his eyes and tried to concentrate, as though being able to see in the rain and darkness would somehow help him arrive at a solution. He certainly wasn't going to rub two wet sticks together to build a fire. The little sermon he'd given the group months before about the importance of learning to build a fire now came back to mock him.

His mind was drifting. *When I taught them how to build a fire, did I encourage them to pray?* He shook his head as though to clear his confusion. *I've survived all this, and still I haven't learned to pray when faced with a problem.* He turned his face up toward the darkened sky and whispered, "Lord, help me!"

Although he considered it an exercise in futility, he dragged the stolen pack into the meager shelter of the cliff and began groping through it, desperately searching for matches. Then he realized that the firewood he′d gathered was getting wet. He stepped out into the pouring rain and gathered as much of it as he could before retreating back under the overhang. He needed something that would burn easily and he needed some way to ignite it. Jonathan had once said that he was a man with dynamite ideas.

"No dynamite ideas tonight," he mumbled.

He shook his head in an effort to clear the cobwebs. *Dynamite? Something about dynamite? Of course!* He reached into his knapsack, tore open a plastic bag, and pulled out a stick of the precious explosive. Cutting through the covering with his knife, he gingerly carved a small quantity of the compound from the inside of the cylinder. He molded it into a small mound, laid it on a flat rock, inserted a blasting cap, and piled some small, dry pieces of wood on top. Then he attached wires from the magneto to the detonator, cranked it up, and clicked the switch. There was a loud report, like a fire cracker exploding, something hot stung his cheek, and burning powder and twigs went flying everywhere.

He couldn't see for a moment, dazzled as he was by the intense light after the prolonged darkness. His cheek seemed to be on fire, and he swept up some wet leaves to brush the flaming glob from his face. The pain was intense, but he couldn't take time to tend to his burn. Fire meant life. Right now he needed it to survive, whatever the cost to his features.

He grabbed a piece of wood to which some of the fiercely burning substance had stuck, placed it on the flat rock, and gathered other smoldering pieces of wood which he laid on top of it. Then he blew on them until the flame took hold. He attempted to shield the fire from the rain by leaning over it, but he found himself choking uncontrollably on the acrid smoke.

First water in my lungs, he thought, *now smoke. It will be a wonder if I don't come down with pneumonia.* He grimaced. *Correction. The way things are going, I'm not apt to survive long enough to contract a fatal disease.*

What a fool I was, he realized. *I knew that a small amount of the dynamite would burn as long as it wasn't tightly enclosed, but I forgot that the blasting cap would explode. The least I should have done was run out a few yards of wire so that I was further away.* Then he realized that self-recrimination was a waste of time. His very survival was still in doubt, and he needed to focus on the task at hand, not on the mistakes of the past.

He kept feeding wood to the tiny blaze until the fire seemed strong enough to sustain itself, but the heat brought agony to his inflamed cheek, and he had to turn his face away. It was soon obvious, however, that his fire wasn't going to survive the increasingly heavy downpour.

But he had even more immediate problems. His cheek hurt so badly that his eye was closing. He looked away from the flames to regain his night vision, then gathered some of the leaves that had been blown down into the hole during the past autumn. When he had a good handful, he tipped his head to apply a poultice of the wet leaves against his burning cheek. The cooling effect was marvelous.

At that moment he noticed a shadow in the cliff face. Feeling his way over, he discovered a shallow cave barely deep enough to enable him to get completely out of the rain. With some effort, he was able to pick up the thin flat rock on which he′d laid his small fire. Grunting with the effort, he managed to keep from dumping the burning wood as he moved it beneath the overhang.

He set the rock on the ground by the back wall of the cave, and then went to gather more wood. He tried to ignore the pain in his cheek, and managed to stay upwind of the choking smoke. He no longer gave any thought to his enemies. It seemed unlikely that they would be keeping careful watch this miserable night.

While the fire at the back of the cave grew in intensity, he pulled his own pack out of the larger one he'd liberated from the bad guys, and searched through it for his first-aid kit. He found a little plastic packet of salve, ripped it open with his teeth, and gently rubbed the contents onto his wounded cheek. He experienced immediate relief.

That done, he boiled some water for instant coffee, heated an MRE that he found in the bottom of the pack he'd confiscated, and quickly devoured it. For the next half-hour he sat with his uninjured cheek turned toward the fire, enjoying the heat radiating off the rock wall, sipping a cup of hot coffee, and worrying about the false sense of well-being he was experiencing.

He used a fresh evergreen branch to sweep some of the flaming coals from his fire over the rock floor at the back of the cave. Steam rose from the slab as the incandescent coals burned the dampness away. When the embers turned gray, he swept the spent coals out into the rain. Then he slid the flat rock on which he'd built his fire as far from the back wall of the cave as he could without it being doused by the rain, and heaped on additional sticks to build up the fire.

Now he had a warm, dry area between the fire and the back wall of the cave. Allowing a few more minutes for any errant embers to cool, he spread his sleeping bag on the warm, dry stone floor, and lay down. After a few minutes, the warmth quelled his shaking and he slept.

He awoke about an hour later, again shivering. He stirred up the few remaining coals, threw on the wood which he'd stacked beside the fire to dry, and heated another can of stew. He ate quickly, then left the cave, abandoning everything but his gun, knife, and the smaller backpack containing the explosives.

Executing the Plan

Vermont Highway 19
April 30th, 11:59 p.m.

The rain had stopped, but the sky was overcast and it was very dark. He walked back toward the bottleneck, following along the base of the southeastern escarpment, his misery increased by the constant dripping from the branches above. Using his red headlamp to search for places to plant the explosives, he climbed carefully up the steep slope of broken and slippery rock until he reached the actual cliff face, about fifty feet above the valley floor.

Moving slowly along the base of the cliff, he found a deep crack in the rock where he was sure he would be able to place several sticks of dynamite. He bundled three sticks together using duct tape, and inserted blasting caps in two of the three sticks. Then he fastened the end of the thin cable on his wire reel to the wires protruding from the two blasting caps. Working very carefully, he slipped the bundle of explosives deep into the crack, taking care not to jar the sensitive detonators. Finally he made his way back down the shifting gravel to the valley floor, carefully unwinding the thin cable as he went.

Reaching the base of the slope of scree, CC took a small pair of wire cutters and severed the cable that ran from the reel up the mountain of scree to the explosives he'd just buried. Then he hung the loose end of that cable from a tree limb.

Hopefully, he thought, *I'll be able to locate the wire when I return. If I return...*

He planned to splice the end of that cable to the longer cable that would ultimately stretch from the far side of the valley's entrance all the way back to where he was standing, and from there on up the south side of the valley to McCord's cave. Seen from above, it would lay on the ground like a giant J that hooked around the east end of the valley.

He took a moment to get his bearings, and continued down the valley, finally moving north around the lower end of the lake.

Keeping as far from the lake and the mouth of the dreaded culvert pipe as he could, he crossed the dirt road that ran the length of the canyon. The cliff on the northeast corner of the bottleneck loomed above him in the darkness.

Since he couldn't see very far using his headlamp, he tried to envision what he remembered of the mountainside. The almost sheer cliffs on the northeast corner of the valley's entrance were closer to the lake than those on the southeast corner. He remembered driving his tractor-trailer around the north side of the lake a year earlier, and watching in the mirror as the rear wheels of the trailer almost slid down into the lake. At this point, the distance between the stream bank and the huge piles of scree that lay at the base of the cliffs couldn't be much more than twenty-five feet. There was just enough space for the old logging road to wind between the slope of scree and the lake.

This is where I have to bring down enough debris to create an earth dam and to plug the culvert, he thought.

Here, the actual cliff was almost vertical, and the road was clear of debris.

He moved gingerly among the rocks that lay at the base of the cliff, concerned that he might trip and sprain an ankle. As he turned the corner from the narrow bottleneck and started back west into the widening valley, he discovered a shallow cave on his right at the foot of the cliff. The rock here was rotten, split with numerous fissures. There were small piles of crushed stone and sand laying on the cave floor testifying to its instability.

The cliff rose sheer for about a hundred feet above him, and the entire place appeared ready to collapse over his head. *Which makes it ideal for my purposes,* he reasoned, as fear gnawed at his stomach.

He pressed the button on his headlamp repeatedly until the light changed from red to a bright white. Focusing the beam, he found a particularly rotten-looking fissure that ran up the back wall of the cave. Using his hunting knife, he began to dig out the soft detritus. It took only a few minutes to scrape out a hole about the depth of his forearm and larger than the diameter of his fist.

He was withdrawing the knife from the hole, intending to scrape away any remaining loose dirt with his fingers, when suddenly the massive rock face to the left of his blade slid to the right, not slowly, but with a terrifying thud. The shifting rock closed the hole, locking the blade in place, and leaving his hand, still gripping the handle, just clear of the stone, his knuckles scraped and bleeding.

Dirt and small sharp rocks exploded out as the fissure closed, one of them striking his forehead and drawing blood. The movement was followed by other rumblings and cracking sounds as the rock walls around and above him adjusted themselves, but the sounds seemed as nothing compared to the pounding of his heart and his rasping breath.

He back-pedaled away from the cave wall, and when the noise ceased, he found himself standing well outside the cave, his breath coming in gasps, waiting for the mountain to fall on him.

"I can't allow myself to think about this," he said aloud. "I just have to get it done."

Very slowly, he baby-stepped back into the cave, and – like a man playing Russian roulette – he gripped the knife handle that was wedged in the rock and began to wiggle it up and down. After a moment, he was able to work it out of the crack.

"Ah," he smiled with an ironic twist to his lips. "Just like young Arthur drawing Excalibur from the stone."

With the crevice now tightly closed, he studied the cave wall until he found a narrower crack that didn't travel so far up. His heart pounding, he was far more careful as he slowly dug out the crushed and broken debris. When the hole was large enough, and the rock still seemed stable, he moved to his right about six feet and dug into another crevice.

The rock around this hole looked far more solid, and he was able to pry a relatively small rock out of the crack. Then he scraped away the aggregate, reaching deeply into the hole with his hand, praying that there'd not be another cave in to crush his arm or worse.

He took out six of his remaining nine sticks of dynamite, three for each hole, wrapped the individual bundles with duct tape, very carefully inserted two blasting caps into each bundle, attached the wires to each detonator, and slid one bundle into each of the two holes. "Redundancy counts when you're working with explosives," Jonathan had cautioned him. "Two blasting caps are always better than one."

"Well, Jonathan," he said aloud, "I wouldn't know what I'd be doing without your counsel."

With that accomplished, he backed slowly out of the cave and made his way to the bank of the lake. Kneeling, he scooped up handfuls of sticky clay and carried it back to the cave where he carefully packed it around the dynamite, then completely filled the holes in which he'd buried the charges. Jonathan had impressed on him the importance of this step in order to make certain that most of the explosive energy didn't simply escape out of the holes.

And that's something I failed to do when I was working on the south face, he realized. With regret *I didn't pack the holes with clay.* Then he thought, *There was no clay. But I might have used little stones.*

He remembered the conversation. "Ideally," the boy had told him, "you would drill holes several feet deep and push the explosives deep into the cliff, but you lack both the equipment and the skill."

His thoughts returned to the job at hand. Following more of Jonathan's instructions, he very carefully ran the wires down the cave wall, leaving plenty of slack. When the wires reached the floor, he lay them in a shallow fissure that ran out the cave's entrance. This would hopefully protect them from falling stones, and might even hide them from a chance passer-by.

Again, following Jonathan's instructions, he planned to uncoil the wire as he walked back around the end of the valley, laying it loosely on the ground. When he reached the south side of the lake, he would splice in the wires from the explosives he′d already planted there.

He had backed out of the cave, alternately picking up and setting down the larger backpack, carefully arranging the detonator wire between larger rocks on the valley floor, when he heard an ominous rumbling. He looked up, but could see nothing in the darkness. Then the volume increased, a massive crunching and shifting high above him. Having almost lost his hand a few moments earlier, he reacted instantly. With the handle of the cable spool forgotten in one hand, and his pack in the other, he began back-pedaling urgently away from the cave.

He′d gotten perhaps ten yards from the cave's mouth when there was a violent noise, like a cannon going off. That was followed initially by the relatively harmless sound of dirt sifting down the cliff face, and then by more rumbling, which in turn became the massive, terrifying sound of a landslide. Exhausted and cold, with seemingly no adrenalin left in his system, he was nevertheless again filled with terror.

Pivoting, he ran another few yards, stopping only when he reached the edge of the lake, then turned sideways to run along the bank toward McCord′s corner of the valley. The ground vibrated beneath him, there was the crashing sound of the landslide, and rocks, large and small, started raining down around him.

Grateful that the LED on his forehead was lighting his way, he ran across the bottleneck toward the south wall, unaware that the detonator wire was still unwinding smoothly from the reel. The tumbling earth seemed to be following him, but he was not about to launch himself into the lake′s swollen waters. As the noise subsided, he found himself standing still, with about an inch of dirt covering his boots, and the air around him full of choking dust.

He could hear the earth shifting as the cliff seemed to settle itself. For a moment there was a silence that seemed all the more profound because of what had preceded it, but then he found himself doubled up with a violent coughing spasm. He couldn't get it under control, and therefore didn't hear the sound of a massive boulder falling from high above. It bounced in great sweeping arcs as it descended, almost parting his hair as it passed over his bent form, and finally dropping into the lake just a few yards out from him, soaking him thoroughly.

He stood there for a moment, staring blankly at the boulder, its top rising about a foot above the surface of the deep water at the end of the lake. The only remaining sign of its movement were the concentric rings spreading out over the troubled surface which sparkled in the intermittent starlight. He just stood there dumbly staring at the top of the massive boulder.

After what seemed an age, he noticed the coil of wire at his feet, and bent down to pick it up. Holding it to his chest, he tried to command his hands to stop shaking.

He suddenly realized that he had been repeating something over and over, like a litany. *Praise the Lord! Praise the Lord! Praise the Lord!*

The moon had risen, but it was obscured by the thick clouds of dust, and when he looked up, he could feel the grit in his eyes, and was barely able to see. Turning back, he imagined a vast dark gap where the upper cliff on the northeast corner of the valley's entrance once stood. Now it appeared that huge piles of earth were heaped at its base. In some places the piles rose forty and fifty feet above the valley floor, sloping down steeply until ending quite literally at his feet.

For over one hundred feet of its length, the old logging road through the bottleneck was buried in rock, effectively halting all vehicular traffic in and out of the valley. He laughed.

With God's help, and without detonating one stick of dynamite, I've already succeeded in blocking the bottleneck with nothing more than a hunting knife. Then he was brought up short. *Correction!* he thought. *In spite of my efforts, God has already blocked much of the bottleneck.*

Then he thought of how fragile that cliff had been, and realized how it might have collapsed while he was driving the truck past it a year earlier, leaving him buried beneath the rubble.

Too bad I lack the faith, he thought, *or I'd say to this mountain, "be removed into this lake," and it would be moved.* He bit his lip. *Too bad I don't have the faith.* Then his mind returned to what he considered more practical matters.

It would be wonderful if all we needed to do was keep vehicles out, he thought, *but we still need to flood this end of the valley so that the enemy won't be able to get men in unless they have helicopters or boats.* His thoughts raced on. *And to flood the valley,* he concluded, *we need to plug the culvert pipe.*

Then he turned his head into the darkness and asked, "Right, Lord?"

His words were met only by the sounds of the shifting sands as they settled quietly in place.

Staring through the murk, he tried to assess the situation. He realized that he′d have to blow down a lot more of these cliffs if he hoped to stop up that enormous culvert pipe.

He looked back toward where he had just planted the charges in that shallow cave. It was now buried beneath thousands of tons of rock and dirt.

No doubt, he reasoned, *the detonator wires were severed by the falling rock, and as a result the dynamite won't go off when I try to trigger it.*

Then he turned to look toward the cliff that rose above him on the opposite corner of the bottleneck. It appeared that it was still intact.

Combined with these, maybe the explosives that I set high up on the south side will bring down enough rubble to seal the culvert. I can only pray.

He moved back past the southeastern corner and began slowly making his way west back along the base of the canyon's south wall toward McCord′s cave, continuing to unreel what he considered the now-useless detonator wire.

Someone might accuse me of negativism, he thought, *but I'm negative about my capabilities, not God's. As long as He lends me breath, I'll keep trying.* He laughed. *It's still true,* he thought: *"Man proposes, but God disposes."*

When he thought he had reached the point along the canyon wall where he'd set the first charge of dynamite, he wandered in circles in the wet grass. The futility of this exercise quickly became obvious to him, and he was ready to give up his search when the wire he'd hung from the tree limb happened to brush against his burned cheek. The discovery of the wire, combined with the renewed pain to his face, left him with mixed feelings. While he spliced the wires together, he had time to ruminate over some words of Charles Spurgeon, something about God's blessings coming down to us in letters of gold enclosed in envelopes of black.

After another five minutes he found his way back to the shallow cave where he'd sheltered earlier. He moved his rifle and backpack outside, then went to the back wall of the cave where he dug the scree out of a crevice, and inserted the last three sticks of dynamite. Leaving the cave, he made his way to the upper end of the small lake where he put handfuls of less-than-satisfactory mud into the smaller knapsack, and returned to the cave to pack the holes. He then gathered the wires and spliced them into his main cable. His fingers were so stiff with cold, and the grit under his fingernails so painful, that he could barely complete the simple chore.

The main detonator cable now extended behind him all the way to the northeast corner of the valley, where it lay beneath the fallen cliff that had almost buried him. At each stop from there to here, he'd spliced a tee into the main cable, uniting the wires in parallel that connected the charges he'd planted along the way. He would continue to unwind the cable from the reel until he settled himself in McCord's cave. At that point he would finally attach the magneto and, in theory anyway, be ready to detonate all the charges at once.

CC discarded the smaller of the two backpacks because it was filthy from carrying the mud. Then he settled the larger one over his shoulders, slung his rifle, picked up the spool, and continued unreeling the remaining cable as he moved slowly along the base of the cliff where he hoped to discover McCord's luxurious cave.

In spite of the burn on his cheek and the cut on his forehead, he realized that he was not in too bad shape. His back and shoulders ached, but all-in-all he hadn't suffered too badly from his experiences, and he continued to trudge stubbornly onward.

The batteries on his headlamp were nearly exhausted, and he was unable to see much by the aid of the waning moonlight. So he was startled when an empty tin can rattled beneath his feet. It took a moment before he realized that this must have been the place where McCord had discarded his trash.

Looking up to his left, he spotted a shadow on the cliff wall. Trailing the wire behind him, he climbed a steep slope that led to a narrow ledge. He realized that he'd finally reached McCord's highly touted cave. He used his headlamp to check the time, but his watch had stopped. It had been irreparably damaged during his journey downstream.

How, he wondered, could he synchronize the timing of his detonations with Jonathan's destruction of the dam when he didn't even know the time? He shook his head, trying to clear away the cobwebs, trying to decide when to fire the charges. He didn't dare wait too long, for if someone discovered his explosives, they would cut the wires, and then follow the cables back to this hiding place. And if Jonathan leveled the dam before he successfully caved in the canyon walls, the resultant flood might wash away his wires.

And what if the stones Jonathan blasts from the dam wind up blocking the underground river that drains the cavern? I hadn't thought of that. Would they all drown?

He worried about that for a moment, then realized that they should be safe. *First,* he reasoned, *the two tunnels below the underground dam should drain off most of the flow, but if they didn't, his little company should have enough time to escape through the back of the mountain before the waters below the dam pooled high enough to flood the tunnels.*

He snorted. *They might be okay, but I won't be. I'll be stuck down here with a flooded valley and enemy soldiers between me and my friends.*

Realizing that he would be at risk of someone noticing his light, he turned on the almost invisible red LED, and began searching through the large backpack. He discovered some canned heat. And in a little plastic baggie next to the canned heat he found a box of wooden matches. *Well, I'm grateful to find them now,* he thought with chagrin as he gingerly touched the burned spot on his face, *but I can't help wishing I'd found them earlier.*

With shaking hands he removed the lid from the canned heat and lit the fuel. Now he had a tiny but intense cooking fire. He opened a can of beef stew, and propped it above the flame. In about five minutes, he found himself salivating from the odor. He pulled a plastic spoon from the pack, and bent over the can, carefully spooning out the precious meal. It warped the spoon and burned his lips, so he decided to wait for it to cool. *It shouldn't take long in this cold,* he thought.

Then he rummaged through his backpack and discovered a cello-pack of oatmeal-raisin cookies. He tore it open and wolfed them down. He'd never felt so hungry. It was amazing how he could almost feel the food being converted into energy as it warmed him up. When he checked the temperature of the stew, he found he could lift the can in his hands, so he half-drank, half-spooned the contents.

He looked west, up the valley, trying to fathom whether Jonathan might be ready. Had the boy heard him at what seemed an age ago when he shouted that he wanted him to detonate the charges at five a.m.? Indeed, would he have set the charges in the dam, or had Jim taken control and frustrated their plans?

It doesn't matter! he thought. *I came here to do this, and I will do it.* Questions raced through his mind. *Is it anywhere near time,* he wondered. *Will the soldiers locate both of us before we're ready? How long do I dare wait?*

CC reached down for the cable reel. There was still maybe a hundred feet of wire wrapped around it, but it was designed so that the actual end of the cable protruded out the side of the reel. He stripped the two ends, then attached them one at a time to the contacts on the magneto. Then he cranked the handle to build the fateful charge of electricity.

According to Jonathan, all he had to do now was turn the lever on the magneto to release 40,000 volts of low amperage electricity that would flow the length of the wire in less than a second and, theoretically, set off the fulminate of mercury in all the blasting caps. Those small explosions would in turn detonate the dynamite.

CC sat staring up at the dark sky, the magneto nestled in his lap. After a few minutes, he leaned back against a large boulder, said brief prayer, and closed his eyes.

Corking the Bottle

McCord's Cave
May 1st, 5:01 AM

His dreams were troubled. First, a house consumed by flames was washed away by a river in full flood, while a congregation sang and prayed in the background. Then a tall bearded man – Lincoln? – was speaking to a multitude.

CC watched as each person's face seemed to morph into a gravestone, and as the speaker himself seemed to be drawn down into the earth, his last words echoing across a star-strewn sky:

"*...that we here highly resolve that these dead shall not have died in vain–that this nation, under God, shall have a new birth* *of freedom–and that government of the people, by the people, for the people, shall not perish from the earth."*

CC awoke exhausted and nauseous, unable to recall the dreams, and wondering what had disturbed his sleep. He blinked his eyes several times, and tried to stare out into the darkness. About three hundred yards away, across the stream, he saw fireflies twinkling among the trees. His eyes burned, his back ached, and he just wanted to go back to sleep, but he willed his mind to be clear.

The night was very still, not even the cicadas singing, but he could hear the beat of a drum – a slow cadence.

A drum? He continued staring in disbelief.

Those aren't fireflies! he realized. *They're flashlights!*

He blinked his eyes again in an attempt to clear his vision. Now he saw them, shadowy figures moving slowly up the wood road from the bottleneck, marching to the beat of a drummer. *This is surreal,* he thought, shaking his head. He tried to count them, but it was impossible with the flashlights bobbing in the darkness, and he lost count at three dozen.

What am I doing here? he wondered, and the answer came. *I'm here to help see that "...this nation, under God, shall have a new birth of freedom...!"* He sat up abruptly and squared his shoulders.

Where did that come from? he wondered. But with those words resonating in his mind came the memory of the responsibility he bore and the realization that he couldn't wait much longer to try to fulfill it.

The large group of men moving up the valley joined the few who were gathered around a campfire near the swimming hole. They appeared to be busying themselves setting up camp and making coffee. *That should give me a breather,* he thought.

What time is it? he wondered. He looked to the east, and could see the pre-dawn glow in the sky. *It must be at least 5 a.m.,* he thought. *If we don't do something soon, those guys will be on top of Jonathan in the caverns and it will be too late.*

Then he heard something else. It sounded like a muffled explosion. Had the teen blown the dam, after all? If so, CC needed to hurry to do his part. If he couldn't block the conduit at the end of the lake, any water that Jonathan released would just flow on through the bottleneck. It wouldn't back up and flood the valley, and everything they'd been through would have been in vain.

He reached for the magneto, but it had fallen to the floor of the cave while he'd slept. He scrambled around in the darkness, dragging his fingers over the rough floor, feeling for it. His fingers caught one of the wires and accidentally pulled it loose.

There's no help for it, he thought. *I have to have light.* He reached to his forehead and fumbled for the switch on his headlamp. The white light came on, and a moment later there was a shout from across the river.

He bent for the magneto just as a rifle bullet ricocheted off the cave wall near his shoulder. Kneeling on the floor he held the magneto in one hand and the loose wire in the other. With fingers still stiff from the cold, and a mind numb from lack of sleep, he clumsily wrapped the bare end of the wire around the electrode and screwed the wing nut down. Then, without hesitating, he twisted the detonator.

Nothing happened.

He felt the wind in his hair as another bullet passed by him at a nominal 1,200 feet per second, followed a split-second later by the actual sound of the discharge. He dove for the floor and immediately turned off the headlamp.

What now? If they shoot enough times, one of their bullets is bound to ricochet off a cave wall and hit me.

He stared between a couple of boulders and could see at least a dozen powerful flashlight beams aimed in his direction. He thought he could hear laughing. They were having target practice, and he was the target. He had to work fast. The bullets were coming so rapidly now that he couldn't count them. He tried to focus on the task at hand.

He thought that the magneto could be defective, but then he realized that the stored charge might also have leaked away while he slept. He had no idea whether he could repair the thing, but it didn′t matter. There was no time.

Another bullet struck near the mouth of the cave, but without his light to serve as a target, the shooters weren′t so accurate. It didn′t really matter. With that rate of fire, they were bound to get him sooner or later. For the moment, he figured that they couldn′t decide whether he was a target of opportunity, or not worth bothering with. They might decide to pass him by. But if a couple of them moved around to his side of the lake, he′d be in big trouble.

With that unhappy thought, his eyes turned toward the bottleneck at the east end of the valley, and he saw a few men carrying flashlights change course and start walking up his side of the canyon. He laughed at the irony, but the sound came out as a near-hysterical giggle.

Trying to ignore the rifle fire, he gripped the magneto firmly with one hand, twisted the charging crank with the other, and immediately pressed the detonator button. Again, nothing happened. He slumped forward, supporting his forehead on his fist, realizing that after all he′d been through, he'd failed.

He began to chide himself. *Maybe I didn't properly set the detonators in the dynamite. Maybe I broke a wire. Maybe the enemy found the charges. Maybe...* He bent down to reach for the wires, to recheck the connections, to try just one more time.

He again cranked the charger on the device and twisted the lever. A heartbeat later he felt a dull shock through the rock on which he was lying. It was followed a split second later by the sound of a several distinct explosions.

The cave floor shook beneath him, and after a second or two he heard a crashing sound. He risked lifting his head to see what was going on. The men across the stream had ceased shooting at him and were now pointing their flashlights down the valley toward the sources of the multiple explosions. CC's eyes followed their beams.

Several hundred yards down the valley, above the cave where he'd taken shelter from the rain, the air seemed to actually be wavering. *It must be some sort of optical illusion,* he thought. But, no! Here and there stones and waves of sand began dropping from the cliff face. Then an enormous section of the canyon wall broke loose and seemed to hang suspended before it suddenly plunged down into the valley.

At the same instant, a dull report echoed back from across the canyon. His eyes turned toward the southeast corner of the bottleneck where he could sense rather than see another immense section of the cliff crash into the gap near the culvert pipe. Now the sun seemed to be rising behind the tops of the trees that stood in the bottleneck, and the sky took on a brighter glow.

The entire cliff wall on the northeast corner of the valley appeared to quiver in the growing light. The eroded rock began to drift slowly away from the roots of the mountain and crumble before his eyes. Like a great slice of gray wedding cake, it seemed to stand there, then it began to tip, and finally fall, crashing to the valley floor below, burying a dozen men who had turned to run back through the bottleneck.

It was awesome. The dynamite had begun the work, but it was the old rotten rock of the mountain that seemed to be tearing itself apart, it's own mass yielding to the gravity that brought it crashing to the valley floor. The boulder on which CC was perched was vibrating with the shock waves, and he wondered whether the roof of the cave might come down on his head. When a few small pieces of the ceiling broke loose and dropped around him, he decided it was time to move. He caught up his rifle, grabbed a strap on his pack, and toddled across the vibrating shelf of rock to get outside the cave entrance and take shelter on the ledge.

The air was filling with dust, and the incipient sunrise was turning into a strange kind of twilight as a result of the growing clouds of dust spreading across the valley. The dust was so thick that he couldn't tell whether he'd succeeded in blocking either the conduit or the bottleneck. Keeping well up the slope from the valley floor, CC left the cave and began slowly making his way west along the side of the canyon toward the Sennett farm. Then, as the rising morning breeze began to clear the dust away, he saw what looked like a great irregular earth bank across the end of the canyon. He blinked his eyes. The far end of the little lake was filled with earth, with rock piled three and four stories high across the entire bottleneck.

A thrill went through him. It looked like they had done what they set out to do. By God′s grace, he had been able to plug the bottleneck. He started to laugh and found himself singing some half-remembered hymn.

He sat down on the top of a flat boulder, his legs hanging out over its edge, staring down the valley at the earth dam, and trying to clear the ringing sound from ears that were still throbbing with the deafening roar of the explosions.

He turned to see what the soldiers were doing.

Funny! he thought. *They are all running around over there, and no one's paying attention to me anymore.* And then he heard another sound, a dull roaring that was in contrast to the hollow ringing in his ears.

He looked up the valley. It was the sound of a flood set loose. Jonathan had been able to destroy the dam! And the result was incredible. The enormous pressure from within the caverns was causing the water to shoot out through the underground tunnel like a stream from a gigantic fire hose. But there was a second, even larger stream of water bursting out of the side of the cliff just above the first, and CC realized it was the overflow tunnel adding its volume to the river that regularly rushed down the canyon.

The stream, in spring flood, had already been overflowing its steep banks, in places covering the road and reaching out toward the walls on either side of the valley, and the normal flow had begun pooling behind CC′s newly created earth dam.

But now a wall of muddy water, perhaps four feet high, and spreading across the west end of the valley, glowed dirtily in the first rays of the morning sun as it began its relentless roll down the length of the valley. It was sweeping up everything in its path – trees, rocks, fence railings, and soldiers – and carrying them away in its surge. What CC had once considered immovable boulders were being rolled along by the monstrous current, creating a racket that defied description.

"My God!" he exclaimed in wonder. "What have we done?"

The crest of the flood seemed to roll majestically toward him, but when it swept past, it was moving at a dizzying speed, and only a moment later it smashed into the wall of earth downstream. Then, as though angered that its stubborn career had been frustrated by the earthen dam, the water swept high into the air, its muddy foam fouling the morning light, then falling back, defeated by the obstruction, to swirl and swell behind the makeshift dam.

The water level rose so rapidly that CC considered deserting his place on the edge of the boulder, and to retreat up the slope behind Sennett's cave. The water leveled off so close to his perch that he could almost reach the surface with his toes, and he found himself estimating that the rough trail he'd followed to reach McCord's cave was already under at least twenty feet of water.

CC noticed a couple of soldiers caught on the edge of the flood, trying to swim against the impossible current. Their efforts appeared feeble, and they finally disappeared in the raging tide. As the depth of the water increased, it changed the entire appearance of the valley. Even on the far side, where its builders had kept the winding log road on the high ground, it had all but disappeared. The entire lower end of the valley was now underwater. He estimated that the lake had risen at least thirty feet above its normal level.

The swelling stream climbed rapidly up the loose earth dam that impounded it, then its growing depth seemed to slow as it required ever greater volume to spread out across the valley. CC sat there watching the turgid water rise, dyed brown by the thousands of tons of soil it had ripped from the valley floor. The perimeter of the little lake at the end of the valley had grown until it reached across the entire east end of the valley.

Then the water rose above the banks of the flume upstream from the lake, and though he could still see the turbidity of the flume and the waterfalls in the center of the valley, the original stream had become a submerged river. His eyes moved far up the valley where he saw just the tops of the huge rock monoliths marking what had once been his swimming hole.

And then it all came back to him, his first swim, the bath, the catharsis, the yielding to God. He stood to his feet, raised his hands to heaven, and cried out, "Praise God!" CC stood there for several minutes, giving thanks.

When he looked out across the valley again, he saw a single surviving soldier. The man was seated on a boulder on the far side of the valley, isolated from the far cliffs by perhaps fifty yards of roiling water. Even at nearly a quarter-mile distance, CC knew that the man was watching him. The man rose to his feet, and lifted something in his arms – his rifle?

Is he going to shoot at me? CC wondered. The man held the weapon in front of him in his two hands, then pushed it away, as though repudiating it, tossing it out over the water where it instantly disappeared from sight. Then he raised one hand and pointed to the sky. Was CC imagining it? Was he raising his index finger toward the heavens? Was he also an errant believer come home again? When the man waved at him, CC was certain he was right. He raised his hand and waved back.

The two of them had surely witnessed a work of God, a drowning of Pharaoh's army in a Red Sea. It was a miracle, a stamp of approval for those who believed in the right to life, liberty, and the pursuit of happiness, and based those beliefs on God's Word.

He thought of the farm′s livestock, and hoped that the domestic animals were at the west end of the valley, safely above water level.

He turned to the right and directed his attention once again to the earth dam that sealed off the bottleneck. It had served its purpose. The flood waters had reached the top and begun to flow over the lip. CC saw the rivulet that cut through the top of the embankment grow until it became a small stream. The stream in turn widened and soon became a torrent that ripped through the softer earth at the top of the dam, but failed to move the enormous slabs of rock that made up the heart of the earth dam.

The overflowing water had coursed down the center of the bottleneck and over what had been the entry road, tearing a new stream bed as it swept toward the main highway, even ripping out some of the stately old trees by their roots, scouring up the earth alongside the buried culvert pipe, and carving out a deep channel well below the surface of the old log road over which he′d entered the valley.

CC couldn't see it, but the initial flow that had reached the end of the valley began to run down the side of State Highway 19, between the rocky escarpment and the pavement, following the swale on the edge of the road, and ripping out the culverts. Within minutes the blacktop was stripped away and whole sections of the mountain highway were washed into the valley below.

The ledge on which CC had dismounted from his log just a few hours before was gone. In fact, the highway above it was gone. The flow of water over the top of the waterfall had cut away the highway, its lip now fifty feet closer to the entrance of the bottleneck. The huge corrugated culvert pipe that once crossed beneath the highway, now lay twisted over the edge of the newly sculpted cliff, and hung limply suspended out over the valley below. The wood road through the bottleneck had become an almost impassable ravine, and anyone who wished to enter the valley from the ruined highway could only do so by climbing sideways across several hundred feet of cliff using ropes and pitons.

The state road up the mountain was destroyed. It would be years, perhaps never, before anyone would replace that major north-south route.

No one would get into the valley, let alone into or out of the bottleneck, except by helicopter. And because the valley was full of mud and water, it was unlikely that even a helicopter could land until the water level dropped.

CC knew nothing of the havoc they had produced, let alone how effective they had been in achieving their goal. But he smiled with grim satisfaction at the destruction he could see. It represented a small victory ... and a far greater defeat. For that was all it was. It would not change things. Perhaps it would give them a brief respite, but little more.

His mind flashed back to the day they had learned that Elizabeth had been a curator at a Boston museum, and how, on the day the war began, the *Declaration of Independence* and the *Constitution of the United States* were to be put on display. As the only survivor on the museum staff, and with the city under attack, she'd rescued the invaluable documents and carried them with her into the mountains of Vermont.

Now their little group was destined to leave this place, to try to take America's great state papers to some other hideaway. And, perhaps some day they would see those documents once again ensconced in a fitting place of memorial.

Memorial? No! He thought. *These are living documents, perhaps not inspired in the biblical sense, but prayerfully produced under His guidance, and acknowledging the One True God. The only item that excelled them for the raw impact they had upon humanity was the Book from which their inherent truths flowed – "The Holy Bible."*

But those documents might not reach a place of safe-keeping for many years into the future, and it would only happen if dedicated men and women were able to stay ahead of America's enemies and somehow remain alive.

He picked up his rifle and began making his way carefully over the banks of scree and falling rock toward the Sennett Farm. There was no risk of anyone shooting him in the growing daylight. In fact, apart from the one soldier who'd thrown his rifle away, there appeared to be no one left alive to mount such an attack. As far as he could tell, every one of his unwelcome visitors had been drowned in the flood.

Shaking his head, he looked for a way along the canyon wall. He would have to find a path that would enable him to reach the west end of the valley.

With God's help, he could find the back entrance to the caverns and hopefully hook up with his little company.

Shared Experiences

The Caverns
May 2nd, 3:25 a.m

No one spoke. They were all gathered around the pale glow of a kerosene lantern, and the gloom of the surrounding cavern was made even more impenetrable by the effect of its glare on their tired eyes.

Their exhaustion was evident. When they looked around at one another, each mirrored the worn expression of his neighbor. Every face was dirt-grimed, lined and haggard. Their hair was matted, and their unwashed bodies had not become a cause for personal embarrassment only because they all shared the same problem.

Their circumstances seemed all the more dismal because, over the preceding months, each of them had enjoyed a hot shower and a change of underclothes every day, and they all realized that it might be a long time, if ever, before they again bathed in hot water.

It had taken CC several hours to make his way back to them. With a helicopter flying up and down the valley searching for survivors, he had been forced to lie up in a damp shallow cave to avoid detection. He wasn't able to reenter the main caverns and locate his little company until after darkness had forced the Chinese to call off their futile search.

While CC had been in the valley exulting in their achievement, the group had no idea that he had even survived, much less succeeded. In fact, they believed that CC had perished, and that they had simply reduced the likelihood of their enemies using the caverns as a base of operations

So while CC had been hiding from the Chinese, Jonathan had been leading the four surviving members of their tiny band along a confusing series of passages to the agreed on rendezvous point, well back inside the mountain. These were live caverns that had been carved by nature, not by the hands of man. And Jim, who'd tried to keep track of the complex twistings and turnings they had made, realized that he could never hope to find his way back to the dam, much less to the place of escape on the west side of the mountain that had been hinted at by Jonathan.

It was, in fact, the place that CC and Jonathan had agreed upon, but with the likelihood of CC's death, Jonathan had only gone there because they all needed rest, and because he harbored the stubborn hope that CC had somehow survived and would show up. But even now, he was determined to move on before daylight.

Where these two tunnels crossed, the roof was just out of reach, but the floor area was large enough for all of them to sit or lie down without crowding. They group was resting at the junction of two natural tunnels when CC had stepped out of the murk. He'd found his way back only moments before, and now sat propped against one of the tunnel walls, his arms locked around his legs, his head resting on upraised knees, the stereotype of a

Mexican enjoying his siesta. Instead of being warm and well-fed, however, CC was cold, hungry, and exhausted.

He raised his eyes to see how Jonathan was faring, and the look that he received in return made it clear that the teen still considered him their leader. It was a role for which he′d once believed he lacked the qualifications, not to mention the ambition, but the past twenty-four hours had somehow altered that conviction.

He had originally assumed the mantle of leadership because it was thrust upon him. This was his home, and as the first and only adult, he had become responsible for Sarah and Jonathan. When the other three adults had arrived, he had considered them simply his guests, individuals unable to survive for any length of time on their own.

When McCord had challenged him over his qualifications months before, he had concluded that he might not be much of a leader, but unfortunately, he was the best available. Now, overnight, CC had become convinced that he was God′s man for the job.

His eyes flicked from person to person. Rachel was handing a roll of gauze to Elizabeth. They hadn′t been able to bring much in the way of food or medical supplies, simply because they did not have the capacity among them to carry more. So their dwindling medical supplies had become far more precious than gold.

As Elizabeth worked over Jim in the dim light, her cheeks were two bright spots. It was clear that anger festered near the surface, but she held her tongue. She reached out for a bandage, her face shining with perspiration, the humidity of the caverns compounding the exhausting activities of the past day. She caught Rachel′s eyes with her own and offered just the hint of a smile.

It was Rachel's steady loving ways that had kept them all together through many difficult times, and CC had ceased to wonder whether it was all some sort of an act. Rachel was simply

Rachel, and she was the best medicine in the world for a group like theirs.

She continued digging through a pack in search of something, while Elizabeth held a compress against Jim's forehead in an effort to staunch the flow of blood. He was clearly in pain and did not move or speak.

Jonathan was sitting across the tunnel a few feet away. His back was also to the wall, his rifle across his thighs, and his arms locked about his knees, a grim caricature of CC. Behind him, out of sight in the darkness, his adoring shadow, Sarah, lay curled up in a sleeping bag.

CC pointed at Jim, demanding an account. "What happened?"

Jim stared at him from sunken eyes, but remained sullenly silent.

Rachel turned to Jonathan, anticipating that he would explain, but his only reaction was to move the muzzle of his weapon slightly so that it was pointed at McCord.

So Rachel took the initiative, and began in halting phrases to tell the story.

"When you and Jonathan were in the water beneath the dam, and you were trying to swim toward one another, Jim took hold of the rope that was serving as Jonathan′s lifeline, and yanked him away from you. After you were out of Jonathan′s reach, Jim let go of the rope, allowing the current to pull Jonathan back toward the whirlpool. Then he began untying the end of the rope, and it seemed obvious that he didn′t care if you both drowned."

The teen muttered something, and CC turned to him. "What did you say, Jonathan?"

"I said, it wasn′t that Jim didn′t care whether or not we drowned." The boy tipped his rifle barrel in McCord′s direction. "He tried to murder us."

CC′s turned to Rachel. She bit her lip, but nodded quickly and decisively.

Elizabeth picked up the story. "He seemed insane. We had to stop him, no matter what. I was on his blind side, so I pushed him as hard as I could toward the edge of the dam. He fell and started to roll beneath the railing, so he was forced to let go of the rope in order to grab for one of the posts."

She looked down into McCord's eyes, and suddenly remembered who it was she was helping. Her anger became venomous. McCord moaned as she ripped the blood-encrusted gauze from his wound, then threw it to the floor.

CC thought, *She's judged him, and when she threw the bandage down, it was her way of putting an exclamation point on the end of her sentence.*

Her next words summed up her feelings.

"He managed to hang on to the railing to keep from falling over the side. I wish I'd stamped on his hands."

"It's probably just as well you didn't kick him over the side," Rachel remarked. "He would have tried to snatch the rope away from Jonathan in order to save himself."

She looked at CC to see whether he understood what she was talking about.

"The loose end of the rope was sliding over the top rail, and I just managed to catch it before it dropped to the pool below. In the meantime, Jim's legs were dangling over the edge of the dam, and his hold on the stanchion was all that kept him from dropping into the pool. He managed to pull himself back onto the top of the dam, and started crawling toward Elizabeth who now had her back to him. I couldn't help her because it took all of my strength to hold onto the rope to keep Jonathan from being swept away."

Elizabeth again took up the tale.

"I joined Rachel on the end of the rope, and then Jim tried to tackle me. But we were able to make our way across the top of the dam, all the while dragging Jonathan diagonally across the pool below so that he could climb up onto the ledge near the water wheel."

Elizabeth glanced up at CC.

"I'd been trying to keep track of your position in the water, and as soon as we knew that Jonathan had dragged himself onto the ledge and was safe, I shouted at him to let loose of the rope. It took him only a moment. As soon as it was free, I started to pull it back in order to throw it to you. I'd have done it too, but, just before you were sucked under by the whirlpool, Jim slapped the rope away and spoiled my aim. Then he reached around me and punched Rachel, almost knocking her off the dam. Then he turned on me again."

"That was Jim's big mistake," Rachel said, touching the dark bruise beneath her left eye. "Jonathan couldn't help us because he was lying on the ledge below, trying to catch his breath. But it wasn't too late for me to help Elizabeth."

"That's for sure," Elizabeth laughed. "Rachel picked up a length of the broken iron railing that lay atop the dam, and just as Jim was about to push me over the side, she hit him over the head with it."

"Yeah," Jonathan added, satisfaction in his voice, "I couldn't hear the pipe hit him from where I was down on the ledge, but I sure saw him drop like a rock."

McCord made a guttural sound, his loathing fixed on Jonathan, but he said nothing.

Rachel ignored McCord and turned back to CC.

"I was wondering what you had shouted to Jonathan when you passed the rope to him, and I asked Elizabeth if she'd heard you. She hadn't, but Jonathan had. And after he'd climbed back to the top of the dam, he told us that wanted us to blow up the dam at 5 am."

Elizabeth picked up the account. "When Jim came to, he lay there with his eyes closed, pretending to be unconscious. But in the meantime, Jonathan had used the rope to tie him. When Jim realized that he was trussed up like a Christmas goose, and that we were discussing how to go about dynamiting the dam, he was beside himself with rage. He tried to get to his feet, but discovered that not only were his wrists tied together, but that his ankles were tied to the base of the railing."

"Yes," Jonathan laughed. "We'd dragged him between the railing and the edge of the dam, and if he wiggled too much, he'd find himself hanging upside down, suspended over the edge of the dam. First he swore at us. Then he threatened us. And when he realized that threats wouldn't work, he started his old routine, and began whining that we should *reason* with him."

There was silence for a moment. Then Elizabeth added, "He called Jonathan a liar about your telling him to blow up the dam, swearing that you never said any such thing."

Rachel commented, "We'd all been listening to his lies and half-truths for months, and his word no longer meant a thing to us."

Jim had remained silent, listening to their denunciations. He opened his mouth with the obvious intention of refuting their charges, but subsided when Rachel uncharacteristically slapped him where, just moments before, she'd been holding a cold compress.

Elizabeth's lips curled in a tight smile, but she spoke as though nothing untoward had occurred. Pointing at Jim, she said, "He kept repeating that you'd given up on the idea of destroying the dam." She shook her head, her face a sardonic mask. "He just wouldn't give up! You had been down in the water, shouting to Jonathan, while Jim was at the top of the dam with us. And he had the gall to suggest that he'd heard what you'd said above the roar of the water."

"And so," Rachel interrupted, "when we continued to discuss what had to be done to accomplish the task of blowing up the dam, he began to bluster that he wouldn't let us. He insisted that – with you dead and him being the oldest man left – he was unquestionably in charge." His words really frightened Sarah, She started jumping up and down, crying, 'No, no! CC's not dead. I know it. He just can't be.' The poor kid started to weep hysterically. 'He's alive!' she kept crying. 'I know he's alive!' I'll never forget how frantic she was, nor forgive Jim for frightening her."

"We hated to scare Sarah," Rachel added, "but I had to shout to the others in order to be heard above the waterfall. I told them that we had to face reality and base our decisions on the worst possible scenario. I had to admit that I didn't think you had much of a chance."

CC nodded his head. "I didn't have a chance in the world. The fact of my survival is otherworldly. There's no doubt about it."

Rachel looked up from her efforts to bandage Jim's head. She mused, "He's been bleeding like a stuck pig. He should probably have a few stitches."

"Don't denigrate pigs by comparing them with him," Elizabeth snorted. "And don't waste any more of our scarce medical supplies on him. Besides, scalp wounds always bleed a lot."

CC ignored the exchange. "Things might have been different if Jonathan didn't feel he had to act like a hero by leaping into the pool," he commented.

The boy looked down, pained at receiving CC's public censure.

Surprisingly, Elizabeth took the teen's side. "There's no point in being angry at Jonathan for what he did. He'd been under tremendous pressure for a boy his age. He'd already lost so much."

Her words took on a shade of melancholy, and they all sat brooding for a moment, each remembering something of their own personal losses. She looked around the circle, and with a lightness that belied her earlier words, she tallied the score.

"He was doing what he could for his friends. And look at what he achieved by leaping into the pool. If CC hadn't followed Jonathan into the water, the valley would never have been flooded. So God worked things out using Jonathan as part of his plan."

"More than that." All eyes turned to Rachel. "Jonathan felt that he *had* to do it."

"Huh? What do you mean, I had to do it?" Jonathan demanded.

"We all knew that you mistakenly believed you had betrayed your parents by not obeying them, and that if you'd gone with them to church the night the war started, you might have convinced them and some of the other members at the all-night prayer meeting to take shelter in your father's mushroom caves. But because you instead went to the caves and survived, while they insisted on remaining at the church where they died from radiation poisoning, you felt guilty. You had to make amends. You couldn't bring them back, but when you dove into the pool, trying to do CC's job, you were also trying to redeem yourself by offering yourself to save us."

She paused to reflect on her own words. Then she turned to the others. "I think that if Jonathan hadn't done that, he would never again have been able to look at himself in a mirror."

"Hey," the boy remonstrated. "You're talking about me, and I'm sitting right here." They all turned to him and after a moment, he added, "Besides, I know that I could never get rid of my guilt. No one can. It took Jesus to wash my sins away."

Someone said, "Amen," and for a few minutes after that, no one spoke.

Elizabeth returned to the account.

"All that time we were talking, Jim was lying there watching and listening. I asked him why he kept us from throwing the rope to you. He denied that he had. I couldn't believe his gall. He actually said that we were so confused by the stress of the situation that we didn't know what we were talking about."

She turned to CC. "Then Jonathan told us that Jim had actually pushed you off the top of the dam."

"He what?"

She spoke slowly, deliberately, in a steady cadence: "Jonathan said that Jim pushed you off the dam."

CC looked over at Jonathan, and the boy nodded. He hadn't really needed confirmation of her statement, for he'd already suspected that was the case, but when he caught Jonathan's eye, he winked conspiratorially at the boy. He received a dazzling smile in return.

Elizabeth's statement explained the hard bump he'd received when he was standing on the edge of the dam staring down at the boy in the water, and his subsequent fall from the top of the dam into the pool below.

"Jonathan saw it from the water," she explained. He was floating on his back, and you and Jim were silhouetted in the light.

McCord mumbled something.

"What did you say?" Jonathan challenged.

"I said, 'That's nonsense!'"

Elizabeth held up her hand again, as though to slap him, and he subsided, but everyone else simply ignored him. She turned back to CC. "After you were dragged under by the whirlpool, and in spite of his betrayal, Mr. McCord continued to try to persuade us to let him take over, even though he was all trussed up."

"Yes," CC observed dryly. "You've got to give him high marks for persistence."

"I think we should give him an 'L,' for liar," Rachel commented.

"Or an 'A' for attempted murderer," Elizabeth added.

"Anyway, we ignored Jim, and instead went about trying to get Jonathan warm and dry."

"But," Rachel interrupted, "Jonathan didn't want to waste any time. He said we needed to get right to work setting the explosives on the dam. Then Jim recommended that Jonathan take a little nap. It was the first suggestion he'd made that sounded halfway sensible to us, but Jonathan would have none of it. He told us that anything Jim might suggest has to be taken with a grain of salt. Then he added that we probably ought to do the opposite without even discussing it. We all laughed at that."

"So," Elizabeth continued, "Jonathan's decision prevailed. He insisted that since we didn't know whether we had enough time left to accomplish what was required, we needed to get started. 'I'll rest later,' he told us."

"What I said was, make hay while the sun shines," the boy interrupted. "That's what I told you. I learned that from CC."

Rachel again picked up the account. "We thought we'd risk letting Jim up off the cold wet floor. He said he needed to go to the bathroom, so we untied his feet and tied his hands in front of him, but as soon as we turned our backs, he reached down and started dragging the backpack containing the explosives toward the underground lake. I yelled at him to stop, and he shouted he wanted to get it out of harm's way where it wouldn't get wet."

"When I ran after him, and grabbed the backpack, we had a little tug of war, with him trying to toss both me and the explosives into the river. Jonathan and Rachel ran to my assistance and tripped him up. We retied his feet, and Jonathan told Jim that he'd lost his bathroom privileges." Jim demanded to know what he was to do, and Jonathan told him to work things out the best he could."

Elizabeth laughed. "It was about then that Rachel and I realized that Jonathan had really taken on the responsibilities of leadership. After he had changed into warm, dry clothes, he and I crawled around the base of the dam setting the charges. It went well because the dam was really massive, and we were working where there were wide gaps between some of the huge stones that formed the outer layer of the dam. It enabled us to push the explosives back into the face of the dam a couple of feet.

"In the meantime," Rachel added, "I stayed up above, caring for Sarah, and keeping an eye on Jim."

"Yes," Elizabeth laughed, "but Jim had stopped giving us trouble by then."

"What do you mean?" CC asked. "He gave you more trouble?"

Rachel snorted. "He tried. Jonathan and Elizabeth had retrieved her portfolio from wherever you and she had hidden it. When she brought it back, she leaned it against the wall of the cave about fifty feet upstream from the dam. When no one was looking, Jim somehow got free and grabbed the portfolio. And when I caught up with him a second time, he knocked me down. I wrestled with him for it, and he slapped me down again." Rachel pointed to the purple mark beneath her eye.

Elizabeth picked up the story. "Jonathan and I had returned to the top of the dam to get the remainder of the blasting supplies. I was concerned because Jonathan was really exhausted. He wasn't able to keep dry because of the clouds of vapor around the base of the dam. His lips were actually blue, and he was shaking so violently that I was frightened of his trying to handle the blasting caps."

"Yes," Rachel cut in, "and because he was cold and tired, Jim didn't consider him a threat to his plans. That was his big mistake."

Elizabeth laughed. "You've heard what a great striker Jonathan was in high school soccer. Well, when Jim was about to hit Rachel again, Jonathan came racing up from the dam, the sounds of his footsteps masked by the waterfall, and he gave Jim one of his famous kicks, right in the you-know-where, lifting him clear off the ground."

"Jim was bent over making all sorts of funny noises for several minutes," Rachel continued, but Jonathan just seemed to get angrier, and he kicked him in the kneecap, all the time repeating, 'How dare you strike a lady!'"

When Rachel laughed, the bruising to her cheek made her grimace. Nonetheless, she added, "It was really something to see!"

"Then," Elizabeth continued, "Jim turned on Jonathan, and Rachel, our resident female martial arts expert, decked him. Jim was out cold for all of three minutes, and that gave us ample time to properly tie him up again. This time we wrapped his wrists and ankles with plastic wire wraps. We haven't had any trouble from him since."

CC turned to Jonathan, but the teenager's attention was fixed on McCord, though there didn't seem much to observe unless it was to watch the man slowly breathing in and out. The women's account gave CC one of his few occasions for smiling in the past twenty-four hours.

It would have been something to have seen young Jonathan crush Jim's enormous ego, he thought, but the thought made him feel a little ashamed.

Such thoughts of revenge seem sophomoric and uncharitable, and definitely unChristian. On the other hand, he thought, *this man tried to murder several of us, and came very near succeeding. So although he's temporarily under restraint, he is certainly more dangerous than we had ever imagined.*

He stared at McCord, trying to discern his motives and his loyalties.

Then Elizabeth said something that made him feel as though she had been reading his mind.

"There are a lot of unexplained questions that need answering," she told CC. "You've been nothing but kind and generous to Jim. Yet he has persisted in trying to harm all of us. His motives certainly go beyond petty jealousy. I wish I knew his angle."

CC nodded his agreement. "So do I." Then he clarified the situation. "It would be better to know his motives, but not absolutely imperative."

"What is imperative?" Elizabeth asked.

"The facts. He has attempted murder a number of times. It's not necessary to know a rabid dog's motives; it's only necessary to make certain that he cannot satisfy them."

CC realized that he did not have the time to search for any additional information. In spite of the realization that McCord must have been working with the enemy, the urgency of the moment demanded his complete attention. Time simply didn't permit him to dwell on the McCord mystery. What they had to do, he realized, was to escape from the caverns without having to do McCord any more harm than necessary, and without suffering any harm from him in turn. That meant that they somehow had to keep him from following them, or telling anyone where they'd gone. If they couldn't accomplish that without undue sacrifice, then they would have to deal more severely with McCord.

In the meantime, CC had wanted to thank Jonathan for helping to hold things together during his absence. When, however, he had attempted to do so, he'd failed dismally. Earlier, for example, he'd turned to the boy with a forced humor. "Why Jonathan...your attack on Jim doesn't sound like the merciful act of a brother in Christ."

Jonathan looked defensive, then seemed to realize he was being ribbed. He grinned at CC. "I guess I reverted to Old Testament doctrine."

"How so?"

"You know, '...an eye for an eye...?'"

Jim had given them a sour look, and cursed under his breath. "I could have killed you all, any time I wanted."

Jonathan's voice had grown cold as he turned his attention to Jim. "You wanted to kill us, you tried to kill us, and you failed to kill us," he replied.

"Well, it isn't over until it's over," McCord had snapped back. "And this isn't the first shot we've taken at this guy," he said, nodding at CC.

"What's that supposed to mean," CC had demanded, suddenly very alert and very involved in the conversation. "And who is the *we* you referred to?

"You'll find out in due time," McCord had promised.

"We'll take that as another serious threat," Jonathan snapped.

"Take it as a promise," McCord spat back.

Rachel was securing a bandage to McCord's head. She said, "You had plenty of other opportunities to hurt us. Why didn't you?"

"Because, I had nowhere else I'd dare go at the time, and no one else I wanted to be with."

"That's crazy!" Jonathan stated flatly.

McCord turned to him with a strange look in his eyes, but snapped his mouth closed without responding.

CC wanted to say, *And maybe, Jonathan, you're not so far from the truth.* Instead he took a shot in the dark. "Yes, crazy like a fox."

That got everyone's attention. "The truth is, McCord," he continued, "it's not just we five who are unhappy with you, is it?" And CC took another verbal shot in the dark. "You're beginning to realize that your former associates are disillusioned with you because of your failures, and you're afraid to find out just how disillusioned they are."

The truth of his remark struck a common chord in all of them.

McCord mumbled, "Yeah, and you're one of my failures," but he didn't speak loud enough for anyone to make out his words.

When CC asked him to repeat himself, McCord dissembled, and attempted to change the subject. "You're on a fishing expedition!" he challenged, but his words held no conviction. To the others, it appeared to be just another one of his innumerable attempts to mislead and confuse them. He looked from person to person, a smug smile on his face, and shrugged his shoulders. "You don't know a thing."

CC ground his teeth. "You don't understand, Jim McCord, or whatever your real name is."

Oddly, those impulsive words seemed to strike home, and McCord was momentarily speechless, though he recovered quickly and attempted to guide the conversation in another direction.

"What did you mean when you said, 'I don't understand?'"

"I mean that we, the five of us here, don't have to prove a thing." His voice turned to steel. "To anybody."

Everyone was now giving full attention to CC.

"America is lawless. And it's not simply because we have been invaded by several enemies. Powerful people right here in the United States have worked for years to foment anarchy, and they have succeeded." He turned to McCord. "You appear to be among them – an anarchist. You have helped destroy our way of life and the laws under which we labored to assure the right to life, liberty, and the pursuit of happiness for every citizen."

McCord laughed. "And what if I have?"

"So, until one of these foreign powers takes control, and begins ruling with a fist of iron, you too are subject to the laws of anarchy."

"There are no laws of anarchy!"

"Exactly!"

"I don't understand."

"Isn't that what I just told you? You don't understand. So let me explain."

"Anarchy might be defined as every man for himself, or the survival of the fittest. It's like playing survivor at its lowest common denominator."

"And I'm always ready to play."

"I don't think so."

"Why not?"

"We allowed you into our little independent community, a community in which we live by the fewest 'laws' compatible with biblical values."

"So?"

"So, you repeatedly violated those few simple laws, and you violated our trust."

"Again, so what?"

"We've already agreed that the world around us is in a state of anarchy. And I've tried to explain that we are an independent community."

"So, now I'm going to leave your independent community."

"Actually, you are not."

"What's that supposed to mean?"

"Once you become part of any community, you are subject to the laws of that community."

"I think you just said that."

"You violated our laws."

McCord laughed. "So what?"

"Now you will be judged under the laws of our little community."

"And if I choose not to recognize those laws?"

"That's irrelevant. You seem to love the idea that might makes right."

"So?"

"So the community now has you bound in ropes. We have the might. We are free to take action. You are helpless. Your failure to recognize and abide by our laws is the issue at hand. And we are about to judge you for your crimes."

"Crimes?"

"Yes, crimes! In a world gone made, as long as we can maintain our little community, we can also define crimes that threaten it, and dictate their appropriate punishment."

McCord swore, but CC ignored him.

"Together we are your judge, jury, and executioner. You stand condemned for trying to kill Jonathan and me. You've betrayed us all more than once. For all we know, we've lost this home because of you. And, as far as we're concerned, your life is forfeit."

"You can't kill me."

"Really? Give me one reason why not? You admitted that you tried to murder us. You are still threatening us with mortal harm. So it's clear that you are extremely dangerous, a real and present danger to this community. What's more, it appears that some of your associates are about to enter these caverns with the intention of finishing us off."

McCord locked eyes with him, but finally turned away and CC continued.

"You are under our absolute control and, tragically, I don't believe you've left us any alternative."

McCord did not respond, but his eyes began shifting about in desperation, as though looking for a way of escape.

Jonathan walked over to McCord and took a cloth bandana from his pocket.

"What are you going to do with that?" McCord asked.

Jonathan ignored him, and turned to CC with his explanation. "If someone is nearby, and he yells out, they'll find us," Jonathan replied.

With that, Jim tried to shout, but Jonathan slapped him on the wounded side of the head, and when he continued to struggle, Jonathan grabbed his long hair, pulled his head back, and jammed the balled-up bandana into McCord's mouth. Elizabeth then took a nylon scarf from her coat pocket, drew it across his mouth to keep Jim from spitting out the gag, yanked the ends of her scarf around the back of his head, pulled it tight, and tied it securely.

Now there was real fear in McCord's eyes.

CC gave him a look of contempt. *It's always that way with the worst of men,* he thought. *They'll commit every manner of atrocity, but when they are faced with personal danger, most are cowards at heart.*

"Relax, Jim" CC told him. "If we can find a way out of this, we won't harm you, even though you've demonstrated that you wouldn't show us any mercy at all."

McCord simply glared at him. It was clear that he thought CC was purposely trying to put him at ease until he was ready to strike. That was, after all, exactly what he would have done if their situations were reversed.

Jonathan was all business, studiously ignoring the conversations around him while field-stripping his rifle. He lined up the components on a blanket, then carefully cleaned and oiled them one at a time. McCord seemed somewhat relieved that the weapon was no longer being leveled at him. He heard a throaty little laugh, and looked into the shadows, and realized that his sense of relief was premature. Elizabeth now had her rifle leveled at him.

That exchange had occurred a half-hour earlier, and then CC had sat quietly, trying to think out the situation. He turned to Rachel, and she resumed her account. "I'll tell you the rest, but I think we need to be careful about discussing any further plans in front of Jim."

They all nodded in agreement.

Dynamiting the Dam

The Caverns
May 2nd, about 3 am

"After you were swept down into the whirlpool, and we finished our work placing the explosives on the dam, we decided to move back into the tunnel by the side of the underground lake. Jonathan followed us, uncoiling the detonator wire, and laying it in the deep shadows against the base of the cave wall. He had given us directions to a side tunnel where we'd be protected from the blast. He was following us, and he'd almost reached the side tunnel when he heard loud voices from back near the dam."

"It turned out a blessing," Jonathan interrupted, "that I was unable to carry a flashlight while uncoiling the detonator wire." He shook his head as he smiled at the two women. "My "big sisters" were so intent on their conversation that they'd moved way up the tunnel ahead of me, carrying their flashlights with them. I had been about to shout to them that I couldn't see where I was going, but, thank God, I didn't. When I turned to look back,

I saw two soldiers carrying flashlights. They were about a hundred feet from me. I was petrified that they might see Rachel's light, but she and Elizabeth had already turned into the branch tunnel, so everything was in darkness."

"How'd you find your way without falling into the underground river?"

"I held the wire in my right hand and slid my left along the rock wall so that I wouldn't find myself drifting across the ledge." He went on. "I could hear the soldiers shouting to one another above the roar of the falls, and I was shocked by their words."

"What did they say?"

"One of them said, 'Just remember, we are to take McCord alive.' The other replied, 'Yeah, if we can. Personally, I could care less.'"

"About then," Elizabeth cut in, "I noticed that Jonathan hadn't kept up, so I turned around and started back to look for him. But he was already turning the corner, waving his hand and hissing at me to shut off my light. What impresses me most right now," she went on, "is that Jonathan had the foresight to leave the electrical power on, but to remove all the light bulbs above the dam so that it would make it far more difficult for any unwanted visitors to see anything."

"Why would he leave the power on?" CC asked.

Elizabeth cut in, obviously a little piqued at Rachel's frequent interruptions. "Since you had the only detonator, Jonathan had to contrive a means for detonating the explosives, and he connected his wires to an electrical outlet."

"He what?"

"And this is where it really got scary," Rachel interjected, again interrupting Elizabeth and again receiving a nasty look as her reward.

"Yes, really scary," Elizabeth parroted, with more than a little sarcasm for Rachel evident in her voice. She followed it with a smile that may or may not have been added to remove the sting.

"Jonathan had already tried to explain to us how he'd wired the dynamite so that if anything happened to him, one of us might still set it off. I really didn't understand except that he had somehow run what he called a ground wire from the electrical outlet at the top the dam to the blasting caps in the face of the dam. Then he ran another wire from the blasting caps back to his reel of wire. And that's where I got confused."

"Well, I didn't," Rachel said to Elizabeth's growing annoyance. "Without touching the ends together, Jonathan ran those two wires all the way from the explosives at the dam to this tunnel."

"Oh, right," Elizabeth interrupted. "He planned to touch the tips of the two wires together when it was time to set off the dynamite."

"Right!" Rachel affirmed. "He told us that as long as there was current flowing from the generator to that outlet box, all we'd need to do would be to unreel the wire, then strip the ends of the two wires at this end, and touch them together."

"And that's the scary part," Rachel interjected.

"Do you mind?" asked Elizabeth, glaring at Rachel.

Rachel simply rolled her eyes in reply. It was clear that they were all on edge from the tension and lack of sleep.

"So," CC asked, "what was scary?"

"Once he touched those two ends together, he would complete a circuit between the electrical outlet and the explosives. In other words, *BOOM!* And the two ends he held were wrapped around the tin can he was using as a reel. One of them was "hot," and both stuck out the side of the can. He was unrolling the wire as he walked up the tunnel..."

"Ah," CC said, almost sounding indifferent, but only because the time of danger was passed. He smiled. "The light dawns. If there had been any bare surfaces on either of the wires touching the tin can, or if the ends of the two wires had touched one another, they'd have shorted out...."

"...and the dynamite would have gone off, blowing up the dam and killing anyone near it," Rachel finished for him.

"Correct!" Elizabeth agreed. She went on: "Jonathan later told us that he should have unreeled the cable back through the tunnels, checked that the bare ends of the two wires were snipped off and taped over, then gone back down to the dam to hook up the other ends."

"But as it turned out," CC finished for her, "someone was obviously watching over him."

"Not only were we in danger from the explosives," Elizabeth agreed, a bit of irony in her voice, "but if he had taken time to run the cable down the tunnel in the preferred manner, and then gone back to connect them at the dam, he′d have been there when the bad guys showed up."

"But as it turned out," CC concluded, "all he had to do was cross the two wires back in the tunnel to short them out and set off the explosives."

"And to short out the bad guys," Rachel added. It was obvious that both women were as giddy over the group′s collective success as they were from lack of sleep.

Jonathan, who had appeared almost asleep, surprised them all by adding to their account.

"When I was coming up the river walk, it was difficult to orient myself because the running water drowned out other sounds and echoed around me, seeming to come from all directions at once. I had just felt my way around the corner when someone flashed a light momentarily, and I could see that I was almost there.

Elizabeth said. "I had my rifle, and had moved back into the main tunnel in case they were following Jonathan.

"And?"

"By then there were five or six of them back on the dam," she continued, "all waving their flashlights around. A couple of them were leaning out over the railing, obviously studying the layout, and it was equally obvious that they were going to trip over

Jonathan′s wires at any moment. I didn′t think there was any time to spare, so I turned to warn him.

That′s when I realized that Jim had somehow gotten hold of a flashlight and, in spite of being bound, had turned it on. He was trying to crawl around the corner past me, his hands still tied behind his back, the flashlight bobbing up and down. I saw his silhouette as he moved between Rachel and me. I thought it was Jonathan on the cave floor preparing to set off the charges, but when he tried to shout a warning to the soldiers, I realized it was Jim, and I rammed my rifle butt between his shoulder blades. He dropped the flashlight, and it went out."

"I could hear him groaning, Rachel added. Then her face darkened. "But it didn′t matter. I was too late. The soldiers had seen his light."

"Yes," Elizabeth added. "They started running toward us, and the echoes from their footsteps made it sound like there were a hundred of them. I could see their lights reflecting off the surface of the lake. We couldn't figure out Jim′s motives, or his relationship with these soldiers, but we knew that they were killers, and we weren't about to give up without a fight. So I put the rifle to my left shoulder, leaned around the corner, pointed it down the tunnel, and pulled the trigger several times." She rubbed her bruised shoulder, a rueful look on her face. "I should have paid more attention when you were showing us how to shoot."

CC frowned. *They weren't very good lessons,* he thought. *We were only pointing and clicking, and these things aren't cameras. I thought at the time that we didn't dare use live ammo because someone might hear us. Now I'm sorry we didn't set up a rifle range in the caverns.*

His mind had been drifting. He seemed bent on despair, and he had to grope to focus on what Elizabeth was saying.

"My bullets went ricocheting along the rock walls, and I guess it made them all dive for cover. I peeked down the tunnel, and I could see a couple of them waving their flashlights from behind the coping on the top of the dam. Then their lights went out. I ducked back and a moment later they returned fire. The racket was terrifying, their bullets chipping away at the walls, the sound rolling up and down the tunnels. They were using automatic weapons, but I had already backed around the corner, and the bullets must have gone right on by, straight up the river walk past me. I knew they'd be coming up the tunnel soon, and I figured it was over for us, but I'd forgotten Jonathan."

"Yes," Rachel added. "I was about to turn off my light because I was afraid the soldiers would see it, but Jonathan shouted, 'Aim it here!' He was standing well around the corner from the river, and my light fell on him holding a wire in each hand. Before I realized what he was doing, he crossed the ends. I was so intent on focusing the light on the wires that I forgot what was supposed to happen."

Elizabeth laughed, but it was Rachel who described the result.

"There was a tremendous explosion and the shockwave knocked us off our feet."

"There were actually two explosions," Elizabeth corrected, "about a second apart. As deafened as we were, we felt the entire cavern vibrating. We could hear the sound of rocks shattering and water rushing." She shook her head. "I thought the tunnel was actually collapsing over us."

"It might well have collapsed over you," CC mused. "You were blessed!"

"Even where we were," Elizabeth added, "the noise was mind-numbing, magnified by the cavern as it reverberated around us. The sound of the explosion must have rolled around for a full thirty seconds."

"The whole place shook," Rachel exclaimed, "and there was dust everywhere. I could taste it and smell it, and when the stench from the dynamite drifted our way, it choked me. It made me think of what it must have been like for the people below the Twin Towers on 911."

Both women had become increasingly excited as they shared the story.

"We were deafened, and couldn't hear one another speak," Elizabeth said. "I still can't hear very well." She put the tip of her finger in her ear as though to clear it. "And I actually felt the vibration through the stone beneath my feet as the water began to race down the channel and through whatever was left of the dam."

"When the dust had settled a bit, and we finally dared walk down the tunnel to see what damage had been done, we all had our rifles ready. In all the excitement we'd forgotten that we'd left Jim bound, gagged, and lying alongside the wall in the side tunnel. Regrettably he was undamaged, though thoroughly terrified. He sounded like he was blubbering, but we ignored him and moved on. When we got near the dam site, all the soldiers were gone, their bodies evidently blown off the ledge into the lake when the dam blew up."

"It was amazing," Elizabeth interjected. "The entire dam was gone. All those guys must have been swept away. We began scolding Jonathan because he was getting close to the collapsed edge of the dam, but he ignored us."

"He explained later that he was not only concerned with the possibility of survivors, but that the stone blocks that made up the dam might have plugged the tunnel that drained the river. He explained that, if that were the case, the water flowing in from the caverns might rise and drown us. When we shined our lights over the place where the dam had stood, it was impossible to see the wreckage because the entire area where the water wheel had stood was now deep under water."

"It was strange," Rachel cut in, "that instead of the level of the underground lake dropping, the area that had been below the dam had filled with water. After a couple of hours, it was still one deep, fast-moving river, still within its banks, the entire surface only a few inches below where it had stood before we took out the dam."

"What we don't understand," Rachel continued, "is where all that water is coming from. The little underground lake couldn't hold that much, so even though the stream ran back into the mountain, we didn't think there'd be that much water. We were obviously wrong. The river seems to be moving as fast as ever."

"Oh, it's fed by the big lake on the back side of the mountain," Jonathan offered, and failed to notice the cold look that CC gave him. Failing to realize that he had revealed more than he should have, Jonathan expanded on his observation.

"The water wheel and generator were gone, maybe even the ledge they had rested on was gone. The level of the lake above and below where the dam had stood were now the same level. It seemed strange to me that the water was so deep, and that the lake hadn't sunk, until I realized that we weren't just draining the underground lake, but we were also trying to drain the huge lake on the far side of the mountain. The fact that the water level was above the mouths of both exit tunnels pretty much proved that. I think that the flow was so powerful that it may have swept some of the stones that were used to build the dam right out through the exit tunnel."

"I thought of that," CC remarked, hoping to divert their thoughts, especially McCord's, from what might lay on the west side of the mountain. "The deep water made me realize that it was a miracle that the explosives went off."

McCord made a sound of derision that was clear in spite of his being gagged.

"What do you mean, a miracle?" the boy asked.

"The spring flood," CC answered.

They all looked confused.

"After Jim shoved me off the dam, I noticed the high water mark on the side wall of the cavern near the water wheel."

"And?"

"I did a poor installation job on the generator. At high spring flood, it would have been underwater. But since you still had electricity when you needed it to blow the dam, it's obvious that the rising water hadn't yet flooded the generator and shorted it out. I consider that a miracle."

"It's funny you should say that," Jonathan replied. "I was afraid that the underground drain would be blocked, and that the water would rise and flood the tunnels above the dam, drowning us, but instead the second big tunnel above the whirlpool was handling the extra flow."

"What was that that Jonathan was saying about the other side of the mountain?" Elizabeth asked.

CC frowned, looking at McCord to see whether he was paying attention. The intensity with which the prisoner was staring back at him indicated that he had picked up on the comment. CC decided he might as well bring it out in the open. He didn't want McCord thinking that the far side of the mountain was of any special importance, much less the forests that lay beyond.

"Jonathan is right," he affirmed. "The reason the water level in the stream hasn't dropped is because there is a large lake on the west side of this mountain, and it's obviously being drained through this underground cavern."

"How do you know that?" Elizabeth asked.

"Because CC and I have been on the other side of the mountain," the boy answered proudly.

"Well, that explains the big fish we've caught in here," Rachel observed, a grin on her face.

Dealing with a Traitor

Deep in the caverns
May 2nd, 4 a.m.

Everyone seemed to run out of questions and comments at the same time. Having shared their own stories, they seemed to draw back into themselves. They had been excited to learn how successful they'd been in slowing up the enemy, but were beginning to realize that they now faced a far greater challenge. They not only had to escape, but they also had to somehow survive over the long-term.

CC knew that he should try to discover Jim's motives, but he was too tired and preoccupied to try. What he did know was that, a year earlier, Jim and Elizabeth, without his having been aware of it, had somehow followed him into the valley on a motorcycle, and that they had had a difficult time surviving. In fact, if they hadn't stumbled on CC's cave during the Christmas eve blizzard, they'd have either frozen or starved.

He, on the other hand, had arrived in this valley with a tractor-trailer full of carefully selected items, including food, clothing, building equipment and materials, books, firearms, appliances, and much more. He'd added to that treasure trove a large electrical generator that he'd picked up when he returned to Black River Junction, plus other items, including a motorhome that he'd found at a farmer's co-op down in the valley. And he'd been enriched by the discovery of the Sennett farm, with its equipment, livestock, and orchards.

Now he would be abandoning this wealth, and accompanied by four other people, including a child, all they would have for their collective survival was what they could carry on their backs. As bad as their prospects were, his immediate concern, however, was figuring out what to do with McCord, and then getting out of these caverns alive.

McCord is dangerous, he thought, *and we can't let him roam around by himself. Our escape has to be uppermost in our minds. We don't dare take him with us, but we can't just leave him here untied or he'll find a way to betray us. And if we tie him up, he might die long before anybody finds him.*

He glanced at McCord and wondered why he should care. But he knew. *We are to do good to those who persecute us. Since that is the case,* CC thought, *then we must assume that God has designed some way for us to safely be rid of this guy without our being hurt in the process. And one way or another, we've got to get out of here, and we've got to leave soon. So we need to figure out what God would have us do, and quickly!*

As though reading CC's mind, Jonathan pointed his rifle at McCord and asked, "What are we going to do about him? He'll eat a lot more than he can carry."

It was obvious that Jonathan had also been giving the situation considerable thought.

He nodded at CC. "Of course, he's your decision," he continued, "but I've been wondering about other things."

CC wiggled his fingers in a *give-me-more* gesture.

"We can't carry any more food than we have in our packs right now, and when we get to where we're going, we'll need some kind of shelter and a lot more food. Even without him," and he tipped the muzzle of his rifle to point it at McCord, "we'll need a total of ten pounds of food per day." Then he added meaningly, "until we are able to grow some crops."

CC nodded, frowning. *Sometimes it's just as well not to be reminded of the truth, even from a kid as smart as Jonathan.*

Regrettably the boy wasn't finished.

"That comes to two tons of food for the next year."

"Yes. I can multiply," CC replied, unable to hide his asperity. He'd already worked out the numbers. Four-thousand pounds of food! It wasn't difficult to compute after having lived here under similar conditions for an entire year.

Ironically they were being forced to abandon a tractor-trailer with enough food to last the five of them a couple of years, plus a farm garden that had already provided an amazing harvest. And a large quantity of things they'd produced, from honey to horseradish, from cheese to cherry jam. And in a world where most farm animals had perished, they possessed a variety of healthy poultry, hogs, sheep, goats, and milk cows, not to mention a dangerous bull that roamed the west end of the valley at will. Oh, and there were the fruit orchards, and even honeybees.

Jonathan hadn't said anything that they weren't all aware of, but his raw numbers brought their plight home to them. Summer was fast-approaching, but summer in central Vermont is very short, especially in the mountains, and a cold and hungry winter would inevitably follow. What made it seem even more daunting was not simply that they were leaving behind a vast store of food, but also a wide variety of other supplies and equipment.

I wonder, CC thought, *if they realize that we are losing our sources of heat and light as well as all the conveniences of home. We're apt to wind up freezing to death, if we don't happen to starve first. After the events of the past year, I understand the dangers all too well.*

He shook his head to clear the cobwebs. *It's one challenge after another,* he thought. *Little food. No shelter. No idea where to go. And some very bad people hunting us.*

He grinned ruefully. *Well, first things first. Right now, we've got to get out of here.*

"Well?" It was Jonathan again, anticipating his thoughts, and demanding answers. "Do you have any ideas?" he persisted.

CC ran his fingers through his hair and frowned.

"Any ideas? Not really. I don't know where we'll go, but it will have to be a good distance from here if we want to avoid the people who will be hunting us." He gazed off into space, assessing their chances. "But I don't want to say anything in front of Jim."

He and Jonathan moved down the tunnel and carried on a whispered conversation.

CC seemed unapologetic. "All I can tell you, Jonathan, is that somehow the Lord has provided our daily bread up to now, and I'm no more capable of assuring our future today than I was a year ago."

"That's not very encouraging," the teen responded.

"No. Not if you're leaning on your own understanding. But we are to exercise faith. That's what got us where we are."

"Where we are is losing everything we have."

"That doesn't sound like the Jonathan I've come to know and love."

"Sorry."

"You know that faith is the substance of things hoped for, the evidence of things not seen."

"I don't know what that means."

"It means being sure of what you hope for and certain of what you do not see."

"I remember. Hebrews chapter 11, verse one, right?"

"Right."

"Sorry. I was out of line."

"Yes, you were. That sort of negativism is deadly."

"I said I was sorry."

"Apology accepted, though it was God, and not me, that you questioned."

The boy looked down, toeing the ground.

Then CC suggested, "Maybe we can find another cave or something. If we can, I might come back here and – if the horses are still here, and if there's any food left – I might be able to take a load back to wherever we've settled."

"That's a lot of ifs," Jonathan whispered back. "By then, the bad guys will probably strip the place of anything of value, and you won't have much reason for coming back."

That's true, Jonathan," CC responded, clearly exasperated. "But it's the best I can come up with at the moment."

"I'm sorry," the boy apologized. "You have always been amazing at solving problems like this."

"Actually, God has always been amazing in providing for us."

"Amen," Elizabeth whispered. She had followed the two of them down the tunnel, after making certain that their whispers couldn't be heard by Jim.

CC smiled, groped in his pocket, then turned back to them. "If something happens to me, you will need one of these." He handed each of them a compass. After you exit the caves, go around the south end of Lake Allison, then head northwest into the forest. It gets pretty rugged back there, but you might find another cave."

"Aren't you going with us?" Elizabeth asked, fear in her voice.

"Of course. This is just in case we get separated."

They nodded their heads in understanding, and the three of them returned to the group.

From time to time someone would stare accusingly at McCord, but then their eyes would fall on his wound and they'd look away with mixed feelings. They understood that he had paid nowhere near the appropriate price for his perverse behavior, but in spite of the horrors they had seen and personally experienced, they remained remarkably forgiving people.

Jim's eyes stared sightlessly at the cave floor, but it seemed to CC that his mind looked inward, and CC didn't believe it was a result of shame. *Jim's undoubtedly thinking of his next move.*

CC turned to the teenager.

"Jonathan."

The others saw the change in CC, and heard the decisiveness in his voice. But while the teen was clearly attentive he never took his eyes off McCord.

"Was the staircase washed away by the flooding?"

The boy was clearly surprised by the question and took a moment to digest it.

"No. The base of the staircase to the cavern above them rested about ten feet from the end of the dam, on a slope of rock several feet above it, and the water never actually reached the stairs."

"So it survived."

"Yes, when the dam blew, a boulder hit one of the treads and smashed it. But I think we can get past the gap if we are careful."

"So, you have to skip one step?"

"Yes."

"Okay. As quickly as you can, you and Elizabeth untie McCord's ankles, take him through the tunnels to the dam site, and walk him up the stairs to the cottage. When you get him there, tie him hand and foot, and lock him up in the dining area."

Jonathan protested. "You know it won't be long before he gets hold of something and cuts himself loose."

"I realize that," but I don't want to be responsible for leaving him here to starve to death. That would be murder."

"He didn't hesitate to try to murder us."

"No," he didn't. "But we are not going to sink to his level."

"I don't like it," the boy replied. I don't really believe in an 'eye for an eye,' but I think we are fools if we let him go."

CC brooded for a moment.

"Okay. Here's what you do. Take him to the cottage. Tie him up. Strip the room of anything that he might use to cut his bonds, even the mirror on the wall. His friends should show up to rescue him before he starves."

"Suppose he gets free and tries to follow us?"

"Tie his hands behind his back, then tie his wrists to his ankles. Anchor his feet to the wood stove so that he can't crawl around. If we can get a thirty-minute lead, I don't think he will be able to find us."

"Suppose the bad guys rescue him before that?"

"Then things might get interesting."

Jonathan looked at him, shook his head ruefully, and said, "Man-o-man."

CC flashed him an angry look. "What was that?"

"I was just saying, *okay*."

"He won't be able to find his way through the caverns to where we're going. And when his former friends find him, he might have some explaining to do. But I think it will be a while before they get back into Hidden Valley, let alone into our cave and on our trail."

"I hope you're right," the boy responded."

"Okay," CC added, "we'd better get this show on the road."

Jonathan turned to Elizabeth. She was already getting to her feet, and he frowned. She just shrugged her shoulders. Then the two of them reached down to pull McCord to his feet.

"If you can fix it so that McCord has to remain there at least a couple of hours, it should provide us with more than adequate time."

"I've got two sticks of dynamite left, and I can fix a booby-trap on the outside of the door of the cottage. If Mr. McCord tried to open it, it will go off."

"Fine. He's been listening to our every word, and he has a pretty good idea of what we're planning, so it's up to him how he responds. And when the bad guys do show up, it will be up to them whether they want to remove the explosives or detonate them. And maybe they will accidentally reduce their own numbers."

The boy laughed. "Yeah, I can hear Mr. Smooth-talker here trying to get them to let him out."

CC was all business now. "We'll wait here until you and Elizabeth get back."

Jonathan looked at McCord and smiled. It wasn't a pleasant look, and CC wondered again what terrible damage this war had done to the souls of its survivors.

"If he gives you any trouble at all on the way to the cottage, shoot him!"

"Gladly."

"You sound eager."

It was Elizabeth who replied. "Oh, come on, CC! He's repeatedly shown how dangerous he is."

"He certainly has," Rachel agreed.

McCord, still bound and gagged, his legs obviously stiff, was leaning against the cave wall, but the way his eyes moved from speaker to speaker revealed his avid interest in the discussion.

He was unable to speak until Jonathan loosened the gag.

CC turned to him. "Someone once said that the quality of mercy is not strained. I feel very strained letting you go."

"Yeah, yeah."

"So we're offering you your life, this one more time."

"And?"

"And if you intrude on our lives again, it will be open season on Jim McCord."

McCord snorted, displaying his contempt.

CC went on. "Just so we understand one another. If we ever see you again, we will shoot to kill. Do you understand that?"

McCord stared at him, malice in his eyes.

"What about a gun?" he demanded.

"You've got to be kidding," Jonathan laughed.

"No gun," CC affirmed flatly. "No nothing!"

"You can't do that," McCord argued. "Those people might kill me."

"Strange," Elizabeth interjected. "We'd have sworn those people were your friends. They certainly share your lack of morals."

Jonathan reached behind McCord. As a test of his bonds, he jerked McCord's arms up to the middle of his back, bringing a cry of pain and forcing McCord to stand free of the wall.

"All right; let's go," the boy ordered.

McCord avoided his eyes.

"I'm a bit wobbly on my feet. I'll have to lean on one of you."

"Not a chance," CC stated flatly. He turned to Elizabeth and Jonathan.

"If he stalls or stumbles, or refuses to get up and go on, shoot him in the knee and leave him there in the dark. He might survive the wound, but one thing is sure, he won't be following us anywhere today."

"I won't fall down," McCord interjected, his fear obvious to all.

"CC ignored him.

"Take a shotgun and make him walk in front of you. Stay about four feet behind him. If he tries anything, anything at all, forget the knees. Shoot to kill. He's dangerous, and we are again risking our lives for him, and he's not worth the trouble."

It was Elizabeth who asked, "Then why are we doing it? Like you said, he's not worth the trouble. So why don't we just put some more wire wraps on his wrists and ankles, hogtie him, and leave him here?"

CC bit his lip. "Much as I'd like to, I just can't bring myself to do that."

"That's why the bad guys always have an advantage," Rachel laughed. "They face no such moral dilemmas."

CC tapped Jonathan on the shoulder, and when he had his complete attention, he reiterated. "You will not touch him, nor will you allow him to touch you. If he falls and cannot or will not immediately stand up, shoot him. If he stops even for a moment, if he hesitates, if he so much as opens his mouth except to ask directions, you are to shoot him." He searched Jonathan's face. "Can you do that?"

"Oh, yeah. I can do that. But he won't be asking any directions. We'll tell him when to turn."

Jonathan turned to McCord, stuffed the gag back into his mouth, and pulled it tight. Then, while the others looked on in surprise or amusement, he bent down behind him and wove several long wire wraps between the bonds on McCord's wrists and those on his ankles, effectively hobbling him and limiting him to short, shuffling steps.

Rising to his feet, Jonathan commanded, "Move it, McCord!" and he punched the muzzle of the shotgun into his kidneys, bringing a muffled cry of pain.

"Let's go," he repeated, his voice cold and hard, and McCord started up the tunnel.

CC was a bit disappointed in himself for not simply following Elizabeth's suggestion to take McCord into a side tunnel and leave him there, tightly bound. He hoped he wouldn't be sorry for his decision. It seemed to him that they should all be making peace with the God they so often ignored, for he did not see much chance of their ultimately evading the malice of their implacable enemies. Nevertheless, he couldn't rid himself of the nagging thought that mercy is better than sacrifice.

Decision Time

The Caverns
May 2nd, 5:05 a.m.

The underground river made a dull rumble as it scoured its way through the mountain's bowels, perhaps a quarter of a mile from their stopping place. Occasionally a bat would squeal as it flew through the hemisphere of light that the lantern cast across its subterranean highway. Water, dripping from the ceiling, seemed to go unnoticed as it made its little plashing sounds on the infant stalagmites, feeding them an ageless diet of dissolved minerals.

They had carried a sleeping Sarah to this new location, and after they'd all eaten some more hot soup, the emotionally exhausted child had again fallen asleep, while Jonathan and the three remaining adults seemed lost in their own thoughts. It wasn't that there was menace in the atmosphere. There was nothing. No hope. No future. No direction. Just despair.

Jonathan and Elizabeth had returned a half-hour earlier, having locked McCord in the cottage.

"I wired a stick of dynamite to the cottage door so that it would explode if it were opened from either side," Jonathan told them. "The bad guys will have to be very careful and take their time while removing the various wires I attached to confuse them, or they'll set off my fireworks."

This comment was met with silence. They were all exhausted. The group knew it was time to move on, and it took Jonathan, with the impetuosity of youth, and the boldness of a much-loved son, to press CC to make a decision.

"CC, what are we going to do?"

CC didn't answer. He was past the point of conversation, lost in deliberations which had long since melded with despair. His thoughts had bled him emotionally dry, leaving him without the capacity to respond to what should have been a simple question. He had no assurances to offer the teen. He believed that he had nothing to offer anyone. He was, after all, thoroughly exhausted after his trials of the past forty-eight hours. He needed a decent meal and a full night's sleep, but he would have neither. Even if he could get his little company out of the caverns and then escape the pursuit of their enemies, they had nowhere to go and little to survive on.

The last thing anyone in this world wants to become, he thought, *is a refugee. And even if we find an acceptable place to live next winter, what will we do for food? Summer is just around the corner, and it's almost too late to find a meadow somewhere and start a garden. We have no tools and only a small assortment of seeds. Worse, even if we dared visit some village or town, most of the food left in the stores and warehouses has been ravaged.*

That thought kept recurring.

Another New England winter is just a few months away. We are bruised and exhausted. What little we have with us will be a burden to carry through the forests, and is unlikely to feed us even until we find some sort of shelter. And it's my decision that we carry a variety of seeds rather than the equivalent weight in extra food that we will so desperately need.

Worse, we have to travel across rugged terrain and through dense forests in order to escape detection from the air. Apart from evading capture, the odds against our finding shelter, food and clothing are astronomical.

He turned to the others. "Dump the contents of all of our backpacks on a blanket, and divide everything equally between us, food, seeds, and other gear."

No one questioned that decision. They understood that if any of them were separated, they'd all be carrying a proportional share of their wealth.

But even as they carried out that task, the boy persisted. "CC, the clock is running."

CC continued staring at the floor and didn't seem to hear him. The teen was worried, and he obviously wasn't alone. The women were fully attuned to the situation. They all knew that this behavior wasn't characteristic of CC. He was generally enthusiastic and optimistic. They should already be out the far side of the mountain and heading into the forests. *What was making him wait?* they wondered. And yet, waiting was obviously what he felt he needed to do.

"Why don't we pray?" a little voice asked plaintively, clearly disappointed that no one else had suggested it.

The smiles that the little girl received in return were embarrassed, not condescending. CC wasn't sure who it was, but one of the women whispered, "...a little child shall lead them."

And CC, visibly embarrassed, seemed to awaken from a drugged sleep.

"Why don't we pray?" he agreed and, gazed off into infinity, as though thinking aloud. "Prayer always seems to be our last recourse, rather than our first and best hope." He looked into the shadows where Sarah lay on her stomach, her chin propped up on her hands. She was gazing at CC, her confidence in him unshaken.

"Sarah," he asked, in a very soft, very serious voice, "You're absolutely right. We must pray. Will you please lead us?"

She slid her knees up between her elbows until she had assumed a kneeling position. Then she clasped her little hands firmly together and squeezed her eyes tightly shut in concentration.

"Dear Lord Jesus," she began, and there were scraping sounds as each of them tardily sank to their knees. They too closed their eyes and bowed their heads, first in deference to this child, and then in respect to the God who they all hoped or feared was listening. And there was an almost-palpable movement in the still dank air, as though a spirit had stirred, or an angel had gently brushed its wings against a cave wall. Sarah's prayer was simple and heartfelt.

"I am a little girl, Lord Jesus. I think we're all supposed to trust you like little children. Please help us, Lord, and show us Your way." She was silent for a moment, then she uttered a quiet, "Amen."

After her prayer, there was a long moment of silence, then the adults added their own hushed amens.

Then Jonathan cleared his throat. "CC?"

When there was no reply, the boy repeated himself in a louder, more assertive voice.

"CC, what are we going to do? Will we use the back door?"

No one else had ever heard mention of a back door, and the expression clearly sounded strange to them, but the easy familiarity of the boy with the man, and his obvious knowledge of the pathways and workings of these mountain passages, immediately created a stirring of hope which caused them all to raise questioning eyes.

CC's angry response only served to encourage them further. "For Pete's sake, Jonathan, keep your voice down."

For a moment, no one spoke, but for some inexplicable reason their eyes darted about, trying to penetrate the darkness. They were all suddenly conscious of the dripping water striking the floor somewhere in the shadows, and they realized belatedly they had been making so much noise that their enemies could easily have crept within a few yards without anyone in the group being aware of their presence.

The boy apologized, whispering sheepishly, "I'm sorry." He'd been told so often to keep his voice down that he knew he was doubly worthy of censure, and he clearly recognized the significance of his blunder. The way these caverns bounced sound around, someone a quarter-mile away might have heard him. Stiff from sitting on the cold floor for so long, Jonathan rose unsteadily to his feet, hands gripping his rifle. He tried to pierce the darkness with eyes and ears, hoping that there had been no unwelcome listener, but he was too late.

The unmistakable sound of a foot scraping the cave floor back in the shadows brought Baron to his feet, a menacing growl belying his age. Then the old dog gave a glad yelp, and like a pup, with feet scrabbling for purchase on the slippery floor, he rushed into the shadows to greet someone whose scent clearly delighted him. Jonathan pointed his rifle toward the place where the dog had disappeared, but a deep voice brought him up with a quiet warning.

"You wouldn't want to discharge that firearm in this cave, son. A ricochet could be fatal to anyone."

The Surprise Visitor

The West Side of the Caverns
May 2nd, 5:25 a.m.

The unexpected visitor halted in the gloom just outside the lamplight, the dog capering about him, his tail wagging joyfully.

Rachel had been sitting next to Elizabeth on the opposite edge of their little circle, her legs crossed under her, but at the sound of his voice her face lost its color and she scrambled backwards into the shadows, using her arms like oars and kicking away with her feet. She looked something like a rowboat back-watering out of a warship's path.

Elizabeth also seemed shocked, but her response was far different.

"Oh, my God, it's him!" she whispered.

Her voice caught the unwanted visitor's attention, and he stepped out of the shadows, whereupon she exploded into action with a shout of rage. She leapt to her feet, ran straight toward him, and began raining blows on his chest. Although he seemed momentarily surprised by the assault, he didn't seem unduly troubled.

CC, who had just seen Rachel react to this man's presence by back-watering like a rowboat under the bow of a racing battleship, was now oddly bemused by Elizabeth's reaction. He thought that her efforts were akin to a single termite attacking a giant oak. He realized that she would not have liked his alluding to her as a termite. *On the other hand,* he thought, *termites had been known to bring down some pretty large trees – given sufficient time and numbers – and if the trees weren't fighting back.*

Somewhere along there, the metaphor broke down. *This man is not a tree, and Elizabeth is definitely not a termite!* And with that thought, CC wondered how his mind could wander so far afield when faced with extreme danger. Then something clicked. He didn't believe that this man represented danger to them.

As he was reaching this conclusion, the man was enfolding Elizabeth in his arms and spinning her around so that he held her helpless in a loose hammer-lock.

"Look, lady," he said. "A year ago, I saved your life, and all the thanks I got was to have you try to fracture my skull and leave me a victim of our enemies. What's with you?"

With those words, she hissed at him, "Is that what you were doing? Freeing me?"

"Wasn't it obvious?" He tipped his head to look down at her. "You appear to be long on beauty and short on brains." His statement left her momentarily speechless, an unusual condition for Elizabeth.

"And after I cut you loose," he continued, "you not only repaid me by hitting me over the head, but you ran off with, of all people, Jim McCord."

CC exclaimed, "You know McCord?" but his words were lost as the two of them argued back and forth. In the meantime, he was trying to correlate Rachel's strange reactions with Elizabeth's wrath.

Up close, the man was even more formidable than at a distance, and his presence here should have seemed ominous. CC had no difficulty identifying him as *GI Joe,* the man who had wandered into their cave months before, and who, using only a knife for a weapon, had attacked and killed several armed soldiers in broad daylight, and had helped Jonathan escape from his crow's nest in the oak tree.

CC wanted to ask him how he'd somehow escaped unscathed when the enemy officer threw a hand grenade down into that pothole, and why he'd even tried to save him when he was being swept down the river, but this didn't seem the proper moment for those questions.

One thing is certain, he thought. *His ability to locate us in these caverns proves that he knows a great deal about Hidden Valley. He might not be a friend, but after the assistance he's rendered us, it's impossible to picture him as an enemy. He's obviously not a stranger to the women. And the dog obviously loves him. Rachel knows him, but doesn't want him to recognize her. And Elizabeth seems confused about her relationship with him.*

The pieces of the puzzle were being dropped on the table too rapidly for CC to fit them into any order. He instead sat there astonished by the incredible coincidence that had brought them all together deep inside a mountain in central Vermont, for he sensed that somewhere, at some time in his own forgotten lifetime, his path too might have crossed with that of this man. As a result, he was somehow sure that they need not feel threatened by his presence.

The man started to back into the darkness, dragging Elizabeth with him, her wrist raised painfully between her shoulder blades, while his rifle was easily gripped in his massive right hand, his finger upon the trigger. He suddenly twisted her head around, kissed her on the lips, then thrust her away so that she went pirouetting across the cavern before sprawling onto the floor in the center of their little circle. Their eyes had followed her movements, and by the time they looked up again, he had disappeared, and Elizabeth was crawling back to kneel next to Rachel.

She was breathing hard from her ordeal, and it seemed incongruous when she whispered, "I can't believe I'm saying this, but he's cute."

Rachel looked at her in amazement. "I can't believe that you're saying it either."

Elizabeth immediately mistook her words to mean that she was jealous or angry, but Rachel's next words disabused her.

"I can't believe that 'Elizabeth Cool' would lose her cool over a stranger that she'd once cold-cocked with a chunk of firewood."

"Well," she confessed, "I can't either. It must be the product of a lifetime of abstinence."

"A lifetime?"

Elizabeth colored. "In spite of popular opinion, yes, an entire lifetime of abstinence."

"So we have something else in common," Rachel observed.

"Really?" Elizabeth asked, obviously surprised.

"Really."

In the silence that followed, Rachel whispered, "You called him cute? I might call him a hunk, but not cute," a hint of laughter in her voice."

"Well, I'll go along with that. He's definitely a hunk, but I think he's cute too."

"I never thought of him as cute," Rachel intoned.

"From what I read in the papers," Elizabeth commented, "he not only had women falling all over him, but he's a notorious bad guy."

"Haven't you ever heard that you shouldn't believe everything you read in the papers?"

"Like you know anything more about him than I do," Elizabeth challenged.

"I know that he did have women falling all over him, as you said, but that he's essentially a good and decent man."

"Good one! You've known him for all of, what, two minutes?"

"A little longer than that."

"Oh, really. And how was that, dear friend of mine?"

"He was my fiancée."

"Ha, ha. Good one! I'm glad you're feeling well enough to crack jokes. When I first met you, you didn't have much of a sense of humor. You've come a long way."

"Yes, a very long way," Rachel agreed, her voice trailing off. Then she spoke in a choked voice.

"He rescued you from the enemy. Just don't let him leave you waiting at the altar."

Elizabeth turned to her, and the grin on her face faded as she noticed tears shining in Rachel's eyes. She was trying to find words with which to respond when his voice, filled with amazement, came from the shadows.

"Rachel?" There was a pause. "Oh, my God! Rachel, is that you? You're alive?"

His stunned audience remained silent, but Elizabeth's shocked eyes were fixed on Rachel's face,

The big man started to move toward her, but stopped abruptly when he realized that he might be putting himself in peril by stepping back into the light.

"Rachel, I'm so sorry. Please forgive me." His cry was met with dead silence. "I had no choice...," but even as he spoke the words, he seemed to realize that his attempt to justify himself was ridiculous, and his voice trailed off.

They were all caught up in the strange exchange, and, except for the sound of the dripping water, the tunnel had become as silent as a tomb. Elizabeth continued to stare at Rachel, and understanding began to dawn in her eyes.

Finally, Rachel responded, and her words were dry, like ashes.

"It's all right, Joseph. I've had a lot of time to consider our relationship, and I know now that things have worked out for the best."

"You can't mean that?"

Her failure to respond seemed to encourage him.

"Rachel?"

"Yes, Joseph, I do mean it. I knew it was over the minute I stood alone in that cavern and heard alarm bells instead of wedding bells, and you weren't by my side. And since then the Lord has repeatedly confirmed it."

"The Lord? You're walking with the Lord now?"

"Yes. I could only have survived this long because of answered prayer."

CC's mind had been in a ferment since the strange discussion had begun, but his confusion was slowly giving way to understanding. One thing was obvious. This man had jilted Rachel, and their past relationship couldn't help but impact what would transpire over the next few minutes.

Elizabeth, on the other hand, was thunderstruck. A deep and growing affection for Rachel was being tossed to and fro by her irrational feelings toward this towering man. She couldn't explain it because she didn't understand it herself, but she realized that she might have already fallen in love with him. And it had suddenly become clear to her that he really had risked his own life for her when he'd tried to rescue her from the looter's camp.

So apart from the fact that his actions appeared to have brought the enemy into their midst, with the consequence that they were now being forced to flee for their lives, and that she was unlikely to ever see him again, she couldn't deny her feelings for him any more than she could betray her dearest friend.

She made her choice. Determined to demonstrate her solidarity and to comfort Rachel, she slid her arm around the other woman's shoulders and hugged her. Rachel glanced at her in understanding, but couldn't help notice the tears of regret now shining in Elizabeth's eyes.

When Elizabeth looked back at her, Rachel whispered, "Hey, dummy...."

"Why are you calling me a dummy?" she responded, clearly hurt.

"You're a dummy if you think that my past relationship with Joseph will harm any possible future relationship you might have with him, or with me."

Elizabeth was stunned. "Really?"

"Truly."

She stared into Rachel's eyes, trying to detect whether her friend was speaking the truth. But of course, she was. Her friend seemed incapable of a lie.

Rachel smiled at Elizabeth, a grin on her face. "Say, 'Thank you, Rachel.'"

Elizabeth smiled uncertainly. After a moment, she replied in a whisper, "Thank you, Rachel."

This interplay went unnoticed by CC, for he was at that moment ruminating over whether any of the others still felt threatened by the big man's presence. It was obvious that he hadn't come here expecting to find either of these women, so he had come for some other reason, and it was that purpose that would probably form the tipping point in their relationship. Just as he began half-hoping that the big man had decided to move on, his voice again boomed out of the darkness.

"I have a number of questions for you."

"Questions for us?"

"Yes."

"And if we don't choose to answer them?"

"I think you would find that a costly mistake."

Jonathan held his weapon leveled across his hip, aimed into the shadows. His eyes turned questioningly to CC who responded by shaking his head almost imperceptibly. Jonathan reacted by lowering the muzzle of his rifle slightly.

The man's voice sounded very calm as it resonated through the passage. "That's better. Now, suppose we talk. I'll ask the questions and you provide the answers."

No one else spoke. In fact, except for CC, they were all staring down at the floor of the cave, their plight again brought home to them, defeat registering on their faces. It was CC who finally responded.

"How about I've got a question for you?"

"I'll allow one question."

"What's with the major's insignia on your collar points? Isn't that insignia U.S. Army issue?"

"That wasn't the question I was expecting, and in fact, you asked two questions, but I'll answer them. First, the People's Revolutionary Army has declared that the U.S. Army no longer exists as a viable entity, so the insignia I'm wearing only has significance as they apply it. Second, because the Chinese communists have experienced a lot of controversy over the past century as to whether they should issue rank to their own people, they certainly wouldn't honor us *big nose* Americans by allowing us to wear their uniforms or symbols of rank. But they consider me a quisling, a turncoat, a typical untrustworthy American who is nevertheless at least temporarily useful to them, and I have therefore been issued these leaves."

He appeared indifferent to the loathing in their eyes.

"I hope you are satisfied with that explanation because now I expect answers to my own questions."

"What questions?"

"First, I'm looking for some cans of coffee."

They looked from one to another in obvious confusion.

"I followed you here last winter from the co-op. I have reason to believe that you removed a knapsack containing several pounds of coffee from the cellar. I want those cans!"

CC was incredulous. "You've caused us to lose our home, and now you're harassing us for a couple of pounds of coffee?

You can't be serious!" CC's question dripped with sarcasm. "Are you insane?"

"If you had tried to brew it, you'd understand."

CC turned to Jonathan and the boy shrugged. "I stacked those cans on the pantry shelf behind all the other coffee. *FIFO.* It's your rule. 'First in, first out.' Save the freshest for last, you always say."

The man stepped out of the shadows and spoke directly to the boy. "Then you never opened the cans?"

Jonathan didn't reply until he had received a nod from CC.

"No." He was respectful, but clearly unafraid, his face guileless as he expanded on his answer. "As far as I know, the coffee cans are still where I put them."

CC was furious. Their relatively luxurious home was irretrievably lost and this idiot was looking for cans of coffee. Except, he realized, whatever was in those cans wasn't coffee. And this man was anything but an idiot. And these were crazy days, so he tried to match his voice to their assailant's apparent calm.

"This conversation is just getting a bit difficult for me to deal with," he ground out. "And under the circumstances, all this sweetness and light is a little much." He pointed at the intruder.

"You lead a pack of thieves and killers to our hideaway, blow away our security, manhandle a lady, threaten our lives, and all for a couple of cans of coffee? Why don't you tell us what's really going on?"

The man laughed. "You'd like to know the facts, huh?" He stepped completely out of the shadows. "Well, why not?" He leaned nonchalantly against the cave wall, his assault weapon casually pointed at them. "It's very simple, really. Those red plastic coffee cans contain several pounds of pure cocaine. Cocaine is now impossible to get, even on the black market, and it is, not surprisingly, more valuable than ever. Its sale will help provide the resources I require to assure a certain amount of comfort and security in the days ahead."

"Cocaine?" CC was speechless. "You destroyed our home, and any hope we have for our own futures, for a couple of pounds of cocaine?"

At the frustration and anger in CC's voice, the man slowly swung his rifle to cover him. "You'd better get this straight. I didn't lead them here. I followed them."

CC realized that this could well be the truth.

"But I would have come here anyway," he continued. "There are several rich and powerful people who have everything else they want, but still put a lot of value on drugs. That, along with my getting my hands on the jewels and the missing documents, is very important to me."

"What jewels? What documents?"

"We shan't play games."

CC noted that both his vocabulary and pronunciation made him sound more like an Ivy Leaguer than a G.I. Joe. The man's voice was dry, almost bored, but it was all the more menacing because of it.

"I want those papers," he persisted. "Where are they?"

CC held the stare of his assailant, his own demeanor changing dramatically. His anger was no longer evident, his emotions under tight control, his face cold and expressionless. He was putting things into perspective, putting a value on the items mentioned.

As far as he was concerned, the cocaine was a non-issue. As were any jewels. This guy, whoever he was, was welcome to them, and good riddance. But he realized that the demand for the drugs was a smokescreen to cover his real interest. The "papers" he was alluding to were an entirely different matter. CC didn't need to appraise the faces of those around his little circle to realize that they were in one accord. He was certain that their feelings would be much the same as his. Their continued possession of the *papers* was not open to negotiations.

Things have changed, he realized. *Yes, we are losing our home, but we did take a serious toll of the enemy, both in lives and in temporarily frustrating their purposes. And if there are any bands of Americans out there in America, working against the invaders, what we accomplished will have enormous propaganda value. And that suddenly seems very important. And we accomplished it by God's grace, without losing a single life. What's more, we just rid ourselves of an enemy who has betrayed us. So, CC* decided, *we may be down, but we're definitely not out. And we might have lost this battle, and lost our home, but we haven't lost the war, and we will somehow gain strength by passing through these ordeals.*

Most importantly, he somehow understood that his entire little company was in agreement with him. The preservation of these documents was far more important to each of them than their own survival.

For CC's part, God had delivered him from death so often over the past year that, whatever happened, he considered his future secure. If he lived, he anticipated a continual struggle serving God and his people. If he died, he expected to immediately be with the Lord. It was all the same to him.

He searched the faces of his friends, and realized that their dread, like his own, had been replaced by indignation and a mutual self-righteous anger. Instead of shrinking in fear, their eyes now focused on their assailant.

CC couldn't help but smile. The intensity of each gaze brought an enormous sense of respect and pride to his heart. *But their courage,* he thought, *won't stop a bullet.* Playing for time, he turned the man's demands around. "What papers?"

"Don't waste my time!" the man replied, casually brushing at some dried mud on his camouflage uniform. "I want the documents that Ross stole from the museum in Boston, and I want them now."

The absence of the word, "we," resulted in a silent exchange between CC and Jonathan, for now they were reasonably certain that this man was indeed working alone. The boy's knuckles were bloodless as he gripped the stock of his rifle tightly, again aiming it at their assailant.

The man had not missed the exchange, or the slight movement of the weapon. He responded with a sharp command.

"Drop the rifle. Now! If you do not drop the rifle, I will shoot the girl in the knee." He pointed his weapon at Elizabeth, who surprisingly responded with a laugh.

"You wouldn't shoot the woman you're going to marry," she asked, "would you?"

He simply stared at her, a bemused look on his face, but the muzzle of his rifle dipped almost imperceptibly.

CC turned to her for an instant and was surprised to see that she was still smiling. They were all smiling. He heard a slight scuffling, and when he turned back toward their assailant, he'd again disappeared into the shadows.

He hadn't injured anyone yet and had, in fact, provided them substantial assistance in the past. There was, however, no discounting his spoken threat. In spite of her laugh, Elizabeth shivered, realizing how a bullet would cripple her and, under the circumstances, probably result in her death. She nevertheless raised her own weapon and pointed it into the shadows. "Shooting my future husband is probably not the best way to start a romance, but if it's necessary..."

"Start a romance? Would you stop saying that?"

"Hey, you're the one who just kissed me. And you're the one who saved my life at the looters' camp. So now, according to some old legend, I belong to you."

Rachel couldn't help herself. The laughter she'd been restraining went rolling across the cavern.

"You think this is funny, Rachel?" he demanded.

"Oh, boy, do I," she laughed. "And I'll tell you something else, Joseph."

"What's that?"

"If Elizabeth Cool has set her cap for you, your bachelor days are numbered."

"Let's just say that my days are numbered and leave it at that."

For some reason, that wiped the smile off her face.

"Okay, I'll tell you something else," she said, her voice sobering.

"I'm listening."

"Give up on the documents!"

Before this exchange had occurred, Jonathan had been ready to acquiesce and lay his weapon on the cave floor as the man had ordered him. When he noted the look of determination on Elizabeth's and Rachel's faces, however, he instead stood to his feet, pulled his weapon into his shoulder and aimed at the last spot he'd seen the man. Then, because he'd researched this interesting weapon that they'd taken from the farmer's co-op, he flicked a lever near the trigger housing. That tiny sound reverberated around the cave.

Stalemate

Deep in the Mountain
May 2nd, 6:10 a.m.

The clicking noise brought an immediate response from the darkness.

"Hey, kid. What kind of weapon do you have there?"

Before he could respond, a similar clicking sound came from Elizabeth's assault rifle.

It was CC who answered. He casually bent down and picked up his own rifle and, as he lifted it, he too twisted a little lever.

"This, as I think you know, is an M16, and the three of us have just set our firing options at full automatic." His voice sounded almost indifferent. "Sure, if you pull that trigger you might get one or two of us." CC couldn't believe how cavalier he was sounding. Maybe it was the exhaustion. Maybe it was an "I don't give a darn" kind of reaction. Whatever it was, he no longer cared.

"I refer you," he went on almost glibly, "to the Department of the Army *Field Manual FM 23-9*. It states that, when we squeeze these triggers, the three of us will empty three 30-round magazines in your general direction in less than twenty seconds. That's a total of ninety rounds.

Rachel, who'd been standing in the shadows, interrupted him. "Make that four 30-round magazines. One-hundred-and-twenty rounds. And my shooting might not be so random," she warned. "I still have love for you, Joseph, but I won't hesitate to take your life in order to save the documents. And even though you're standing back in the darkness, and in spite of what you and I have shared, I think you should know that I have a night-vision scope on my rifle, and I have you centered in my sights."

Elizabeth let her pack slip to the floor, the portfolio strapped to it, and stepped boldly toward the man, placing herself between it and him.

He stepped back into the light, but oddly seemed to take little interest in the bundle she'd dropped.

Everyone realized they had reached a stalemate, and each of them took this opportunity to study him more carefully. The big, square-jawed man that CC had studied through the field glasses had a mass of dark, loose curls, and was still dressed entirely in camouflage clothing. There was an unmistakeable aura of power about him. As he moved forward in the flickering light, he cast a giant shadow on the cave wall behind him, and his unshaven and haggard face produced an almost cadaverous appearance. His mien was made even more singular and incongruous by the presence of a silver cross sticking out from beneath the fold of his jacket collar.

Jonathan blurted, "Isn't it just a bit of a contradiction to be wearing those Commie anti-Christ insignias on your collar while you've got a cross half-hidden by your lapel?"

The man turned to him, but instead of exploding in anger, he tipped his head as in thought, and after a moment agreed, "Yes, it might present a bit of a philosophical problem, but I'll worry about it later."

"You'd better hurry; you might not have a *later.*"

"Don't push it, kid."

Jonathan was wise enough to venture no additional comment.

In the meantime, the man's eyes had returned to the portfolio, but it was clear that he was still very much aware of their movements and of the grave danger that they represented to him.

"It's not really the documents that you want, is it," CC asked.

"That's an interesting observation," the man replied. "Why would you surmise that?"

"A hunch."

"I haven't made up my mind as to whether I'll take them with me."

"Not that you have any say in the matter, but why vacillate?"

"I'm trying to decide where they'll be safest."

"What's that supposed to mean?"

"Exactly what I said."

CC nodded his head, in sudden understanding.

The man again pointed his rifle at Elizabeth, who was standing boldly in the lamplight. She was trying to slip a small vinyl satchel into the backpack to which the large portfolio was fastened. "You surely are beautiful," he said appreciatively.

"As are you," she replied. "But as Conrad wrote, *Handsome is, as handsome does,* and we will soon discover whether you have attained the sort of character required in a true hero."

"And you live up to the publicity," he responded.

"What publicity?"

"Keenly intelligent. Tough. Dedicated. And..."

"And what," she asked, a husky sound in her voice.

"Why, beautiful, of course."

"Well, thank you, kind sir."

Then his demeanor changed, and he was all business again.

"What's in the small package?"

She hesitated.

"Well?"

"These are supplies that I need to maintain the documents."

"If that were the case," he replied, a smile on his face, "shouldn't they have been kept together with the documents?"

"No. I wouldn't want the liquids to accidentally spill on them."

"Well, whether or not I take the documents, I'll want your so-called supplies."

"You wouldn't know how to use them," she replied, her laugh sounding artificial.

"Perhaps your hearing has been damaged, but even I can hear that your liquids are rattling," he observed dryly. "They sound sort of like loose jewelry."

She dropped the small bundle to the ground, fumbled the portfolio loose from the backpack, and hugged it to her.

He looked at CC "Have you got any idea what kind of supplies she has in that little satchel?"

CC was suddenly enjoying the interrogation, and smiled as he remembered the newspaper clipping that Jonathan had shoved into his pocket.

"Oh, I have a pretty good idea what that little satchel contains. And as far as I'm concerned, it's negotiable." Then CC's face became stern. "But the documents are not."

"Your situation is hopeless. I can take what I want."

"If that's the way you bluff, you must have been a very poor poker player."

He made no response, so CC continued.

"Aren't you a bit presumptuous in inferring you will get anything at all from us, or have you forgotten that there are several automatic weapons aimed at you?"

"If you pull those triggers, those weapons will start spraying bullets all over the place, and a lot of them will come ricocheting back at you. Besides," he smiled, "I don't think even one of you has the guts to shoot."

"Don't bet your life on it," CC replied. "Over the past twenty-four hours, this group has been through fire and water. And even if you're willing to trade your life for ours, it's not a very profitable exchange."

"Maybe not. It's a trade you'll have to decide on."

"Oh, I think I can speak for all of us when I say that we've already made that decision. We're all willing to die to preserve the contents of that portfolio."

"Well, I'm actually glad to hear you say that, but I wasn't figuring on shooting all of you."

"Oh, really," CC smiled. "Have you considered how angry the other survivors might be if you were to shoot even one of us?"

"I wouldn't shoot just anyone. I'd shoot you."

"Then what?"

"They'd probably figure that with you gone, they'd have no chance of survival at all."

"Well," CC laughed, "they know how to lay a campfire, build a lean-to, and even a little about living off the land. And as far as marksmanship is concerned, even our teenager is fast and accurate."

"Anyone can shoot a target when it's not shooting back. Besides, I'm faster and more accurate."

"Perhaps you need to stop bluffing."

"Bluffing? I never bluff. But to get back to my question, have you got any idea what kind of supplies she has in that little satchel?"

"In fact," CC offered, reaching into his pocket, "I believe that I have an inventory of her 'maintenance supplies' right here. And," he added, "this might be of as much interest to your Chinese or Muslim friends as the documents you were demanding." He unfolded the newspaper article and began to read.

> **Boston**. The extraordinarily display of precious gems at the Back Bay Museum of Art will close tomorrow.
>
> These gem stones have been the most popular exhibit in the museum's history, with visitors sometimes queuing up for blocks in the falling snow to view them.
>
> Included in the presentation, is the 45-carat Hope diamond. Its history is clouded with the legend of a curse that follows its owners, and is valued at two hundred million dollars. Other notable stones include the Logan Sapphire (423 carats), and numerous other famous diamonds, emeralds and sapphires worth well over one hundred million dollars.
>
> The gemstones, loaned by the Smithsonian, will be returned to Washington this week, and the exhibit will be replaced by one featuring the original manuscripts of both the *Declaration of Independence* and *The Constitution of the United States*.

CC folded the article and slipped it back into his pocket. Elizabeth, her face ashen, simply stared at him.

"That little packet of maintenance supplies might come in handy," the man remarked with a smile, but oddly enough, he seemed to have lost interest in the satchel that now lay neglected on the cave floor. Then he said something that sounded very strange and out of character with what had gone before.

"Whoever has the responsibility for protecting those documents will require substantial resources."

He turned to CC, and an unexpected quality in his voice arrested their attention. It wasn't exactly pleading, but there was s definite hunger to learn something. The radical change in the direction of the conversation surprised all of them.

"I walked over to that old farm, and I found two graves out behind the ruins of the house."

What's he fishing for? CC wondered.

"Do you know what happened to those people, how they died?"

Elizabeth's eyebrows drew together as she looked to Rachel for some hint of what was going on, but Rachel simply shrugged her shoulders.

CC hesitated, then decided, *Why not answer him? What can it hurt?*

"They were good people who obviously preferred the seclusion of this valley to the confusion of the world outside."

"Then you met them?" the man demanded. "You talked with them?"

"Sort of."

"What do you mean, 'Sort of?'" His formerly tentative interest was rapidly turning into an impatient series of demands, revealing that this discussion possessed a significance above mere curiosity.

"You either spoke with them or you didn't."

Attempting to frame a response, CC watched as the man's impatience turned to anger.

"I spoke with her for just a moment, but I really learned about them by examining their home and their possessions."

"You mean you are a pillager? Did you hurt the woman?"

"Of course not," CC replied flatly.

The man pondered that, then demanded, "Go on."

"In spite of the fact that they were obviously woodsmen and farmers, they had the same sensitivity to their world that inspired 19th Century naturalists, artists and poets like Jefferson and Franklin." CC seemed to be gazing at some far-off scene as he went on.

The man shifted his feet, clearly dissatisfied with this oblique answer to his question. "Get to the point!"

"I am," CC answered, almost losing his own temper. "Since I don't know what you're asking me, or why, I don't really know how to answer your question." He pulled some thoughts out of the air. "They had a large library, and it was obvious from the notes they made in the margins of their books that they read voraciously. And they were gifted writers."

His next words caused the big man's eyes to shine. "They were well-educated, culturally refined, and it's clear they had been great Christian leaders."He gnawed his lip trying to remember anything else. "They were elderly, but probably not too old to be your parents."

The man snapped, "Get to the point," and CC wondered whether he'd inadvertently touched a raw spot. What he had said certainly didn't justify the shouted reply. The man's anger increased the tension, and seemed to rattle Rachel. Everyone's knuckles were white from gripping their weapons so tightly, their fingers tensing on the triggers.

Then the man said something strange. "No one here needs to be hurt. Let's all just calm down so that I can get my questions answered."

"Whether anyone gets hurt here," CC responded, "depends on how hard you push to possess things that don't belong to you. But I don't mind answering a few questions."

And though the words weren't particularly calming, some change in both men's demeanor encouraged a slight relaxation in the atmosphere.

CC went on. "When I arrived at the farm," he began, "the old man had already passed on." Unmistakable sorrow shadowed his face. "I buried him that afternoon. He tipped his head toward Baron. "The dog had stayed by the man's side, and had barely survived, but I fed him and kept giving him water, and by the next day he seemed much better. He led me to a cavern that housed an amazing underground barn packed with livestock. I found the man's wife there. She passed on as we were speaking."

"Radiation poisoning?"

"Yes. And probably a broken heart."

"I like how you said, 'passed on,' instead of 'died.'"

"Yes, I believe that we all have somewhere to go after we are finished here."

As their would-be assailant continued to stare at him, CC continued his account. "He left a diary."

There was a new spark of interest, as though all that had come before was expected.

"Where is this diary?"

Strange question. Why does he care? Then the dawn broke. *Of course. How stupid of me! He knows his way around this valley and around these caverns. Rachel knows him, and Elizabeth is afraid of him. He's very interested in the Sennetts.*

"Well?" the man demanded, bringing CC back.

"The diary is back in our motorhome."

"Where?"

"There's a bookcase."

He nodded, satisfied.

Then CC prodded him. "Why are you so interested? Do you think there's a map to buried treasure in that diary?" He immediately realized he should not have been flippant. T*his is obviously a sensitive matter, and certainly nothing to joke about.*

But instead of growing angry, the man pretended to stifle a yawn, refusing to answer directly. "I'm trying to find some answers. It doesn't concern you, but maybe I'll take a look at it after I'm done with you. His voice, though still polite, began to take on a brittle tone, and CC decided not to push him further.

CC, in turn, was pretty desperate. Time was slipping away. He glanced quickly at his watch, and realized that McCord might be freed from their cottage at any moment, and it was a tossup as to whether he would go out into the valley to contact their enemies, or pick up one of the extra firearms they'd been forced to leave behind and follow them back into the mountain. Either way, time was of the essence. So in order to break this deadlock, CC decided to prime the pump with additional information, hoping that perhaps he might rattle the man and learn something of value.

"Their name was Sennett," CC continued, watching carefully to see whether the name might strike some chord, but although the man's lips seemed to draw into a tight line, he remained impassive. When he remained silent, CC went on.

It was ironic. The two women knew precisely who this man was, but CC was still groping.

"The old man was away from home when the bombs fell," he continued.

There was an increase in interest. The big man appeared to lean forward as though he didn't want to miss a single word.

"He made it back home," CC continued, "but he'd suffered a great deal of exposure to the radioactivity, and he passed away before his wife."

Now his listener seemed to be having a little difficulty controlling his emotions and was clearly hanging on every word. And though the horror of the past few months had left many people calloused and indifferent to such accounts, there were few who weren't occasionally touched by the pain and suffering around them. Their assailant was now staring at the ground, absentmindedly kicking at a small stalagmite, but he looked up at an unexpected question.

"Do you know what impressed me most about this couple?"

The man remained silent, staring at CC from beneath hooded brows, his shaggy head lowered like a wounded bull just before the toreador administers the coup-de-gråce.

"It was the way the two of them remained focused on one another in spite of their horrible illness."

"What do you mean?" he asked, his voice gruff.

"Radiation poisoning causes an individual to become disoriented and confused–indifferent to the needs of others. Yet somehow this old man managed to overcome the effects, and continued to extend his love to her. He even recorded an account of their last day."

Even Jonathan was caught up in the exchange now, somehow sensing the high drama, and wondering if it might possibly hold the key to their own future. None had heard this story before, and everything else–their grimy hair and filthy clothes, even the portfolio at Elizabeth's feet–was momentarily forgotten.

"And the old man...? What happened to the old man?" their interrogator persisted.

"I found him on his bed, his dog lying there on the floor beside him. The animal didn′t want to leave him. I wrapped the old man in his bedding, took him out back, and buried him." CC couldn′t think of any reason to describe his advanced state of decomposition, but his inquisitor probably guessed. His fingers relaxed, the rifle′s muzzle no longer pointing at CC.

CC had also become indifferent to any peril and again challenged him.

"They wrote of a son. They were, and I quote, ′hoping for better things from him.′ It was their dream that he might someday return from what they called '...his prodigal and fruitless search after futility, and help lead the world to the Lord.' They were sorry that he hadn't returned before their deaths."

"Yeah. Well, that's neither here nor there." He cleared his throat. "I was just curious, that's all."

"Sure. Glad to help."

He shot CC a suspicious glance, as if trying to decide whether irony or sarcasm underlay his response, but he was evidently satisfied that he was being ingenuous.

He cleared his throat again. "All right. One more thing. We heard that there might have been a little girl at that farm." His mouthed tightened, there was a look of desperation in his eyes. "Did you find her?"

They all remained stone-faced, and no one replied.

Their assailant turned his head aside, and brushed his nose with the back of his hand. CC almost relented, for the man must have known about the child and therefore concluded that she had also died, a presumption that seemed supported by the fact that he didn't pursue the subject further.

"O.K.," he said, almost indifferently. "I'll take the documents. "Then he added with some irony, "Oh, and the 'cleaning supplies,' Then you can all go."

The others had fanned out across the cave during the conversation. Now, as though on cue, they collectively laughed.

"Fat chance," was Jonathan's comment.

"That's the trouble with kids," their visitor commented sardonically. "They don't have sense enough to keep their mouths shut or to understand how permanent death is."

The boy repeated himself. "Again, fat chance. And where do you get off telling me I don't know about death? I've seen plenty."

And all of them carefully sighted their weapons at the man, their fingers taking up any slack in their triggers. *Are we really only a hairbreadth from slaughter?* CC wondered. He'd been trying to keep up his end of the conversation even as he was plotting how to handle the situation.

"Some of us will survive this," he suddenly declared.

The man's eyes moved from person to person, then back in CC's direction.

Jonathan warned, "Don't do it, mister. It's four against one now."

The man smiled. "You know what, boy? I respect you for wanting to help your friends, but I don't think you have the nerve to shoot anyone. And I can kill all of you before any of you gets a shot off."

"Mister, you may shoot me, but I won't go down until I put a round in you. I shot down an airplane with a 22, and I don't think I'll have any trouble hitting you at five yards." His voice communicated both pride and a fatalistic determination.

And his words had an impact on the man. His strained mouth almost shaped a smile. "So that's what happened," he muttered. And he thought, *With enough people like this, maybe America does still have a chance.*

CC sensed the change in the atmosphere and was immensely proud of all of them. And the broad smile on his face showed it. He suddenly appreciated something of the nature of their forefathers who had hammered out those coveted documents in the first place. For with this fearless manifestation of his little company's determination, CC suddenly understood with a sense of both joy and sorrow, that each of them, independent of one another, had determined to offer their lives to save these God inspired documents that represented the birth of the greatest nation in history. He looked at the man and realized that he had come to the same conclusion, and was even more surprised to see that he seemed pleased by his epiphany.

Indeed, he had a similar thought. *These four people, from diverse walks of life, have one thing in common. They are real Americans.* Nevertheless, he persisted in challenging them. "If you try to leave, I'll have to shoot."

They heard the words, but they had all noticed the change. Instead of insisting on them giving him the documents, now he was warning them that they could not leave.

"It's obvious that you are not insane," CC replied in a matter-of-fact voice, "and it's equally obvious that we are all prepared to die to save these documents." He took a step toward the man. "The real question is, are you prepared to die?" It was a challenge that was delivered matter-of-factly, in a conversational tone.

When there was no answer, CC continued.

"No, I don't think you'll take anything from here." There was iron in his voice, and though he didn't know where it had come from, he could sense a new confidence manifesting itself.

They were all watching the man to see whether he sensed the change in their determination, and for some indication, some movement, some word that would act as a signal and trigger an overwhelming response. CC didn't realize that his tone had brought hope to the others, while at the same time hardening his own resolve. It had been a spiritual metamorphosis. Each of them had obviously gone through some sort of a moral crisis, a process that converted them from limpid puddles of molten metal, into coiled springs of hardened steel. They had all independently resolved to protect the papers, certain somehow that it was their destinies to do so, and they would do so, even at the cost of their own lives.

The fact that they were fanned out around the man placed him in a difficult, if not impossible situation. And, while there was no perceptible movement, they all seemed to anchor themselves where they were. And he was struck by the fact that Rachel, with her night-vision scope, hadn′t slid back into the darkness where she would have had an overwhelming advantage, but was indifferent to the added danger she faced out in the open.

Their unwanted visitor couldn′t know it, but they′d each committed their destinies to the Lord, and in the next few moments, they would either be delivered into the Lord′s presence or free of this danger. They were confident, and they were clearly at peace with themselves and with God. Like the three in the fiery furnace, they had become invincible. Live or die, they knew that they would live forever.

Their assailant did not miss the change in the atmosphere. Earlier, while he was still hidden from view, and he′d heard Jonathan's plaintive voice speaking about an escape from the mountain, he had sensed the despair and division that gripped them. Suddenly, their realization of the importance of the papers they possessed had changed all that. They were unified, and they each carried a very lethal weapon. They couldn′t know it, but that realization pleased him immensely.

Even now it was obvious that they were all preparing to strike out at him, and he knew that he could no longer intimidate them. In fact, any additional threats would probably trigger an overwhelming response. He realized that he might not get out of there at all, but when he considered his future, such a death at this time would probably be a blessing. *But I have a mission too,* he reminded himself, *and they may unwittingly help me fulfill it. In fact, they may outlive me and accomplish what I could not.*

At the same time, CC didn't understand that the man had become as indifferent to the growing threat from his little band as they were of him. It was not that they really wanted to hurt him, he understood, not even Rachel, though he realized that the man had done her injury. Of course, they didn't want to be hurt either, but CC had reached the inescapable conclusion that they would all try to kill him if that was what it would take to keep those documents out of his hands.

What's more, he sensed that they had suddenly come to the conclusion that the they had a mission, and that their mission was transcendent, a task for which they were all willing to sacrifice their lives. So, even if the man were still inclined to seize the documents, he would have to kill them all. At the same time, CC realized that they had independently resolved that they wouldn't let him succeed, no matter what.

What they didn't know, could not have accepted, was that he'd planned to seize the documents because he believed that they would be safer in his hands. Now he realized that this was not the case. For he too had recognized a dramatic change in these individuals whom he'd initially considered his potential adversaries.

Some nebulous ideas had coalesced, had crystalized. If anything, his little dialogue had strengthened their resolve to resist him. He suddenly understood where they stood. Not only were they as determined as he to save the papers for future generations of Americans, but there was strength in their numbers. Apart from that, Elizabeth possessed the knowledge to preserve the documents which he lacked.

No, he realized. *Everything has changed.*

His mind raced. *These people are aiming very sophisticated weapons at me. And they're determined. Now I can really understand why those who have been ambitious to subvert America struggled so hard to disarm the population. Maybe the majority of our early American forefathers had little formal education, but they understood issues like freedom. And how to fight to preserve them, including how to load and shoot a rifle.* He looked up, his demeanor markedly changed.

"Did you know that during the American revolution, nearly every citizen owned a weapon that was comparable to, or even superior, to those carried by British soldiers, and in many cases the Americans were better marksmen?"

They were all surprised at this radical turn in the conversation, but CC surprised himself by answering in kind.

"It's true that most had muskets, and many had rifles, but few had bayonets."

"That's true. Nonetheless, the British attempted to disarm their American subjects. And it was over the issue of forced disarmament–as much as taxation–that British regulars met the American militia on Lexington Green where the shot heard round the world was fired. And it was the professional soldier, the Red Coat, and not the Minute Man, who suffered terrible losses that day."

"Yes," CC replied. "I think that we all know that."

The assailant went on as though he were thinking out loud, as though CC hadn't spoken.

"That day, each American was equipped with his personal weapon, plus the little powder and ball he could afford to own. There was no federal army to fight his wars for him, nor to supply his needs. Those men had become expert marksmen because they had to be. They were in large part poor men who lived hand-to-mouth. When they went hunting for meat, they didn't dare miss because they couldn't afford the extra powder and lead if they missed their targets." He looked from face to face, and realized that they were bemused at this turn in the conversation. But he persisted.

"And even though the British had significant advantages – the greatest navy in the world, trained and seasoned troops, artillery, mounted cavalry, comfortable quarters, warm clothes, sufficient food, and medical supplies – it was nonetheless that rag-tag Continental army of starving patriots that ultimately prevailed."

They eyed one another, confusion on their faces, as he continued.

What's his point? Elizabeth wondered. *Have I fallen for a crazy man?*

His smile made her think that he might have somehow read her thoughts, but his response seemed disjointed and irrelevant.

"Most Americans were afraid of big government because so many of them, or their forbearers, had escaped to the New World to be free of its evils. They'd seen how monarchies and totalitarian governments were inevitably arbitrary, capricious and oppressive. George Washington, the father of our country, later summed it up with these words: 'Government is not reason; it is not eloquent; it is force. Like fire, it is a dangerous servant and a fearful master.'"

CC stood there stunned by this philosophical turn in the conversation. And although he agreed completely with the points the man was making, he wondered how these high-sounding phrases squared with his demand that they turn over the state papers, the jewels and the drugs. The next sentence didn't clarify matters.

"And so was born the Second Amendment to the Constitution, *The right of the people to keep and bear arms shall not be infringed; a well armed and well regulated militia being the best security of a free country....*"

"CC waved the muzzle of his weapon up and down slightly to get the man's attention, and when he had it, he became quite outspoken.

"You're not making any sense."

"What doesn't make sense?"

"You are suddenly implying that your concern is for the *Constitution*."

"Don't be misled. My concern right along has been for the documents you have in your possession, but I didn't think that my motives were your concern. Now I see that its a growing conviction with you."

"Well, if you think these flowery sentiments make us any more prone to surrender these documents to you, you are sorely mistaken."

The man's only response was to raise his eyes and stare at CC, a slight smile on his face. Moving his jaw like a fish slipping a hook, he finally spoke.

"I wasn't really speaking to you. I was repeating some words that I'd once heard from that old man you buried. Remembering them kind of set me head-over-heels and made me revise my thoughts about you."

"I don't understand," CC replied candidly. He still felt uncomfortable with the man, and couldn't imagine him having come this far only to suddenly reverse his intentions. "So," he demanded, "if you want to protect the state papers, why your interest in the cocaine and the jewels."

The man laughed aloud, a deep laugh that seemed to fill the tunnel and shake the walls.

"It's simple, really. You know the old saying, 'Money talks.'"

His listeners looked even more confused, though Rachel was familiar with his often convoluted approach to introducing an idea.

"Oh, come on!" he laughed. "It's really very simple. "I need things to barter, things that have great value. If I can trade drugs or jewels for my freedom or even my life...." His voice trailed off. He saw their looks of confusion.

"You really don't get it?" he asked in obvious surprise. "It will take money to maintain possession of these documents, to protect them, and primarily to keep yourselves alive. The drugs and jewels are as good as money and, like money, they will talk."

Now they were all nodding their heads in understanding. He didn't wait for their affirmation, but simply continued on in his oblique fashion, again changing direction so rapidly that he again left them confused.

"If I asked you to quote the president's oath of office, you probably wouldn't be able to recite the words, but I think you would agree with the sentiment."

Now they looked even more perplexed.

"Your determination to protect these documents indicates that you would have no trouble affirming that oath."

The words flowed through the big man's mind. He put himself not in the place of a president, but of an 18th Century citizen soldier, intent on securing his nation's freedom from tyranny. For some reason, the words came readily to mind. He looked from person to person, commanding their attention. Then he said something surprising.

"Repeat after me."

CC looked at him in surprise. "You're kidding, right?"

"Not at all. Please humor me."

"Unless you ask us to say something with which we don't agree...."

"I won't."

"All right. We'll humor you."

"I, please state your name...."

And each of them, forgetting their danger, raised their right hands from the triggers on their weapons, and repeated their names.

"... do solemnly swear that I will support and defend the Constitution of the United States...."

When he realized that no one was repeating his words, he stopped short. His next words startled them.

"If you wish to assume responsibility for and have authority over these documents, please repeat after me."

CC was about to say, *We already have responsibility and authority for these documents,* but for some reason, he felt constrained to go along with the man. The others looked at him, and he shrugged his shoulders. When the man began again, they all repeated his words.

"I," and they stated their names, "do solemnly swear that I will support and defend the Constitution of the United States against all enemies, foreign and domestic; that I will bear true faith and...," he hesitated. "I'm sorry, I can't remember the ending except for the most important words... So help me God."

Oddly enough, they found themselves repeating the words after him, their voices rising, their agreement manifest, their eyes aglow.

He laughed aloud, and they all stared at him as though they were sure he was mad. But then they suddenly realized that everyone of them subscribed to the same ideals, and what he had just demanded of them, what they had done, had focused their convictions and raised their dedication to the highest plane. What had been a nebulous commitment to safeguard those old parchments had suddenly become a very real commitment "...to support and defend the Constitution of the United States against all enemies...," even if it cost them their lives. It was not merely a matter of agreeing with its ideals, but a sacred promise to physically protect the actual document. Their sense of wonder was immediately replaced with the awareness that they had assumed an almost impossible burden.

And for GI Joe's part, it was amazing. He felt like a man coming out of the shadows, like a blind man who'd suddenly regained his sight, like a Nebuchadnezzar who'd had his reason restored. Suddenly he felt lighter than air, no longer in conflict within himself. He had given more than casual thought to saving the state papers, but now he realized how ill-equipped he really was to do so, and what a profoundly important responsibility it was. And with that realization, he'd found something bigger than himself, something worth fighting for, even dying for, as these people were prepared to do. And he was absolutely astonished by the realization.

He didn't even seem to notice that he'd let the muzzle of his weapon dip until it actually dropped into a shallow pool of water on the floor of the cave. And, contrary to habit, he left it there, immersed in the mineral water, no longer a threat to them...nor to himself.

With a voice filled with amazed delight, he shouted, "You have just pledged yourselves to defend the actual *Constitution* of the United States, even if it costs you your lives!"

"And *The Declaration of Independence,*" Elizabeth added, a smile on her face.

"Really?" His smile broadened. "You actually saved *The Declaration* too?

They had watched as he lowered his weapon, and as one they realized that the crisis was over. And they all began to smile, first in relief, then in excitement. CC didn't know what effect those smiles had on their unwanted visitor, but they had a strange influence on him.

"Get your things," he said, turning to the others. "We have to get out of here."

One by one, they bent to gather their belongings. They ignored their assailant as though he was of no further danger, but Elizabeth was still confused. She looked over at him, a question in her eyes. He understood her confusion.

Touching his hand to his head, he said, "You swing a mean log."

"I'll make up for it."

"I'm afraid there will be no opportunity for that."

"I don't know why, but I'm convinced that you're wrong."

Rachel turned toward them, her pack on her back. "You'd better listen to her, Joseph. She's a very determined woman."

"I don't understand your attitude. You don't mind? Her and me?"

"No. I don't mind. I thought I loved you, and in a way, I do, but God has shown me that he didn't intend us for one another."

"But people don't fall in love this way...in one minute."

"Oh, I wouldn't be too sure of that. You two certainly look as though you have."

Elizabeth smiled shyly at him. "You really did save my life, didn't you?"

"Yes. I slit open the roof of your tent and cut the ropes off your wrists and ankles so that you could escape. And then you cracked me on the skull."

She looked as though she were about to cry, but all she could find to say was an inane, "Oh, I'm so sorry." And then something clicked. "Thank you." Then she made her choice. Placing her toe beneath the edge of the little satchel, she kicked it lightly, and watched as it slithered to within a foot or so of Joseph's feet.

He stared blankly down at it for a moment, then raised his eyes to search hers. With a quirky little smile, he shook his head slowly in negation. "They're part of the package. God provided you with those jewels as a resource to help you protect the documents."

Then he turned abruptly and walked back up the tunnel, and they suddenly understood that he was no longer interested in possessing coffee cans, rare jewels, or state documents.

A Strange Turn

The West Side of the Caverns
May 2nd, 5:25 a.m.

CC had felt like a spectator as he'd listened to the odd conversations play out. For some reason a rarely sung verse from the *Star Spangled Banner* had come to mind, and he began to hum it. Everyone looked at him as though he were slightly daft, and, he had to admit to himself, *Maybe I am, but a little reckless bravado certainly won't do any harm.* And the words that tumbled from his mouth seemed somehow to be terribly appropriate. So he continued to sing them in his hoarse, off-key tenor.

"Then conquer we must, when our cause it is just; and this be our motto: 'In God is our trust!'"

None of them remained unmoved by the lyrics. Jonathan wondered whether the words were actually part of the National Anthem, for he'd never heard them sung before, but it helped them all to understand that somehow this was their moment. Recent events had shown them that an individual's life may not seem to count for much in this world. But now, seeing both how cheap and yet how incalculably dear life could be, they had each been forced to decide whether they were willing to invest their own in the most meaningful way. Perhaps they didn't have a lot to die for, but they now realized that they had a great deal to live for.

But from reckless bravado, CC slipped into abject despair. It all seemed so hopeless.

Even if we have rescued these documents from this one man, he thought, w*ho's to say that we can keep them undamaged and safe from other predators? The papers could be gone in the next hour. And how will we ever deliver them into the hands of some authority who might ultimately protect and preserve them?*

But he did not allow his uncertainty to be seen by the others, and as he continued to sing, he felt his confidence begin to grow again. When he'd finished singing the verse, Elizabeth's clear voice picked up the words of "My Country 'tis of Thee."

CC found himself praying because he realized that the song is actually a prayer.

Elizabeth went on singing, and concluded with the verse, "To Thee, O God, for you are the Source of liberty, the God of our country."

And as this realization came home to him, he realized that they also sensed its truth. Rachel and Jonathan joined Elizabeth, their voices at first low and rasping, but then gaining power and confidence and pride.

CC had a hunch, so he thought he'd take a long shot. He spoke into the hollow darkness of the cavern where the man had disappeared.

"They wrote of a son; they were hoping for better things from him...*that he might someday return from his prodigal and fruitless chasing after futility, and lead the world to higher values.*" He had altered his voice as he quoted their words.

The man was still standing in the shadows, staring at him now, unable to hide his anguish.

Jonathan looked at him, a flash of intuition lighting his eyes. "What were those people's names? "he wondered aloud.

But the man's eyes were locked on CC's, and everyone else seemed frozen in place. CC felt the name taking shape on his own tongue, but before he could speak it, the man snapped at them, "You'd better hurry. Move out!"

Jonathan kept his eyes on the man, but his rifle was now slung over his shoulder. He stooped to catch up the satchel of jewels that had been left laying on the floor of the cave.

When the man voice came from the shadows, it was not threatening, but humble. "Thank you for seeing that they were both properly buried. I owe you for that."

The others quietly caught up their belongings, not wanting to break the spell that seemed to hold them all in its thrall. They knew that he was still nearby, for they could hear the Baron's light pantings coming from behind them. They were prepared to leave in a moment, and without a word they began to move away up the tunnel.

Jonathan led the way, Elizabeth following, grasping her large portfolio, looking back once into the shadows, a strange longing in her eyes. Rachel had picked up Elizabeth's few personal things, then bent to shake Sarah awake. She put herself between the child and the man who had confronted them, but from where he stood in the darkness, he must have noticed her furtive movements.

Sennett Meets Sennett

The Caverns
May 2nd, 6:25 a.m.

Hold it!" he commanded. His voice echoed down the tunnel. "You didn't tell me you had a child here."

"No," CC answered evenly, "we didn't." He and Rachel were alone now with the child, and he was far less confident that they could resist this man′s strength.

"Who is she?"

A sleepy Sarah peeked around Rachel to peer at the man, but the light was poor and both of their faces were hidden in the shadows.

"She's just a little girl," CC responded. That's all you need to know."

Turning to CC, he said, "You have no idea how important this is to me. No one walks out of here until I see that little girl."

Then he started doing some verbal math. "She's didn′t come with McCord; he wouldn′t have taken care of a child. She wasn′t with Rachel either; I know her. She wasn't with Ross when I met her at the camp. And I know enough about you to state unequivocally that she's not your child."

CC wanted to interrupt him and ask what he knew about him, but the man went on without hesitation.

"And as sure as God made little green apples, she's not that teen-age boy′s daughter."

"Why not?" Jonathan stepped forward, having run back down the tunnel. "Maybe she's my little sister."

"Nice try, kid," he said, dismissing Jonathan's argument. "Now bring her over here so that I can get a look at her."

But before anyone realized what she planned, Sarah ducked around Rachel and ran to where the dim light from the lantern was brightest. She had sensed the growing menace in the air and was now wide awake. Fists on her hips and elbows spread wide, she leaned back and stared into the shadows, examining the face that was illuminated by the lantern, her young eyes sharper than theirs. With the fearlessness of a David rebuking a Goliath, she slung her words at him as though they were stones.

"Now you listen here, mister. We're not afraid of you." She extended her arm to shake her finger in his face, a diminutive school teacher disciplining a towering teen. "You've hurt just about all the people you're going to hurt around here. You've been very bad and God is not pleased with you."

She was talking very rapidly, but she wasn't quite finished. "Don't you remember the Ten Commandments?" And she commenced to quote a couple. "*Thou shalt not steal, Thou shalt not kill*, and....'" Biting her lip as though she were deciding whether there were any other commandments that might be applicable, she ordered imperiously, "Now, you just turn right around and march out of here."

"And just who might you be, and how old are you, my feisty little theologian?"

"Again the hands went to her hips, elbows akimbo in her characteristic pose, and she replied, "I am Sarah Sennett, and I am almost eight years old."

She was like a bantam rooster charging a mastiff. And she drove him off. His resistance simply melted away under her onslaught, and it was clear that he had all he could do to keep from laughing in delight. There was no question as to her identity. He didn't need to look in a mirror to see the resemblance. He knew precisely who this little girl was. If she had not turned away so quickly, she might have seen him trying to mask the smile of amazement and pride that swept over his face, for there was no mistaking the family resemblance in that determined little face, much less in her demeanor.

"I wonder, honey," he asked in a husky voice, "would you mind if I hugged you?"

"No!" Rachel gasped, but she was too late, for Sarah had already spun around, her arms raised, totally unafraid.

He sank to his knees, and very gently put his arms around her and held her tightly to him. Then he leaned forward, parted her hair with his fingers, and kissed her on the top of her head. She leaned back, and studied his face. Then she leaned forward, put one small hand on each of his ears, kissed him firmly on the lips, and hugged him again. As he released his embrace, she stared into his eyes and said very cheerfully, "Don't worry, everything is going to be okay." Then she turned and ran back to Rachel's side. He seemed to break, his chest heaved and tears ran down his cheeks.

Sarah took Rachel's outstretched hand and tried to drag her up the tunnel, but the woman hung back for a moment, staring at him, a look of inconsolable grief and sympathy in her eyes. Then the child's insistent jerking on her fingers won her final loyalty, causing her to turn and walk away from him.

The man continued to stand there, caught between shock and delighted surprise. When the lantern light flickered, CC had seen a smile flash across the man's lips, but he also noted the tears pouring from his eyes. Then the man muttered something that sounded ironically like, "And a little child shall lead them."

It was the second time CC had heard those same words in as many hours. And he recalled clearly where he'd read them. It was Isaiah 11:6, a prophecy, and a child was seen to be leading a multitude of pacified animals.

He was no longer shocked that he could remember the precise words. *The wolf also shall dwell with the lamb, and the leopard shall lie down with the kid; and the calf and the young lion and the fatling together; and a little child shall lead them.* They were all safe in the midst of potential predators. And now CC knew that he was safe standing alongside Joseph Sennett, Jr.

Elizabeth, who'd returned with Jonathan, and now had the portfolio strapped to her back, began her second retreat with Jonathan following, both walking slowly away.

A chuckle came from the darkness, and with a choked voice CC heard a wry comment that confirmed Sennett's continued presence. "She's quite a little lady, isn't she?"

His question didn't demand an answer and none was forthcoming.

Then, "It's obvious that you'd fight for her, too."

CC turned toward him. "I'd give my life for her. She's what the Declaration of Independence and the Constitution are all about.... In her case, however, it's more than that. One cannot help but love that very special little child of God."

"And I can see you will give her a better upbringing than anyone available could." There was ineffable sadness in his words.

CC hesitated, his heart suddenly breaking for the man. His words seemed inane. "We'll do our best, sir."

While they were speaking, Rachel and Sarah continued up the tunnel. Rachel asked the child, "Weren't you just a little afraid of that big man?"

"Oh, no."

"But wasn't he kind of scary," Rachel pursued.

"I knew I didn't have to be afraid of him."

"Why not?"

"Because Grandma and Grandpa had his picture on the night table next to their bed, and we prayed for him every night."

Hope for Tomorrow

The Far Side of the Caverns
May 2nd, 6:42 a.m.

CC picked up the kerosene lantern, and held it well out from his side to avoid blinding himself. He was still concerned that he made too good a target in the dripping pall of the cavern, not to Joe Sennett, but to other enemies that might appear. Those walls, which had protected them for so long, had lost their friendly security.

The caverns were no longer home to them, no longer their stronghold. *And, truth be told,* he thought, *I'm a little tired of living in the damp and cold, like a mole. I'll be glad to see the trees and the clouds, and feel the warmth of the sun on my face.*

The caves had become an alien place, a place to be away from, and all the pleasant memories that had been associated with them had vanished as though they'd never existed.

So many lost pasts, so many dead memories, he thought.

The stranger's voice – reverberating in the cave's depths, and sounding even more hollow in the emptying passage – intruded on CC's thoughts.

"One more thing...," Sennett said, and CC was surprised by his tone.

"...why do you persist in calling yourself, 'CC?'"

CC stumbled, then stood frozen in place as the man pursued his odd line of questioning. "Are you running from something that I haven't heard about?"

CC turned around and was startled to find the man standing only a few feet away, his rifle hanging muzzle-down from his shoulder. The corner of his lips were turned up slightly in an ironic smile.

CC couldn't grasp the question. Too much had been happening too rapidly, and he wasn't ready for more verbal sparring, let alone to pursue the secrets of his past.

"It's just a nickname," he answered to cut off the conversation, but found himself unable to turn away. He couldn't resist the possibility that the man might know something about him.

Perhaps it was Sennett's tone, neither indifferent nor antagonistic, but interested, almost helpful. And CC felt certain that he had only rarely taken an interest in other human beings.

For the first time since he awoke in the hospital, CC used the word he dreaded.

"I have amnesia," he replied. The initials, *CC* were engraved in the wedding ring I discovered laying by my clothing when I regained consciousness."

The man laughed, and CC wondered what he found so amusing. "Don't you believe in 'ladies first?" he asked. Or are you the male chauvinist type who always puts his initials before those of his wife?"

Sensing that the man wasn't really making fun of him, CC struggled with the question. Finally the man relented, taking pity on him for his obvious confusion. "You chose the wrong set," he laughed.

When CC still looked confused, he added, "The initials! You chose the wrong set of initials." He laughed again. "The initials for your wife's maiden name were CC, not yours!" Then with a puzzled sound in his voice, "I'm surprised that McCord didn't tell you."

"McCord? McCord knows my name...my wife's name? My wife's name, as in the present tense?"

"Yes. As in, 'You have a wife, and she is alive?'"

CC swayed, and the man stepped forward and caught his arm to steady him. It seemed a long moment before he regained sufficient control to speak. Then the words poured out. "How would you know my name? And how do you know my wife is alive? And what difference does it make to you whether I know my name or not?"

"Take a break!" the man laughed. "It's a long story, and we don't have time for it right now. I just wanted to give you something to chew on, and to provide some information to make you think twice about your so-called friends. First, to answer your questions, yes, you have a wife. Her name is Chris. Yes, she is alive. Or," he added, "she was alive two days ago when I saw her being taken into the Emir's office." He didn't add that she was being dragged into the ruler's office by two bearded men wearing kufis.

"And in her case, it really should be 'ladies first.' I have to hand it to her. She's a real fighter, and she's willing to suffer for what she believes in. Though," he added as an aside, "she might have been a lot better off if she'd played along with those who took an interest in her." He hesitated here, then laughed aloud.

"She's tough, and she's never stopped insisting that you were alive." There was admiration in his voice. "She called you a survivor, and she said the Holy Spirit is protecting you." He shrugged. "She's evidently right about that. Anyway, your kids believe it too."

He turned serious. "Problem is, her confidence in your survival has the Emir searching for you."

"She thinks I'm alive?" he choked.

"She knows it. She caught a glimpse of you the night you were arrested at Butter Creek Tavern, and after I saw you the other day, I told her you were doing fine."

CC couldn't believe this conversation. "My wife saw me? You talked to her?"

"Yes." She'd just been arrested too, and was afraid to let them know she knew you."

"And you told my wife I'm alive?"

Once again, CC imagined he smelled the stench of drenched coals and charred flesh. He had a vision of children's bodies being loaded into ambulances. Everything began to move around him. He could feel his voice cracking as tears began to fill his eyes, memories flooding in. "There was a fire...."

"I'm really sorry about that," the man said. It didn't sound like a confession. He peered at CC through the gloom. "Hey, are you okay?" He again caught CC with his massive hand, and again steadied him.

CC shook his head, as though to clear his thoughts. Things were coming back, maybe too fast. "Our children...." His voice trailed off. "I...we had children...." He looked at the other man, tears pouring unheeded from his eyes. "Now I remember!" He was crying now, choking out the words. "They're dead...in a fire."

"No. They're not dead," the man corrected him. "Your sister-in-law and her two children died in that fire. I guess she brought her kids to your house after she had a fire in her kitchen that forced them to move out. Your wife had already decided to take your kids to her father's farm for the weekend. Providential," he mused. "They were able to survive the war in his old underground fruit cellar. Apart from severe cases of diarrhea from eating so much canned fruit and vegetables, everyone was fine."

"My father-in-law's farm?" He laughed with the realization both that his family was alive and that he was regaining something of his memory. The downside was that he was on an emotional roller coaster. "You mean my wife is here in Vermont?"

"Yes, but not where you can find her."

"What do you mean?" CC challenged. "How do you know all this?"

Sennett paused, pondering whether he had time to reply. "I know because I am, or rather was, an official in the so-called Chinese Transitional Government, the CTG, that claims control of this area. I already told you that I was an officer in the Home Guard." He gestured toward the bronze leaf on the peak of his service cap.

"How did you manage that," CC asked.

"It wasn't difficult getting in. I forged some papers with my step-father's signature on them so that I could approach the military governor for New England."

"Your step-father?"

"He's the governor of New York. Or, rather, he was the governor while there was a New York."

CC remembered the elder Sennett's diary and suddenly made the connection. "What happened?" he asked.

"I was grabbed by a patrol as I was driving toward their headquarters. When I was brought into the commandment's office under guard, he laughed at me. He knew my history well enough to realize that my step-father would never have sent me to Vermont to work with him, but he nevertheless concluded that I was a kindred spirit, so he put me to work. But he was wrong. Most of the notoriety surrounding me was invented by my step-father's public relations people to make me and my real father look bad, while at the same time making the governor look kind and benevolent."

CC nodded his head in understanding. The diaries had made that much clear.

Sennett went on. "The Vermont military governor put me on his staff because he was confident that he could control me and because he was sure that the Chinese would welcome me. He's not the first one to make that mistake. It was going well enough for me until the Emir showed up."

He watched CC's eyes to see whether that brought any reaction. All he received was a look of curiosity, so he went on.

"It's all pretty confusing. I guess the easiest way to explain it is that the Muslim invaders and their American allies have formed a shaky alliance with the Chinese invaders in order to counter the growing Russian threat." The irony rang through his laughter.

"What's so funny?" CC asked.

"Whenever they think that they can get away with it, they snipe at one another, hoping to leave no witnesses."

CC nodded his understanding. "Sort of like Hitler allying himself with Russia while fighting the British?"

"Right. Then turning against the Russians and launching a land war in Asia.

"So we can only hope," CC suggested, "that at some point there's a falling out between the Chinese and the Muslims, and we can stand by while we fight one another."

"I wish it was going to be that easy," Sennett answered, "but I believe a lot of us surviving Americans will have to put our lives on the line if they want to win our country back."

CC noted that he said "our country," and not "their country."

"Anyway," Sennett continued, "the Emir was more interested in locating my real father than he was in any assistance I might offer him in his war for Islamic supremacy. He asked the military governor to leave me alone with him in his office, and he proceeded to question me, then attempted to beat the information out of me.

Since I didn't know what he wanted, his third-degree turned into quite an argument. In fact, he tried to kill me. Fortunately for me, I spent much of my wayward youth taking lessons in martial arts. And I was in a lot better shape than he was. As old as he is, I have to admit that he nearly beat me. I learned later that he was a former instructor in a Libyan terror training camp. Anyway, I was able to hold my own, but the racket we made attracted the attention of the guards in the outer office. Two of them held me, and the Emir had me beaten and then locked in the stockade.

"One of the jailers was an American, a former friend of mine. I don't have many," he added ruefully. "This jailer had originally wanted a part in running this great new society he'd been led to believe they were creating, but after observing their methods, he ultimately decided that he didn't want to see them in charge. So he helped me escape."

"Where is he now?"

Sennett was silent for the better part of a minute. "We tried to escape together. We were riding double on a motorcycle, and when we went past the guard post, they shot him in the back. He didn't make it."

"And my wife?"

"I met her before the Emir showed up, when she was brought in for interrogation. She had been picked up for refusing to cooperate with the authorities."

"Where is she now?"

"In a detention center."

"How can I find her? Can I get her out?"

"You're asking me? Listen, you'd better forget about her for now. You'll be lucky if you get out of these caverns alive." He smiled ruefully. "And, as you pointed out a few minutes ago, you have a higher purpose now."

CC gave him a sour look.

"You do remember, don't you?" Sennett asked, deadly serious. "A higher purpose? Your pledge to save those documents for posterity?" His nose was now only inches from CC's. "Your wife wouldn't hesitate to leave you to your own devices if she had to choose between helping you and fulfilling such a purpose."

CC, trying to imagine what sort of woman he might have married, realized that Sennett was probably right, but smiled and asked, "You don't think that she might hesitate for just a moment."

"Well, all right," Sennett responded in kind, "she might give you a few seconds thought, but she'd still do the right thing."

CC nodded. "Yes, I suppose she would."

"You dare not put these documents in any additional jeopardy. And right now you are responsible for the American state papers as well as the lives of these few courageous people who have placed their trust in you, not to speak of my little girl."

Even as he reminded CC of his charge, Sennett was reminded of Elizabeth Ross and her bald statement that she intended to marry him.

Impossible, of course, even absurd, he thought, *but I wouldn't want anything to happen to her.*

"Yes, of course you're right," CC responded dully, obviously wanting so much to rediscover his past and gather his family, but again trying to focus on the reality of their situation.

The desire to rescue his wife was counteracted by the sudden fear that he might not even recognize her, that too much had changed, and that he really had no memory of her at all. She was almost like a figment of his imagination. Even if he located her and freed her, they'd both be on the run, and she would very likely remain a stranger to him.

It will take a certain amount of normalcy to find normalcy, he realized. *And there is certainly no normalcy in this crazy world.* He said as much to the man, and wondered why he was airing his personal problems with a stranger.

Oddly, Sennett didn't agree with his conclusion. "No, she has been your wife for a lot of years. When the time comes for you to be reunited, you will find your way together in trust and love. The trials you are going through now, and the trials you will be joined in then, will provide opportunities to exercise your faith and enlarge on the things you have in common. You are good people. You will respond accordingly."

Even as CC listened to these encouraging words, he was struck with the realization that it was this particular man who was reminding him of these truths. He thought of the state papers. *They are tangible,* he thought, *and they are temporarily in our care. And, if this man had the character to leave the jewels behind to help us, we must in turn have the character to protect those documents.*

It was as if the other man was reading his mind. "I didn't really want the jewels to provide for my own comfort."

"I understand that now."

"I was going to use them, if necessary, to protect the documents."

"I realized that was why you let us keep them."

"Yes." He hesitated. "But there is something else."

"What's that?"

"The jewels. They are part of our national treasure. If you don't need to use them to keep yourselves alive and to protect the documents, they might one day help finance the restoration of our nation."

"What did you plan to do with the documents?"

"Just what you were doing. I was going to secrete them back in these caverns."

"Ah."

"But that's no longer an acceptable alternative. And when I met you, I realized that your group could be trusted to do a better job taking care of them than I could."

CC smiled. "So, the apple didn't fall so far from the tree, as the world would have us believe."

"Let's say that this apple is trying to find its way back to the orchard."

"Yes, and doing very nicely too." CC was pondering what else he might ask the man, when he heard shouting from up the tunnel.

As if to punctuate the warning, Jonathan raced back down the passage toward them. There was urgency in his voice as the boy took him by the arm and began to pull.

"CC, hurry! We started to go out the back of the cavern, but Sarah thought she heard a helicopter."

The other man shook his head, a look of resignation on his face. "They're coming for us. You'd better hurry."

CC felt oddly relaxed, as though he was somehow not burdened with the responsibility for any further decisions. He knew that he had to get those documents away. It was almost a sense of fatalistic well-being that had been growing in him since they'd faced up to this man.

No, before that, he thought. *It was when I lay half-frozen on that tossing log, and realized that I am immortal, that I will not die without the Lord's permission and only in his time. In fact, I'll never die. I'll just 'pass on' to a better place.*

Although he didn't feel that his decisions and actions were under someone else's absolute control, he did believe that Someone else was guiding and protecting him and would ultimately be in control of the outcome.

And as sure as he was of divine assistance, he was also certain of this man's character. He stared into Sennett's eyes. "Thanks," he said. He put out his hand without thinking, and was surprised when Sennett took it, then gave him one of those quick manly half-hugs. Then CC turned and made his way up the passage, following the weaving glow of Jonathan's dying flashlight, its old batteries merely dusting the limestone as they burned down the last of their power.

As Jonathan moved out of sight, CC felt compelled to stop and turn around. Sennett was kneeling on the ground, his arms wrapped around the dog, his face buried in his mane.

"Why did you tell me all those things?" CC asked.

"I'm not sure." He hesitated. "I was originally sent here to waste you."

"That's a biblical expression."

"We both know that. Don't you care?"

"What," CC laughed. "That it's a biblical expression, or that you were ordered to kill me?"

"That I was ordered to kill you."

"That's a decision you had to make, and one that you'd have had to live with."

"Yes. That's true, but there was never any real danger that of my obeying that order. No, I couldn't kill you," he said with finality. "And if I have anything to say about it, you won't be killed. You're too good a man. Not that I haven't seen good men killed," he added unnecessarily. He was silent for a moment. "You're a good man who's made a difference, and I think you are needed. I, on the other hand...." His voice trailed off as he began to turn away.

CC interrupted him. "You, on the other hand, have made a difference too."

"Ha! How so?"

"You didn't waste me. In fact, you killed a number of those who were hunting us. And you've encouraged us to carry off the documents." His tone changed. "Why don't you come with us?"

"You're not serious!"

"Of course I am."

"This probably sounds melodramatic, but it's too late for me."

"I don't believe that, and I don't believe you mean it either."

"What are you going to do, reform me? Save me from my sins?"

"If you're the son of Joseph Sennett, you know at least as much as I do about salvation. This much I do know; all of us need to be transformed, not reformed." CC smiled. Then he added, "You know, I'm a funny kind of guy."

"How so?"

"I watched the way your dog ran to you, not to speak of how Sarah put herself into your hands. I believe that it's hard to fool a dog. He loves you. You must have been good to him, a best friend. And I can tell you from my own experience that it′s very difficult to fool Sarah. So, if you have that love for a dog, and such love from that little girl, you've got a lot of values hidden away inside. In fact, you just demonstrated them."

"You know, Rev, for an intelligent, honest and sensitive guy, you say some dumb things." He laughed. "But, all in all, you're okay."

CC felt as though he'd received another body blow. He attempted to separate the essence of the conversation from the suddenly familiar title, but he could not. It was not a comfortable or respectful word, this "Rev," but he knew it somehow fit him.

Sennett seemed indifferent to his discomfort, and stuck the needle in again. "You are really a terrible innocent, Rev, incredibly naïve, and far too trusting."

That title again, derisive or intended to inform? And CC retorted.

"Naive? I think not. But I do try not to be stained by the filth I′ve seen. Let me ask you this. Are you suggesting that I was in some sort of ministry?" But again, he already knew the answer. *This is Joseph Sennett, Jr., and he knows who I am,* and CC was chagrined at his tardy insight.

Sennett was too engrossed with his own problems to realize that he′d provided CC with additional significant insights into his background. Both men were caught up with their own identity issues, and Sennett went blithely on.

"When a guy like me starts out, everyone can see that he is flawed, everyone but himself. He has a certain physical charm to women, and a reputation, and even an aura of danger, which makes him more appealing in some perverse way. Things like promotion, money, and girls seem to come easy. Most guys who find everything coming too easy don't find it necessary to strive. They stop searching and they stop stretching. When all is said and done, their lives don't count for much. That's me."

Sennett seemed to be musing, indifferent to the dangers that might lurk in these tunnels for both of them, and he went on.

"A few of us learned to play a dangerous game. I realized that I was playing that game because your God – who incidentally I know to be real – continued to deal with me for a long time. At first he was very gentle, convicting me by contrasting my life with the lives and principles set down in those scriptures that my parents drilled into me as a youngster. Then I watched his judgment occasionally fall on those around me who spurned him. Finally, I felt the bite of his discipline, and sometimes it was so severe that I thought I wasn't being disciplined, but punished. But when I saw the suffering that my parents experienced because of me, I couldn't handle it. How could God allow such a thing to happen to two such wonderful people!" Sennett went on without waiting for an answer.

"I was just a kid, a teenager like that boy you have with you, but I didn't have a friend like you to mentor me. The people who'd taken control of my life used to tell me that my parents had brain-washed me, that their religion had made me guilt-ridden and myth-ridden. They warned me that I was too willing to accept the Christian lie, that I was kidding myself."

He stood there, staring into space, as though weighing his words.

"Kidding myself? Even as a boy, God revealed Himself to me over and over again, and in incredibly powerful ways. And sometimes I even responded to Him. At one time I thought I might even be able to change – to really repent – and maybe I did, but I always backed off from my commitments, just like Pharaoh with Moses.

"I never learned who I really was. After all, I was surrounded by a bunch of very nasty personalities who encouraged me to live a lie, then exercised great care not to let me discover truth. But their thinking was flawed because just being around them caused me to believe there had to be a better alternative.

"As a young scoundrel I couldn't always succeed at their kind of deception, but over time, just like the devil, a person can learn to read body language and behavior patterns, and play to the weaknesses and desires of others. I learned to spot when the most noble soul was subject to temptation, and to manipulate circumstances in order to corrupt them. Many Christians, for example, allow themselves to suffer feelings of guilt simply because they are being tempted – even when they don't surrender to the temptation – but especially if they dwell upon and savor those temptations. The devil can work with that guilt because they are unable or unwilling to take it to God. The proud, the selfish, and the greedy are easier. I saw that in others, and I became a very effective corrupter."

"Look," CC interrupted. "You sound like you take a perverse pride in your depraved accomplishments. If you had a part in corrupting others, certainly you should be ashamed. But I'll tell you this much; you couldn't start a fire if the fuel wasn't there."

CC didn't wait to see what sort of impression his words made on the younger man, but went on. "What interests me more, however, is that you took a strange pride in manipulating others by making them feel guilty, while ironically you are like Bunyan's Pilgrim, and like him you carry your own heavy knapsack of guilt everywhere you go."

"Why not?" he whispered. "These are the only accomplishments I have to take pride in."

"That's not true," CC said. You're letting the five of us walk out of here, not only with the documents, but with a king's ransom in jewels. What's more, I know that you are capable of change. "You could help people instead of hurting them. In fact, you've already begun to do so."

"You're wrong on the first count," Sennett countered, "because you've mistaken my capabilities. Initially, I really did think of bartering these things. But the fact is that it was unlikely that I would have been able to capitalize on the possession of those papers, so why take them? And, since I probably couldn't make use of them, you're wrong on your second point because I didn't make that gesture out of pure motives."

"You said 'probably.' You probably couldn't capitalize on them. So there's room for doubt in your own mind, which means that you did make a righteous gesture and had mixed motives. And when all was said and done, you did the right thing."

"Are we talking 'works-righteousness' here, Rev?" It was a rhetorical question, the words alive with laughing scorn.

"No, of course not! You've been sold a bill of goods. The people that you claim corrupted you have also convinced you that your situation is hopeless." CC bit the words off. "For by grace are you saved through faith; and that not of yourselves: it is the *gift* of God."

"Don't go quoting scripture to me."

"Why not? The scriptures are the reason that I know you can overcome. The words of the Holy Bible promise each of us immediate assistance today as well as hope for tomorrow."

"What makes you think that I can overcome?"

"If the Holy Spirit is still dealing with you, then God obviously hasn't given up on you. Aren't you the one who implied that you regret your evil acts."

"Yeah. So?"

"So, repent and don't do them any more." CC waved his hands in frustration. "Look, you're like Timothy in the Bible. "...from a child you have known the holy scriptures which are able to make you wise through faith which is in Christ Jesus."

"Touché, Rev. Preach it!"

"And why do you keep calling me Rev?" CC asked in frustration. He realized, with unexpected shame, that he had become more intent on winning his point than in pointing Sennett to the Lord, and Sennett was laughing at him because he obviously realized it too.

"Why do I call you Rev? Because they used to introduce your radio program with, "He was no run-of-the-mill pastor, and his was no run-of-the-mill church!"

Program? What program? What church? Again CC's mind was awhirl with another link to his past, but perhaps he, like this man, was afraid to pursue these nebulous possibilities, and so he blundered on.

"Listen!" CC said. "We both know that God is long on forgiveness and short on condemnation. As long as you have one more breath to breathe, you still have a choice. You know that. It's God's work, not ours. What I do know is that, while you live, it's never too late for salvation and the wonderful new life that goes with it."

"Well then, you may finally be getting the point."

"What point?"

"That's the issue–death."

"You're speaking in riddles."

"It's simple. I think you've already figured out that I was supposed to marry Rachel."

CC studied him, more pieces falling in place, confirming his suspicions.

"Yes. I got that. You're the guy who stood her up at the altar?"

Confession is good for the soul

The Caverns
May 2nd, 6:55 a.m.

Sennett lapsed into a brief but incredible account of his childhood, and CC was again shaken by the tale of how government's meddling had actually increased societal problems.

Too often, he thought, they addressed symptoms rather than the underlying causes and the impact they would have in the long run on others. Too often the laws were designed to advance a political agenda, and frequently exacerbated the problems they were supposed to cure. And starry-eyed idealists were too proud, too busy, too selfish, too ignorant, too indifferent, and too ungodly to understand the consequences of their misguided actions. So in the six decades following Lyndon Johnson's *Great Society*, America had increased the number of people living below the poverty level.

CC listened as Sennett told his story, and was struck by the fact that so many of the clippings that he had read in his father's scrapbook didn't conform to what he was now hearing. Obviously, CC realized, the media hadn't reported the truth about Joseph Sennett, Jr, or at least not the whole truth. *But why should I be surprised at that? Toward the end, virtually all media outlets were infested with anti-Christians and pro-socialist reporters.*

In spite of CC's awareness of these facts, Sennett's story was an eye opener.

"I lived in this valley until I was fourteen. That's why I know my way around these caves better than you. My problems weren't caused by my parents," he said. "I was very rebellious, and my father wasn't consistently firm with me. That's right–firm. He traveled a lot, warning Americans that they were rapidly losing their freedoms, trying to make them see that they had to bear responsibility for their own actions if they hoped to continue enjoying authority over their own lives. He maintained that the key to a great nation was limited government, individual responsibility, and a fearful respect for God."

CC found that he had been unconsciously nodding his head in agreement, for he shared those convictions. And as he listened, he felt more of his personal fog lifting.

"I was just a kid," Sennett continued, "selfish, egotistical, and short-sighted, with the narrow-mindedness of most kids–of most Americans. My father used to quote a Proverb to me, 'Train up a child in the way he should go, and when he is old he will not depart from it.' I would laugh at him. I was attending public school – the school bus came right up this valley in those days – and I was paying more attention to the political liberals who dominated the teaching profession than to my own parents."

He began speaking more rapidly, perhaps because CC seemed edgy, rocking from one foot to the other.

"One day I stole some money so that I could sneak into town to see a movie with some friends. Boy, was my father ever mad. Sure, he was upset because I stole the money, but even more so because I lied about it. Then I tried to stonewall, refusing to discuss it with him. Well, I was big–I was already six feet tall when I was fourteen–and when he was going to try to spank me, I laughed at him, and then I slapped him in the face. I broke his glasses, and there was blood on his cheeks."

He stopped talking because he had begun to cry. "I hit my own father, one of the best men who ever lived. Dad just stood there in front of me, blood and tears running down his cheeks, telling me he was sorry he had failed me. Can you imagine? He was sorry he had failed me! I was so ashamed. Anyway, I couldn't stand it, and I ran away."

"I didn't have anywhere to go, and one of my teachers saw me on the street. I knew she hated my father, because she used to talk in class about what a threat Christians were to society, and my father had been a national religious leader. At that time, his books and speeches were very popular with many voters, and especially with Christians, but his enemies were active and they did everything they could to discredit him.

"Anyway, this teacher could see that my shame was eating at me like a disease, and since I didn't want to go home and face my parents, she was able to manipulate me. She said she'd make sure I had a nice place to stay, and I stupidly went along with her suggestions. Without my knowledge, she filed reports of child abuse against my father, and I was never even asked to sign anything. Then they took me away and locked me up in a detention center, telling me they were protecting me from my parents."

"It got to be a national scandal. The governor of New York made a big thing out of Joseph Sennett's son being abused by his preacher father, and for political purposes, he ultimately adopted me. Problem was, he never cared about me. He hired a couple of bodyguards to act as my 'companions,' and he made it crystal clear that if I tried anything–to get away, to talk to the press, or to contact my family–he'd somehow hurt my family and deal severely with me. I was really scared. So I went along, and I was ultimately swept up in his life style because it seemed so glamorous."

"I had just about anything I wanted. And the governor pretended to like me. Maybe he did. I think he recognized me as a kindred spirit. I was turning into his kind of guy, devious and slimy. Anyway, he began to groom me for a political future. It was about two years later that I found out that he and his cronies had thoroughly ruined my father's reputation, had wiped out the non-profit foundation he'd founded, and left him with no alternative but to come back to this valley to live out his years."

Joseph's barking laugh was on the edge of hysteria. "With all that, they couldn't shut dad up. He learned to use a computer, and set up a blog. It was very popular, but he was basically preaching to the choir. He might inspire or challenge them, but he no longer had any real impact on public opinion."

"State officials used the widening of the mountain highway as an excuse to cut off access to this valley. It was easy for them. The powerful politicians in Montpelier and Albany manipulated the local politicians, and got them to take away the zoning variance for his piddling cement mining operation, even though it was grandfathered. They even tried to raise his real estate taxes, but the local authorities wouldn′t let them go that far. They were afraid to help my father, but they wouldn't hurt him any further either."

"So he continued writing books, though only his most loyal followers bought them. After a while, he was unable to get them printed, so he self-published them on a couple of websites as e-books. I learned later that dad also wrote me a lot of letters, but I never received a single one. I found that out when I discovered a stack of his letters while I was searching the governor′s home office."

CC started edging up the tunnel. "You'd better hurry," he told Sennett. "We've got to get out of here."

"Please! Hear me out." The big man was almost pleading.

CC turned to face him. He sensed that Sennett had to get this off his chest, and it seemed to be one of those unique times in life when he would be the only one available, in fact, the only one who′d ever be available, who might, as it were, hear Joseph′s confession. "Okay," he said; "I′m listening."

"When I reached twenty-one, and had finished college, the governor made some kind of deal to get me on the staff of a U.S. senator. That was to be my stepping stone to political office, but he made it pretty clear to me that I was also to serve as a spy for him." Sennett shook his head, as though in disgust. "There was corruption everywhere, and if the corrupt leaders were unable to corrupt others, they destroyed them. And I," he whispered, "I was eager to get my hands on the rotten fruits of that corruption."

"I became involved in a couple of money-making ventures on my own, but nothing like the filth they accused me of in the media. I didn′t, for example, sell drugs or promote prostitution. But I did become involved with a software start-up, and later learned that the venture capitalists who finally came to control it had gotten their investment funds illegally using donations that had been made to my step-father′s political campaigns."

"And by the time it was exposed, my step-father's crowd had been able to float an initial public offering, and had milked it for millions. But I was their goat. They got me off without charges being filed, but I took the blame in the media, and the senator I was working for was politically embarrassed."

"That was really small potatoes compared to what was going on nationwide. About that time the president was having the Federal Reserve print money by the trillions, and much of it was illegally and secretly directed to his political cronies. Overnight America had a whole slew of new billionaires dedicated to using their wealth, more correctly, our taxes, to subvert the country.

"The governor was one of those billionaires. He'd just been re-elected, and with the way the laws were being changed, he figured he'd never have to face the voters again. So he decided to publicly repudiate me and to announce my firing from his staff at a press conference. Before he did so, however, he found out I was in possession of some very incriminating evidence concerning his own depredations, so he changed his mind about trying to ruin me politically, but instead considered arranging an accident for me."

"So he tried to have you killed?" CC asked, not at all doubting the possibility.

"No. My supposed involvement with the stock manipulation hurt me, but my involvement with him was soon forgotten, and they pulled in some favors so that they could spin the story. Since I'd just joined his staff, they pretended to be just as amazed as everyone else to learn what I'd supposedly been doing. Then they remarked that, since I was merely an impetuous young man who'd gotten in with the wrong crowd, all I needed was a proper influence to straighten me out. Any story would work. They controlled the press. Even if I had tried to expose them, I could never have gotten a public hearing, and if I had tried, they would have spun it."

He laughed ironically. "America was all into forgiving the criminal and indicting the victim at the same time, taking from what they labeled the unworthy and self-righteous rich and redistributing the wealth to those they labeled 'victims.' Mostly they were interested in increasing the size of the huge voter base that they'd seduced into relying on government entitlements. Those who were really entitled to a break were the hard-working taxpayers, but they were helpless to keep the government's hands out of their pockets. Most people didn't start waking up until they saw Russian soldiers guarding the halls of Congress, making certain that our *representatives* voted correctly, and by that time, it was too late."

CC frowned. "Why in the world would the New England senator help you?"

"Well," Sennett explained, "It was a simple quid pro quo. The senator wanted something from me that would help guarantee my silence and at the same time save him from political embarrassment." CC's eyebrows rose as Sennett continued to unveil his unsavory tale.

"Looking back, it all seems so sordid," Sennett commented. "None is righteous, no not one," he quoted. "I've been learning that. And I've been learning that there really are evil forces in the world ready and willing to help me destroy myself. Every time I considered crossing over the line into sin, I discovered that I had supernatural encouragement to help dig myself into an ever deeper hole, all the while deluding myself that I was perfectly justified in my actions."

"By supernatural, you mean demonic, right?"

"When I began sinning, yes, the devil and his demons were right there to encourage me. But I can't offer any excuses. Yes, we are all bombarded by the world, the flesh, and the devil." He shook his head in self-condemnation. "But to counter that three-pronged attack, there was always that *still small voice* attempting to gain my attention. And when I occasionally listened, and asked for help – on those rare occasions when I resolved to turn away from sin – I always received incredible assistance and blessing from the Lord."

"Well," CC said, "you seemed ready enough to embrace your guilt and slow to accept Christ's forgiveness. What happened next?"

"The senator learned that his daughter was pregnant, and evidently he considered her boyfriend to be an even worse bozo than me. So he became all sweetness and light, all ready to forgive and forget. And all I had to do was abandon my commitment to Rachel and marry his daughter instead. Oddly enough, it turned out to be unnecessary."

"How so?"

"We were to be married on the same day and hour that I was scheduled to marry Rachel. We were in Albany, and the judge was just beginning the civil ceremony when the governor received a call that America was under attack. He interrupted the wedding to rush us all to a huge shelter near the state campus in Albany."

"Shelter? You mean a bomb shelter?"

"Sure. Didn't you know about that? The big-city politicians always looked out for themselves. But unless you were a politician or a union boss, those New York liberals would rarely do anything for you beyond taxing you to death. They always publicly mocked the concept of civil defense preparedness for the general populace, but they were sure good at caring for themselves."

"I don't understand."

"It's simple. During the Cuban missile crisis, New York State had built a huge bomb shelter near the capital. It was to house elected officials and numerous bureaucrats. In 1987, they rehabilitated it. So there we were, safely underground, while millions across the northeast were dying.

"I don't know why, but the more I thought about it, the angrier I got. At one point they had a couple of guards handcuff me to a lally column. After several days the governor had me thrown out of the shelter. I had nowhere to go, and by the time I crawled into a culvert pipe under the Thruway, I guess it was too late. I'd already suffered too much exposure to the radiation." Sennett gave a sardonic chuckle. "They say it's cancer."

CC began to understand. "How long do you have?"

"Three to six months."

"Who told you that?"

"The doctor who examined me."

"How does he know? Did he find an expiration date printed on the sole of your foot or something?"

"It's not really funny, at least not to me."

"No, but maybe it's funny to the doctor. How do you know he was telling you the truth? What are his motives?"

Sennett pursed his lips as he appeared to give serious thought to CC's question. "It's true that there is no love lost between us, so, yes, his diagnosis might be open to question if there weren't other issues."

"Like what? Are you suffering from indigestion? Are you passing blood? Any pain? Any sores that don't heal?"

"Well, no; not yet."

"So you don't have any symptoms?"

"Well, I tire out more often than I used to."

"That's no surprise. Like most people today, you're undernourished. And you're under enormous emotional stress. So certainly you'd feel tired." CC pursed his lips. "You probably don't sleep as well lying on the cold ground as you did on a plush mattress. I'm guessing that you haven't exactly been enjoying a relaxed life style."

"What's your point?"

"It's been a year since the nuclear weapons were detonated. By now, even after a mild dosage, your teeth should be rotting out of your head. In fact, you should be suffering with any number of problems. But you're not! So if I were you, I don't think I'd give up until I got a second opinion."

"And where am I supposed to get that?"

"Well, there probably aren't a lot of labs left that can run blood tests for you."

"Right!"

"So I guess I'd look to the Lord and try to take a positive attitude."

"You mean I should practice faith healing?"

"Well, that's always a possibility, but I'm thinking that if you believe you have cancer, even if you don't, it could become a self-fulfilling prophecy, and you'll wind up just as dead."

"So?"

"So, start acting and living like you've still got something to live for."

"Such as?"

"Maybe an adorable little seven-year old girl." CC gazed off into the distance and laughed. "And a beautiful strawberry blonde."

"Humph," Sennett snorted, but he was clearly giving the possibility of a wrong diagnosis some serious thought.

"Yeah, 'humph,'" CC retorted. "Nevertheless, as I look back on the past few months, it seems to me that those of us who have survived have had *someone* watching over us, giving us a second chance."

"Are you getting a second chance?"

"It's funny," CC responded, staring off into space, "but I have no idea what my first chance was." He looked up at Sennett, and changed the subject. "So, why not come with us?"

"Weren't you listening? I'd only be a drag on you." He saw the question in CC's eyes, and tried to explain. "It's not just my physical health. This meeting with you and your friends was an epiphany. You are all willing to stand for something noble, while I was wavering, close to the point that I couldn't stand myself anymore." He wore a pained expression. "I betrayed my father, although now I see it was unwittingly. And now I may have unwittingly led these people to you."

CC held up his hand to forestall further comment. "As far as your leading them here, we both know that they'd have found us sooner or later. And as far as your parents are concerned, you were just a kid. Your father's diary makes it clear that he understood what they were doing to you, how they manipulated you, and how they used the power of the press to destroy both you and him. He never held any of it against you. He still loved you. And as certain as God is in His heaven, your father is looking down right now, and he loves you still." CC spread out his hands.

Sennett looked at him. "You really believe that, don't you?"

"You would too, if you had read your father's diaries."

"I meant, about God."

"Well, he left us a pretty good diary too. You might consult that as well. If you get a chance, pick up your father's Bible when you pick up his scrapbook."

"Pick up what?"

"Your father's diary, his well-marked Holy Bible, and the scrapbooks he put together about you. I told you they were in a bookcase, but now I recall that I put them in the cabinet between the twin beds in the back of the RV."

"But I betrayed him," he cried. Then, looking embarrassed, he moderated his tone. "Motives don't matter," he said emphatically. "But actions do."

"Motives do matter," CC snapped. They underlie our actions. And what matters now is that you have the right motives."

CC cleared his throat. "Listen, Joseph. If you were required to somehow make right every mistake you'd ever made, and every sin you've ever committed, you could never get straightened out with God. That's why the concept of a Savior works. We are born with an obligation to live a lifetime of flawless behavior. We ought always to have been perfect, but we inevitably failed. In fact, we are already failures when we are born, as though we carried some deadly virus. And even if Adam hadn't sinned, and even if his sin were not imputed to us, every one of us would have sinned anyway. You certainly understand that. The people you've been dealing with for years are living proof."

CC was speaking in a soft, conversational tone. "The fact that everyone does sin is proof enough. Sooner or later we make the wrong choices and do the wrong things. Often it's a matter of impulse. We don't even have to think about it to act in the wrong way. And when we fail in just one little thing, we ruin a perfect score."

"And since we are unable to live beyond this lifetime to make up for those lapses, for the stain that our sin leaves, and for the damage we do to others, we have an insoluble problem. We can't get rid of our sin. We can't wash it away We can't do good works to make up for it. We can't justify ourselves."

Sennett nodded his head in understanding, and CC went on.

"But thank God that the Lord Jesus Christ solved that problem by offering Himself as a living sacrifice, to take your place and mine, to be our substitute and to suffer for our sins, to cleanse us and make us new, and to go on helping us throughout our lives. And all we have to do is be sorry and ask Him to mark our sins to His account."

"Well," Sennett replied, "it's obvious that I am not one of his chosen ones." He returned to CC's argument about motives and actions. "It's clear I have wrong motives because I've exercised wrong actions."

"That's in the past, right?"

Sennett remained silent.

CC searched Sennett's face. "Your actions from this moment on will reveal your motives."

"Don't preach at me! I've heard enough preaching."

"Indeed? Well then, act on what has already been preached to you!"

"I only know that I didn't finish sinning yesterday. I led them here!"

"That was your job."

"Yes! I mean, no. It had been my job, but I wised up. And I changed my mind. I didn't intend to bring them here. I'd finally had it with all of them. When I found out that the Chinese, Russians, and radical Muslims were all vying with one another to take over America, and that people like my step-father were selling us out for their own short-sighted gains, I decided to come back here and make peace with my real parents. But I was too late."

With tears glistening in his eyes, he clasped his hands together in front of him. It was as though he were begging CC's forgiveness, or at least his understanding.

CC had to reach up to put his hands on the big man's shoulders. "Listen, Joseph. You didn't know there'd be a war. And you couldn't have gotten here in time." He hesitated, then decided to go with his instincts. "Look, we've got to hurry. Come with us. We can help one another."

"You don't make it any easier. I don't want your pity. I don't need your forgiveness. Just get out of here."

"Where will you go?" CC asked.

"Well, first, I intend to get my hands on the books you referred to."

CC nodded in understanding.

"It's something I've got to do. It's my last chance to sort of talk to my father, or to have him speak to me. You understand that, don't you?"

"Yes, I do."

CC shrugged into his own backpack and shouldered his rifle. "Goodbye, Joseph Sennett. I know that your father is proud of you today."

New Hope

The caverns at Hidden Valley
May 2nd, 6:42 a.m.

As he started to turn away, Sennett seemed to relent.

"Wait a minute," he commanded, and stepped into the shadows. He returned carrying a heavy backpack, and set it down between them.

Curious, CC watched him rummage through one of its pouches. Sennett pulled out a stack of papers. Unfolding a topographical map, he beckoned to CC to kneel down beside him. He flooded the map with a flashlight, and CC was able to identify Hidden Valley and the vast forests that surrounded it. Sennett pointed at the chart. "This is where we are now," he said.

CC nodded.

Sennett then drew a circle around a small meadow in the midst of the forest many miles to the northwest.

"You can see by how close together the lines are on this topographic map that the land rises precipitously on the uphill edge of this meadow," he said, and he pointed to a spot perhaps twenty-five miles away.

CC nodded.

"It's a cliff. And in the base of that cliff is a cavern, not as large as this one, but virtually unknown to the world. And in that cavern is a sort of a hunting lodge." He smiled with obvious pride. "I call it 'The Citadel.' I have one friend who knows about it." It's on virgin forest land that was owned by my father, but even he never knew about the cavern."

"I don't understand."

"It's a place for you to go."

"Why are you telling me this?"

"Because," he smiled, "our motives dictate our actions." He looked at CC, his eyes pleading. "Isn't that what you just told me?"

"Yes, that's what I said. And I appreciate this more than you'll ever know, but be careful that you don't find yourself trying to purchase absolution for your sins through good works, 'for there is none other name under heaven given among men, whereby we must be saved,' except that of the Lord Jesus Christ."

"Yes," he said in exasperation. "I know that! And you're wasting precious time." And then he countered, "Didn't you just imply that good works flow out of our faith?"

"Well, yes, of course," CC replied.

"And, besides, there's that little girl you have with you," he persisted. "And Rachel, and that – what did you call her –

beautiful strawberry blonde, not to speak of that teenage boy. I wouldn't want anything to happen to any of them."

"Nor would I."

"About this other cavern. From the age of twelve, I'd go off alone on weekend hunting trips. Dad and mom had inherited an enormous area of land in this area, much of it surrounded by national and state forests. Since it's only commercial value lay in logging, and it was pretty much worthless for anything but hunting and fishing, he ran a few cows on it and harvested a little timber in order to claim it as farmland on his taxes."

"Anyway, when I found the cave, it reminded me of my home here in Hidden Valley. So I began secretly gathering tools and materials. During the two summers before I was removed from my parents, I worked on it a lot. With game so plentiful, I was always able to bring something back from my weekend trips, and mom and dad never suspected what I was really doing with my time and money."

"After I was forced to go and live with the governor, they still let me go on hunting trips. In fact, they were glad to get me away from the capitol. But they wouldn't let me go alone. I always had a couple of body guards with me.

So I found a few acres for sale a couple of miles down an old dirt road from my dad's property.

I didn't tell anyone that my father owned the land just up the road, and since my parents lived so far away, it never occurred to anyone that my dad might own land nearby. The governor gladly bought the small parcel and had a small cabin built."

"He said that it would be a good place for me to stay when I went hunting, and maybe he'd go up there some weekend with me. He never did. I overheard him tell someone that it was like killing two birds with one stone. It was a great way to keep me out of his hair and for me to let off steam. I'd leave on Friday after school, then return Sunday night all worn out, and he didn't have to waste any time with me."

"My bodyguards had to go up there with me, and they were to follow me whenever I went hunting. Well, that first time out, I ran them ragged all day. When we got back to the cabin, they discovered that there was no indoor plumbing and no hot water, and just a wood stove to cook and a kerosene lantern for light. They hated it because it was so primitive. So they tried to be clever and made a deal with me. If I didn't tell my father, they'd leave me alone to hunt wherever I wanted. I argued that it was too dangerous. 'Suppose something happens to me?' I asked."

"They said that they really respected me, and that they knew I'd be okay. Then they bribed me by promising to give me fifty dollars a week if I'd play along. They also gave me a cell phone so that I could call them if I needed them. So almost every weekend, year 'round, they'd leave me at the cabin, and then drive back across the mountain to Butter Creek Tavern, which ironically is only a few miles from Hidden Valley. I guess they sat around the inn and drank every weekend."

"But I didn't care what they did. Their absence allowed me to head for my caverns, and I didn't need to take time to hunt, or to go back and forth each night because there was no one to check on me. I can't imagine what the governor would have done to them if I'd had an accident or if I'd run off. They would have had no idea where to look for me. The best part was that I was able to spend every weekend working on my secret hideaway within the cavern. And I had an extra twenty-six hundred dollars a year, tax free, to invest in my Citadel."

He laughed.

"And my hideaway is not dissimilar to the one you built here." Then he added smugly, "Maybe a bit nicer."

"How'd you get the materials you needed?"

"I was able to shop the local lumber yard and hardware, and I bought two horses and old farm wagon to pack it back into the forest. The horses are still there, grazing in a meadow, and using a small cave as their stable."

Hope was reborn in CC as Sennett continued to describe the cavern.

No wonder I felt I should hang around here longer, CC thought. *That wasn't just depression or intuition. That was God speaking to my heart! He does all things well and in his own time.*

Sennett went on. "The hideaway is pretty big inside, plenty of room for all of you. And it's stocked with food and other supplies, more than enough to last all of you a year. Plus I stacked about six cords of seasoned firewood under a shelving cliff nearby. And it's all hidden in thick trees. There's a good water supply from a nearby spring, and I rigged an inside electric pump. And," he added with a grin, "there are a few other surprises."

Sennett was speaking rapidly now, for they thought they'd heard the sound of footsteps moving up the tunnel.

"The most important thing is that no one knows about it. If you go there, I'll try to get word to you about other safe places you can travel to."

CC didn't know what to say. It sounded far too good to be true, and a mere "Thank you" seemed meaningless.

"There are a couple more things you should know," Sennett added. "If you head up the steep ravine I've marked on this map, you'll come to a dam. Climb up around the dam and follow the stream that feeds that small lake. After several miles, you'll come to an isolated camp. There are two really great guys living there with their families, a cop and fireman. I'm sure they'll help you."

"Okay."

"But one more thing."

"What's that?"

"Be careful that you don't get shot."

"Right. Don't get shot. Got it."

"I'm not joking. Those guys are both dead shots, and they take their freedom seriously."

"I understand. What else?"

"There is power in my cave, too."

That really captured CC's attention.

"I wondered where you got the electricity to power your water pump. Is it like you had here with an underground dam?"

"No." But there's the dam that I mentioned. It's just upstream from the cave. It was built across a ravine, and it impounds a small lake."

"So it doesn't produce much power?"

"On the contrary. It's deceptive. The ravine forms a narrow pond, but it's very deep.

"I don't understand. You built that?"

"No. It's been there for decades, I think the dam was built for flood control by the people of a little hamlet a few miles downstream. The hamlet's long since abandoned, only an old hermit lives there now.

"How do you generate the power?"

"The men who built that dam had installed an iron pipe about twelve inches in diameter at its base to drain the lake if necessary. The inserted a couple of smaller pipes with valves along the side of that large pipe. I guess they might have wanted them to supply water to houses or to irrigate the fields below the dam, but they obviously never used them. Through the years the pipes became buried under soil and leaves."

"Fascinating."

Sennett looked at CC to see whether he was being sarcastic. Evidently satisfied, he continued.

"I happened to stumble across it one day, literally. I was standing beneath the dam, stalking a deer, when I tripped over one of the smaller pipes." He laughed. "The sound of my fall spooked the deer, and I was pretty angry. At first I thought that the mud covered pipe was a broken branch sticking out of the side of a buried log, and I kicked it. I hurt my toe, but I didn't budge it, and when I stepped away, I noticed a mud-filled hole in the end of it. So I dug around it with my hands and discovered it was a pipe. I dug a little deeper and found a gate valve. Then I returned to my cave and got some tools. With a little spray solvent judiciously applied, I was able to turn the handle on the valve. It still worked. The water shot out the end of the pipe like water from a fire hose."

"The next week I did a little research on water pressure. As soon as I could, I bought a few hundred feet of flexible plastic water pipe, rented a small backhoe, drove it back through the woods, and buried my hose in a trench I dug to the cave. I hooked my pipe to the valve at the base of the dam, and I had water at the cave. After I buried my new pipe, I went back and buried the large drain pipe at the base of the dam. In the course of that summer, weeds grew over my fill, and by the time winter came, it was all covered with fallen leaves. No one would ever know the pipe was there."

"Okay. I understand how you got lake water to the cave, but what about electricity?"

"From the base of the dam to where my pipe entered my cave, the hill drops about seventy-five feet. Where the pipe exited the bottom of the dam, the water was over twenty five feet deep, and I calculated that I now had a head of pressure totaling nearly one-hundred feet."

"So," CC calculated quickly, at roughly a half-pound pressure per foot of elevation, you had over fifty pounds of water pressure"

"Exactly! You're pretty good!"

CC ignored the compliment. He didn't know how he knew that. He turned his eyes to look at Sennett. "So?"

"So, I installed a very efficient water turbine and electrical generator. They cost me some serious money, but they were worth it. The water now flows from the base of the dam through the pipe to the cave. It spins the water turbine, and the spent water flows through a drain pipe and out of a crack in the rock. Anyone that might discover the water flowing from the rock would believe that the outflow comes from an underground spring."

"Brilliant. And you use the water turbine to turn a generator and light your subterranean home."

"Yes, but that wasn't my primary concern."

"It wasn't," CC asked.

"The turbine also lights a little underground facility."

"Facility?"

"Well, a sort of shop, a factory really."

"You've got to be kidding."

"No. You'll see it all when you get there. You'll need my journals to understand everything. You'll find them in the desk in my office. They'll explain how the computers operate. Then you'll know what you have there, and how you should proceed."

"Computers?" CC was stunned. "Where'd you get the money for all this?"

"Different places. I earned some, my step-father provided a liberal allowance, and my grandfather had left me a trust fund that the governor never learned about. Oh, and of course my bodyguards put up a couple of thousand a year." With a catch in his throat, he added, "Now that I've returned to the valley, I can see how much my father sacrificed so that I'd have a good start. I kept the funds in a small bank run by a second cousin about twenty miles north of Butter Creek. He's the one who rented the backhoe for me, no questions asked."

"Your father and mother lived well. You needn't be concerned about that. But why did you go to all this trouble, building a hide-away when you could have spent every weekend in Albany living the high life?"

"Because I knew that those radicals were committed to turning North America into a socialist continent, and they were already well on their way."

"So you didn't favor that, even though you were part of the left?"

"I was never part of the left," he replied, anger in his voice. I was adopted against my will by a leader on the left."

"Why are you telling me all this?"

"Where have you been while I've been pouring out my life story?" Sennett exclaimed in frustration. "Even if you can't see it, I've come to realize that you and your little group are the ones

God has called to protect those documents. Apart from that, he's evidently had me preparing for years for I didn't know what, and now maybe you can make use of the fruits of my labor. Not to speak of those with you – that little girl, Rachel, and the strawberry blond."

"I don't understand. So we survive the winter. Then what?"

"It's not going to be easy to save those documents. You'll need to locate people of like mind who will help you. You'll need to help win America back. Isn't that obvious?" Sennett shook his head as in disbelief. "Don't you understand? Everything you've all been through, and in fact everything I've been through, has brought us to this moment. We are allies in war, and you are soldiers!"

As weary as he was, CC's face took on a look of understanding. He hesitated for just a moment, nearly overwhelmed by the magnitude of Sennett's insights. "I'm ashamed to say that I hadn't thought that far ahead. But, yes, I guess so, but...."

"No buts about it! There's no time for more. To find the entrance to the caverns, just go up the canyon and look for two pines that have been burned by lightning. You'll find them next to an east-facing stone escarpment. Their trunks form an X."

"Can't you be more specific?"

"No time. Just go!"

"Why should we trust you?" And he instantly regretted asking the truly a stupid question. But Sennett didn't repeat his earlier arguments.

"You just told me I could start again. Apart from that, what purpose is there in my telling you about this place except to assist you? If I wanted to hurt you, I'd just shoot you right now or turn you in later."

CC shook his head, whispering, "I'm truly sorry."

"You told me that you trusted me enough to invite me to join you. Now I'm offering you a place to go." He pulled a compass from the pack. "Do you know how to use one of these?"

"A little. I can find my way around."

Sennett just shook his head, muttering something about God looking after fools and children.

"I've already got a compass."

"Well, take this one too. Maybe someone else will need it." Sennett had no idea how quickly he would be proven right.

CC took the compass and the folded map and shoved them into his pocket. He held out his hand and Sennett grasped it firmly. Then CC turned and started to walk up the tunnel.

"Not that way," Sennett whispered. "They're coming."

"What can I do?" CC replied. "I've got to catch up with the others."

Sennett pointed the way he was going. "Follow me up here, take the first right, and the tunnel will lead you back to the portal where your friends are waiting."

CC smiled. "Okay, Joe. And thanks! You're a lifesaver."

"I'm trying," he smiled ruefully.

He caught CC by the arm. "One more thing."

CC's impatience had worn thin, but he turned and gave him his undivided attention.

"You must go down the cliff from the ledge and around the south end of the lake."

"Because of the cliffs cutting us off?"

"No! You can't travel north up the east side of the lake because you'd have to swim across an inlet where the lake empties into the underground river. It's a very powerful current, and you wouldn't make it."

"Okay. Go around the south end. Got it!"

Then, almost choking on his words, Sennett said, "Tell Rachel...tell Rachel I'm sorry."

"Sure."

"Oh, and what's her name, the beautiful redhead?"

"You don't remember her name?"

"Well," he smiled, "maybe I do."

"And?"

"Tell her I'm taking her threat seriously."

CC laughed. "I'll tell her that."

Sennett started jogging quietly up the tunnel, and CC followed. When they reached the opening on the right, Sennett pointed his flashlight in that direction. CC turned the corner, then stopped and looked back one last time. He caught Sennett's silhouette in the reflected light. The man was on his knees, hugging Baron, and the dog was again licking his face. Then Sennett pointed back toward CC and said something to him. The dog reluctantly turned and started back up the tunnel where CC waited. CC waved to Sennett, then turned, and moved on.

He had walked another half-dozen yards when Sennett called out in a strangled voice.

"CC?"

He turned back for the last time. "Yes?"

"That little girl?"

"Yes?"

"I never got to meet her before. Tell her...tell her that her daddy loves her, will you?"

CC's voice shook a little when he replied. "I'll tell her she has a good daddy who can't come home to be with her right now; a daddy who loves her very much."

There was no reply, and when he looked back down the tunnel, Sennett was already gone.

End of Days

The Back Door
May 2nd, 7:02 a.m.

Rachel and Elizabeth were deep in conversation as they waited with Jonathan and Sarah near the western entrance to the caverns, so they didn't notice when CC moved up behind them.

"Rachel, I'm so sorry. If I'd had any idea...."

The other woman responded with a smile. "Don't worry about it. I'm grateful that the Lord revealed the truth to me before it was too late. He's just not God's man for me."

"Well, I don't think he's God's man for me either, and I feel such a fool that I allowed myself to be swept up by...what? Hormones? Loneliness?"

"Actually, I do believe in love at first sight, and I think he is the man for you," Rachel told her. "I've never seen him react to another woman the way he responded to you."

"But I could never be interested in the man who jilted you."

Before Elizabeth could respond, CC intruded on their conversation.

"It seems clear that he's not meant for any woman."

They both turned their heads toward him, and both shared a look of annoyance, as though their privacy had been violated. Rachel snapped at him.

"Is it your practice to eavesdrop on private conversations?" she demanded in anger, forgetting her otherwise sterling opinion of CC. "And just what would you know about it, apart from the fact that this damnable war may well prevent Elizabeth from ever seeing him again?"

CC bit back an angry retort, and as calmly as possible, he replied, "Your apparent dilemma is no secret to anyone here. You did, after all, carry on a pretty candid conversation in front of all of us."

Rachel realized that she deserved the rebuke, and nodded her apology, but CC wasn't finished.

"Apart from the fact that our lives are in imminent danger, and I don't have time for domestic diversions –seemingly important or otherwise – I have some information that I thought you'd want me to share." He brushed past them with a cryptic, "You'd better hurry!"

"CC," Elizabeth called after him.

"Yes?" he barked, without turning his head.

"We're sorry."

"Fine," he replied. "We're still in danger." Then he stopped in his tracks. Maybe we need to clear this up before we go any further.

"Clear what up?" Rachel asked.

"Why I had no idea that you both had known him before."

"Rachel did. I didn't," Elizabeth replied curtly.

"Then why....?"

"Why does Elizabeth care?" Rachel asked.

"That would seem to be the question."

"Because she's fallen in love with him."

"Rachel!" she cried, clearly upset at her for divulging the secret.

"That's no surprise," CC said. "Some emotional entanglement was made clear back at our meeting place."

Rachel ignored him and turned to Elizabeth. "Well, admit it. You have."

"All right, I'll admit it. I don't know why, but I've fallen for the guy."

"Actually, I can understand something like that happening," CC said.

"Oh, be quiet!" they both shouted.

"Well, there is something you both need to know," he suggested, tentatively, in a soft voice. Something he just told me."

"I don't think I want to hear this," Elizabeth replied.

"Maybe it's just as well. You almost certainly won't meet him again." CC's words actually sounded sorrowful, and Elizabeth couldn't stay angry at him.

"Please tell me. I have to know."

"He thinks he's dying of radiation poisoning."

"Oh, no. Not now," she wailed. "Not when I've just found him." She knew she sounded like someone out of a soap opera, but she couldn't help herself.

"I'm really sorry," CC said. "If it's any consolation, as unlikely as it seems, he told me that he thinks that he's in love with you too."

"Really?" she asked, smiling from ear to ear.

"See, I told you," Rachel laughed.

"Maybe I can help him," Elizabeth whispered in a desperate voice. "Maybe if I were with him, I could nurse him through it."

"He's already told me in no uncertain terms that he will not join our group."

They were so absorbed in their conversation that Jonathan had to shout twice to get their attention. "You'd better hurry. I think there's something wrong."

The five of them–CC, Sarah, Jonathan, Rachel, and Elizabeth–jogged out of the west end of the cavern just as the sun was rising. They pushed out onto the ledge through the underbrush that CC and Jonathan had transplanted months before to hide the escape tunnel that they hoped they would never need.

CC ran across the ledge and leaned out to scout the lakeshore below. Sarah held tightly to Jonathan's hand as she too looked down over fifty feet to the rocks below, then shivered to demonstrate how brave she was. Jonathan pointed toward the location of a rocky summit far across the lake.

"That's Tower's Rock," Jonathan said. "There's a cave on the far side." CC and I hid a cache of food and weapons inside in case we ever had to run for it."

The two women had been talking quietly, both struck by the grandeur of the lake and forest that surrounded it, but at Jonathan's words, they turned to study the high point of rock on the southwest corner of the lake,.

"If you are all through chattering like a bunch of magpies," CC chided, "we are really in a very dangerous place here."

He and Jonathan retrieved a rolled-up rope ladder from the mouth of the cave, carried it to the edge of the cliff, and fastened the top end to the base of a tree. CC had just kicked the rolled-up ladder over the edge, and they were listening to it uncoil, when they heard the flop-flop of a helicopter's rotor as it flew over the crest of the ridge from the east. Everyone raced for the cave and made it back inside except CC.

He heard the stuttering of a machine gun, and dove for the cover of the rocks, coming down hard and bruising his knee. *It's like deja vu all over again,* he thought, as he remembered the last time he and Jonathan were strafed from the air.

The copter swept by, very close to the ledge, and he could see a vaguely familiar oriental face staring at him from the passenger's seat. CC remembered seeing the man's picture in newspapers and magazines, but suspected that he might have met him in his former life, though the man's name escaped him. If he was right, he was one of the notorious Chinese generals who had grown obscenely wealthy off the sweat and blood of his own people, and had used much of his income to finance terrorist activities around the world.

There was another burst of gunfire and CC crawled behind a larger boulder that gave him a somewhat protected position beneath the cliff's overhang. Bullets, however, were striking and ricocheting all around him. He had left his own rifle leaning against a rock while he'd uncoiled the rope ladder, and he dared not cross the ledge to try to retrieve it.

The helicopter was frighteningly close, hovering just out from the cliff edge on which he lay, not more than thirty feet away, and maybe ten feet above the ledge. He was struck with the realization that at any second he'd probably be shot to death. He was mesmerized by the noise and shock of the attack. The man in the passenger's seat was now studying a large sheet of paper that was whipping in the wind of the open cockpit door. He slapped the pilot's arm, then pointed toward the ledge, and the copter began to move closer to where CC crouched.

With the copter swaying from side to side, and mistakenly believing that he was hidden from view, CC started to scrabble across the ledge toward his rifle. He was about halfway there when he realized that the copter was probably going to set down on the ledge, and probably right on top of him.

As one of its skis came to rest within a few inches of his leg, CC had just sense enough to roll to the side and crouch beneath the whipping blade. He looked up to discover that the general was staring down at him from the passenger seat. He was leaning out the door, waving the muzzle of an Uzi at him, and gesturing for him to climb into the copter. Crouching to stay beneath the blades, CC limped to the machine, stepped up on the ski, and rolled through the side door onto his back, winding up just behind the pilot′s seat. The machine lifted off the ledge while CC's legs were still hanging outside the copter, flailing in space.

The copter swung up and around, and CC was momentarily disoriented, the horizon appearing to spin around him. He pulled himself the rest of the way into the machine, and knelt on a pad behind the seats, hanging on like there was no tomorrow. *And,* he thought, *maybe there isn't a tomorrow for me.*

The copter tipped violently as it swung on its axis, giving them a view of the lake that lay below. While the ledge beneath the cliff still lay in shadow, the rising sun was reflected off a cloud-filled sky, and the lake below was aglow with the blazing sunrise, looking much like a great cauldron of molten steel.

The general shouted something that sounded like the "Dragon′s Cauldron" to the pilot. He looked uneasy, but the pilot shrugged his shoulders, indifferent to the rocks and gleaming water that seemed to be set aflame by the rising sun. To CC, it did indeed look like the lake had been set afire by a dragon′s breath.

The pilot, however, was not moved by the grandeur of the natural splendor, but was well aware of the danger of hovering next to a cliff where rising thermals put his aircraft in danger. Turning to examine the rapt face of his superior, he had sense enough to choose the lesser of the two potential evils, and continued to hover there to please a boss who seemed transfixed by what he obviously considered a disturbing scene below.

The general shivered, and his pilot must have assumed it was the result of the chill morning air. Then Eng turned in his seat, and stared past CC at a bundle of clothing in the far corner of the cargo bay. CC's eyes followed those of his captor. He stared blankly at the clothing, then shifted his gaze back to his unwanted host.

The man's eyes seemed to burn with madness. He twisted in his seat, pointing toward the heap of clothes, and shouting something at CC. Unable to hear him, CC gripped one of the pipes supporting the bucket seat and pulled himself forward, causing the general to aim the muzzle of his machine gun in his face.

"Bring me that coat," the general shouted imperiously.

CC hesitated, then got on his hands and knees and crawled across the vibrating deck to snatch up the garment. He scrabbled back, and again grabbed the support as the helicopter juddered in a gust of wind. CC didn't like heights and was afraid that he might be thrown through the cargo door if the pilot maneuvered suddenly.

The general beamed at CC, his eyes wide. "Thank you," he said, in a silken, yet somehow sinister voice. He unfolded the coat and pulled it slowly over the seat so that his prisoner could see it clearly.

"I was cold," he shouted. "This is not mine," he added with a sly smile, "but it should serve well enough."

He twisted back into a forward-facing position and unfastened his safety harness so that he could slip into the coat, but not before he had made certain that CC had ample opportunity to examine the coat. The general was delighted to see that CC's face had gone white. He had undoubtedly noticed the small pin fastened to the coat's lapel. It was just an inexpensive trinket–a bit of silver fashioned in the shape of a fish, an Ichthus.

The shock of seeing the pin unlocked another closet in CC's mind. He had given a pin exactly like that to his wife for Christmas a few years earlier.

"That's my wife's coat," he whispered aloud, and started to drag himself to a standing position.

The general's eyes had never left him, and there was a malicious smile on his face as he pressed the muzzle of his Uzi against CC's chest and commanded him to sit back down. Although he couldn't be heard about the sound of the aircraft, the threat was implicit.

"Please sit down on that bundle of clothing," he shouted, and shook the weapon in CC's face. Eng then pointed the muzzle at the pile of clothing from which CC had picked up the coat, and CC obediently crawled over and took a sitting position. He jammed his back uncomfortably into the rear corner of the cabin, diagonally opposite his assailant, then braced his feet against a strut that rose from the floor in front of him. Sitting at an angle to the pilot's compartment, he could watch the general's movements through the space between the two seats.

The general had already slipped the coat around himself and was now mechanically trying to button it, at the same time searching the ledge below for any sign of CC's friends. His fingers fumbled with the buttons, unable to slip them into their respective holes.

CC watched his every movement, angry now that the oriental invader was mocking his wife by wearing her coat. He wondered whether this was a message that they had murdered her, or simply an attempt to intimidate him. They obviously knew who he was, but it seemed strange that they'd know him. CC rose to his knees, suddenly determined to attack the man, and maybe to bring down the aircraft, but several things occurred before he could act.

It somehow registered on the Chinese general that he was donning a woman's overcoat, and he had inadvertently pulled the right lapel over the left. As a result, and for the second time in as many minutes, he was swept with an acute sense of foreboding. He realized that this was an American woman's coat and was buttoned on the opposite side as a man's. This was very bad luck.

His fingers began tearing at the buttons, almost in a panic, scrabbling to rip the coat open, when the pilot tapped him on the arm to get his attention. CC followed the pilot's finger as he pointed down at little Sarah, running from the cave entrance, shaking her fist at the copter. She was followed by Jonathan, who scooped her up and turned to run back to the cavern. The general forgot the ominous portent that was implicit in the way he'd buttoned the coat, and instead dragged his assault weapon up from the floor of the copter.

The pilot spun the craft in an effort to offer the general a clear shot through the door, and the radical movement swept CC from his feet. Bruised and disoriented, he rolled uncontrollably across the floor toward the open cargo door. The general, drawn by the disturbance, turned to deal with what he considered the potential threat from CC. Satisfied that his captive had all he could do simply to remain aboard the aircraft, he turned back toward those who had run out of the cave to rescue the child.

He fired a short burst into the cliff wall behind them, hoping to force them further out into the open where he could deal with them at his leisure.

CC lay halfway out the doorway, one hand in a death grip on a stanchion behind the co-pilot′s seat, one foot on the ski that hung beneath the copter, his own plight forgotten as his eyes were fixed on the drama unfolding below.

Sarah was standing stock still, bullets chipping the ledge around her, her eyes wide with terror as she stared up at the helicopter that was now perhaps twenty feet above her. She was deafened by the sound, blinded by the dust, and paralyzed by the unwarranted and deadly attack. Wide-eyed, she had her knuckles in her mouth and appeared to be screaming in terror.

The general raised the muzzle of his weapon, caught up a full magazine, and, as he struggled to slip it into the carrier, he noticed a man standing on the mountainside about fifty feet above the ledge on which the others were now huddled, their arms raised in surrender.

The general turned his attention to the man, his mouth dropping open in amazement. He shouted excitedly, pounding the pilot′s shoulder and causing the helicopter to judder as he jabbed his finger repeatedly toward the ridge. The pilot pulled the nose of the machine around, banking steeply, and they started to climb rapidly toward the top of the cliff that rose above the ledge.

CC was bent at the waist, half-in and half-out of the copter, his hands gripping the vertical stanchion behind the co-pilot's seat, both feet insecurely resting on the ski which was about two feet below the side door. He saw Jonathan waving to the others to run back to the cave.

He was immensely relieved to see them turn back toward the cavern, and was too busy to pay much attention to the reason for the pilot's radical maneuvers, as he was literally hanging on for dear life. His hands ached from their grip on the iron stanchion, but as the copter steadied, he looked up the cliff to see where they were headed.

He saw a man standing on the edge of the escarpment. It was Joe Sennett. He had evidently made his way out of another tunnel to climb to a ledge that was well above the one on which Sarah had just been attacked. Sennett was staring fixedly at the copter with the same look of intensity that its occupants had for him.

CC was caught up in the tableau until the rattle of the general's machine gun refocused his attention on his own plight, and he again attempted to drag himself back into the copter. The Uzi was beating a tattoo on the cliff just beneath Sennett's feet, and Sennett was laughing, the stock of his rifle pulled tightly into his shoulder. He snapped off several rapid shots, seemingly without any concentration.

The general's machine gun had been stitching a path up the face of the cliff toward Sennett, but the ratchet sound of the weapon ceased abruptly, and CC twisted around to stare between the door frame and the seat to see why the general had stopped firing.

He was just in time to see the gun slip from the man's hands, and his body slump sideways out the door. *He didn't refasten the safety belt after putting on my wife's overcoat,* CC realized. Now the general's head was lolling just a few inches from CC's eyes.

He looked strangely shrunken, a dark crimson spot flowering on the back of the coat that just moments before he had frantically been trying to remove. Head akimbo, staring down in terror at the glowing water below, the general's eyes were already losing the shine of life.

With the general leaning out the door, CC could now see the pilot. As he watched, the man slumped forward over the cyclic. His feet slipped free of the vital control pedals, and the helicopter started to spin in a terrifying manner. It tilted dangerously toward the ledge where Jonathan was in the act of snatching Sarah up in his arms, then running with her toward the safety of the cave.

CC was laughing hysterically, for he suddenly realized where the word "chopper" came from. With a tremendous shock, the tip of one blade struck the rock ledge, but instead of just snapping, it acted like a catapult, whipping the helicopter up and over in the opposite direction, throwing it completely out of control. CC reacted by closing his eyes and squeezing the stanchion with all his strength, but the helicopter's movements were so violent and the shock so severe that he couldn't hold on. The machine heaved itself over, jerking violently as it hit the cliff. It leveled for a moment, and then skewed sideways, out and away from the ledge.

CC was already falling free, his grip broken by the explosive shocks, his mouth open in a silent scream. His shoulder struck the branches at the top of a tall evergreen a glancing blow, then he was falling again, bouncing down the shingled layers of its branches. He was momentarily entangled, slowing his fall, then he was again falling free. He tried to get himself into an upright position, hoping that there would be water beneath him, hoping that he would strike a deep spot feet first, but before he could finish that thought, he had cleaved the surface of the lake, the impact so great that it took his breath away, his open mouth flooded with water. He choked and thrashed about, determined that after all he had been through, he wasn't going to drown now.

He was still beneath the surface when a tremendous explosion compressed the water, again crushing the breath from his lungs and almost bursting his eardrums. A lifetime later, he somehow found himself on the surface, struggling to stay afloat, trying to take in enough air to paddle toward the shore, but then flames rolled across the cliff face, nearly engulfing him, and he managed to slip beneath the surface to escape the searing air. After what seemed an eternity, he realized that he was again floating, nearly deaf, and there was just the glare of the rising sun, the muted crackling of a fire on the nearby shore, and the smoke rising from the carnage.

He found himself lying in shallow water on the edge of the lake beneath the ledge, dazedly watching his friends far above as their stricken eyes searched the area of the wreckage for his body. He waved one arm weakly, and Sarah's keen young eyes picked out his movement. She pointed downward as she cheered, drawing everyone's attention to him. Jonathan started down the rope ladder, but it was swinging so wildly that no one would dare to follow until he could reach the shore below and tie the bottom to a tree. That left the rest of them looking for a longer, but safer route down. After a moment, Sarah began to follow the dog as he made his way toward the bottom, and the women chased after her.

CC, however, was gazing further up the cliff, and his eyes seemed to catch those of Joseph Sennett. None of the others could see their rescuer as he moved slowly out from behind a boulder, well above their heads.

CC remained transfixed as Sennett removed something from his pocket and tossed it out over the edge of the cliff. Whatever it was caught the rays of the rising sun, then seemed to separate into a small shower of shining silver, a tiny cloud of confetti-like objects, dazzling in the sun's rays.

Swept apart by a vagrant breeze, the glittering objects spiraled slowly outward and downward until they splashed into the shallow water, dipping and swaying as they slipped beneath the surface. CC watched almost mesmerized as they glided back and forth through the crystal-clear water toward the stones that covered the bottom, just an arm's length away.

Feeling a sense of lassitude, CC lay still for a full minute before paddling slowly toward them. He reached down to scoop one of the shining silver objects from the gravelly bottom, scattering a few inquisitive minnows that had begun inspecting them. Gripping one of them between thumb and forefinger, he lifted it from the water to examine it. It was a small silver cross.

He felt the clasp on the back, and fumbled it open to pin it to his jacket. As he raised his eyes again toward the top of the cliff, Sennett threw something else down. Whatever this was didn't sparkle like the crosses. It too fell near CC, and he easily caught it as it slipped beneath the surface. It only took a glance to see that it was in the shape of a leaf, the insignia of an army major.

CC started to slip it into his pocket as a memento of this day, but something checked his spirit, and he sensed that he was being watched. He looked again toward the top of the cliff and saw Sennett pinning something to the front of his coat. It was one of the silver crosses.

CC could no longer see Joseph very well because he now seemed to stand in the penumbra of a bright star. The silver cross on his lapel was intensely radiant as it reflected the sun's rays, and it almost blinded CC, flashing back a glittering message of Sennett's new loyalty.

Joseph Sennett had made his choice. He had decided Whom he would follow. He had resigned his commission to join the Lord's army.

As the sunlight caught the cross on Sennett's chest, CC raised his arm as far as he could and threw the brass insignia out into the deeper water.

When Sennett finally pushed himself erect, CC noticed a dark stain on his pant leg, but his new friend seemed oblivious to it. He stared down at CC, and their eyes met and locked. Then putting his fingertips to the brim of his hat, Sennett snapped him a casual salute, turned and limped away over the crest.

Also by Frank Becker

The Depression Proof Church

The Depression Proof Church might be characterized as a Christian's survival manual for the end times.

Here's what Paige Patterson – past president of the Southern Baptist Convention, and president of America's largest seminary – wrote about *The Depression Proof Church:* "Frank Becker...has clearly enunciated the one essential, namely, a return to the church of the New Testament."

And Dr. John Kenzy – who co-founded the Teen Challenge Bible Institute with David Wilkerson – called *The Depression Proof Church* "Compelling and timely," and said that it "exposes revelation from God."

Senator Stephen R. Wise, PhD, called the "hard hitting," "inspiring a return to biblical practices that have been forsaken in a lust for ever larger churches."

And the Jacksonville Theological Seminary created a course entitled, The Depression Proof Church, for both seminary students and undergraduates.

You Can Triumph Over Terror

You Can Triumph Over Terror is an emergency preparedness manual for those concerned about the natural and man-made threats to their safety in an ever more dangerous world.

Special Agent Frank Gil (Retired) FECR PD; featured on COPS, Metro-Dade Special Response Team (SWAT) wrote: "Frank's book should be required reading. By preparing, you increase your chances of survival, facilitate our ability to assist you, and reduce your own stress and anxiety."

John, Sipos, Broadcast Journalist and host of "Hour Tampa Bay," wrote, "If you apply the ideas in this book...you and your family will radically improve your prospects for survival."

The Chronicles of CC

The Star Spangled Banner Books

www.frankbecker.com

Now available in paperback and as E-books

War's Desolation

The Heav'n Rescued Land

Freemen Shall Stand

Our Cause It Is Just

In God Is Our Trust